THAT LUCKY FEELING

COLIN R. COOPER

ACKNOWLEDGEMENTS

First and foremost of course, I want to thank my fabulous wife Mary for her belief, her support and her love. Without it, this book would not have happened.

Thanks also to my creative sons, Joel and Aaron for their belief. Joel designed the stylized clover symbol that features on the cover.

Finally the encouragement of all of my family and friends has been a boon.

PROLOGUE

Time to get your fine Irish arse out of here boyo and don't be dragging your feet. The thought repeated persistently in the young man's mind. He had been having a fine time during his sojourn in Marseilles - at least until the events of the night before last. He knew something significant had taken place; knew it in his gut. He just hadn't been able to decide exactly what it meant and what he should do about it. Over the course of the previous day as he tried to think it through, his feelings of unease had blossomed into an irresistible urge to leave the city behind – as quickly and quietly as possible.

The misty rain made the bleak pre-dawn even more dismal. He tugged the brim of his cap low and turned up his collar against the cold. His manner was one of extreme wariness rather than fear; eyes scanning the surrounding darkness as he approached the wharf. Apart from anything else going on, the docks can be a dangerous place in the wee hours of the morning.

Marseilles is an old, old settlement and he could smell in the air the complex soup of aromas. It was a characteristic shared by all ancient cities; as if the buildings, roads and pathways were imbued with the scent of the comings and goings of human-kind across the years.

The cobblestone gutter running alongside the pathway was punctuated by exhaust grills. There was barely a hint of wind and tendrils of rising vapor, made visible by the chill, swirled around his legs as he walked. A loud scream of tires on asphalt in a nearby street shattered the eerie stillness. The sound was like the cry of a banshee straight from a childhood nightmare and it sent a shiver down his spine. He shook off the feeling of dread and continued forward.

Ahead through the gloom, yellow overhead lights reflected off the wet concrete of the docks. As he drew nearer he could make out a team of men transferring cargo from a small freighter to a waiting lorry. He walked past them and went in search of the driver of the truck. He found him lounging on a wooden bench where the overhanging eaves offered some protection from the drizzle. He was taking time out to smoke a cigarette– no doubt a Gauloises - as he waited for loading to finish.

Using a combination of hand gestures and his negligible command of French, he was able to establish that the vehicle would be departing as soon as the consignment of freight was on board, with Paris as its destination - a scenario ideal for his purposes. His request for passage was met with a clear-cut 'non' but he could see the driver waver, a flicker of avarice in his eyes when he proffered a fistful of cash – a very practical tool for negotiation and for overcoming a language barrier. Now it was just a matter of how much it would take to break down the last of the trucker's resistance. He hoped he had enough in his pockets and his thoughts went to the money belt he could feel, warm and heavy under his dungarees. He had to work hard to resist the temptation to reach down and touch it. Secreted in it was more money than he'd ever before had in his possession. More than enough to go back home and start up a new life. Eventually, the transportation deal was done and 30 minutes later he was laying on a makeshift bed in the back of the canvass covered truck as it pulled out on to L'Autoroute du Soleil.

That evening and not far away, two men sat across from each other in the sitting room of a modestly appointed but comfortable suite in a three-star Hotel. Each nursed a large crystal balloon glass that glowed with the deep warm honey-colored hue of fine cognac. The man who sat in the armchair could afford the best room in the best hotel in town but it had been Andre Muller's habit for the past twenty years to be understated in the way that he conducted both himself and his business affairs. Simply put, he did not like to draw attention to himself. More important to him than status and unnecessary trappings of wealth was that his room afforded him a panoramic view of the harbor and was centrally located on the quai des Belges.

Although he was Swiss by birth and still carried that country's passport, he no longer considered that label to be a broad enough description of his nationality. If asked, he referred to himself as 'European' – a more accurate declaration because in running his business he travelled extensively, sharing his time across many of the major cities of Europe - something that had been made much easier by the formation of the European Union. He still returned to his original home soil regularly but not because of any bonds to family or friends. Those links were well in the past and the ties that motivated him now were those of a monetary nature. He maintained his bank accounts in Zurich because, in his opinion, it remained the best place to carry out financial transactions away from prying eyes.

The complexion and coloring of the man who sat on the couch marked him as being of Mediterranean ancestry but it would be a lot harder to narrow down that broad classification to his birthplace of Barcelona. He also travelled extensively throughout Europe and nowadays it was much harder to pin down his accent as being Spanish. He had placed his glass on the coffee-table that occupied the space between them and leaned back on the couch. It was clear from his relaxed demeanor that he was a very close confederate of the man in the armchair. It was also clear that Andre was the one in charge.

Their voices were low, as if to retain symmetry with the lighting in the room. Andre was talking about the financial status of the business. It was a subject that was endlessly fascinating for Andre but one that the man from Barcelona found very dry. His attention drifted. He looked at this man who he thought of as his friend but whose orders he followed. Not for the first time he reflected that they were very different people. The English expression that entered his thoughts was that they were 'like chalk and cheese'. Andre was smooth where he was rough - Andre would be described as distinguished where words like sturdy or solid would be used about him. The aristocrat and the peasant. Their interests and ambitions too, were very different. Sometimes he wondered what kept him attached to Andre after all this time. He knew what had started their association but what was it that had sustained it? It wasn't financial gain – of course that was always welcome but it wasn't the primary motivator. When he was totally honest with himself, he would admit that the driving force was the same now as it was in the beginning. The glue that held him to Andre was remorse and it was still a powerful adhesive. When he could finally forgive himself, then he would be able to move on.

His focus returned to matters at hand when Andre asked for a report of the venture that had brought them to Marseilles. He began with the thing that had been bothering him for the past two days. "It's strange that two should turn up in the same city, at the same gambling house," the man on the couch contended.

"Statistically its occurrence has a low probability I'll grant, but nevertheless still a possibility. It has happened once before, remember – back when we first began this business," said Andre.

At his own reference to that time years ago, a look of deep pain flickered across Andre's face and he gave a short, sharp shake of his head as if to physically deny an unwanted thought access to his consciousness. He recovered and continued with his assessment. "Look at it this way. We know that the Frenchman is local so his presence is expected. As for the other one, Marseille is a melting pot. There are so many travelers, truckers and seaman passing though at any given time that it is a conceivable scenario to have two of the gifted here simultaneously," he reasoned. "As to them being in the same establishment, you forget that even though it is an illegal operation, it is the best known gambling den in the city. When we saw them together, they clearly did not know each other – I don't believe that their type could be good enough actors to fool us about that. No, I'm comfortable that it is co-incidental. It might be a long-shot but we deal in long-shots, eh Josep," he concluded with a slight smile at his self-assessed witticism.

Andre sipped his cognac. He tried to sound casual as he asked his next question so as not to betray his feeling of unease. "So were you able to locate the Irishman?"

"No, he's disappeared. Not that hard to do, even without leaving Marseilles. But I think he has left the city. I think he came in on a freighter so I checked around the docks and the usual hangouts of these riff-raff seamen but no sign. As you said yourself, there are so many boats and trucks coming and going every day, finding transport is easy. And no questions asked, if you have cash."

"And cash was not an issue for him after his big win last night," observed his boss and then added, "From what we saw the gift might be very powerful in him. He would have been an excellent addition."

Again he tasted his cognac and after a slight pause, lifted his gaze. Now his ice-blue eyes bore into the dark eyes of his assistant. "Does he suspect he has a special ability?" He leaned forward slightly as he asked, an air of tension belying his casual tone.

Josep Ferrer knew that they had reached the nub of what was on his boss's mind and sought to reassure his master. He knew that he needed to close-off this train of thought quickly, lest it lead to recriminations against him. Not that he would be in any physical danger but Josep hated feeling like he had let down Andre. "I am certain that he has no idea and I was careful to give no hint as to the real reason for our interest in him," he said. "I approached him with the usual story that I work for a group of wealthy businessmen and I am recruiting a team of highly skilled gamblers. The chosen group was to be well paid to be part of a venture aimed at breaking the bank at big casinos across Europe."

Ferrer tried to inject even more confidence into his voice as he continued, "He suspected absolutely nothing. He is simply a superstitious Irish peasant who believes only that he had a once in a life-time lucky night. My offer scared him because he knows that he is a mediocre player. So he has run away with his tail between his legs, back to whatever backwater potato field he came from."

"Okay Josep. I tend to agree with your evaluation. Spend no more of your time on it. The Frenchman is now your priority. He was the reason that we came here in the first place and he is where you should put your energies. I want you to get him on board. He shouldn't be too hard to convince and I like him as a prospect. He has that hungry and greedy look that makes for a pliable employee."

"You may go now," was how Andre signaled the end of their meeting. His eyes narrowed slightly as he added, "As for the Irishman, if he does start to understand and use his gift, we'll find him. They always go too far and come to notice."

After the door closed behind Ferrer, he turned to his son, Lukas. The young man had been sitting silently on the other side of the room, listening intently. Andre was proud of the boy. At an age of only 20 years old, he already seemed to have mastered the art of knowing when to speak and when to observe – a discipline that many people never seemed to learn. He was showing a strong aptitude when it came to learning his father's business and already Lukas was beginning to value his opinion.

"What do you think Lukas?"

"I agree that the Irishman is unlikely to be a problem. But we should also keep our agents on the alert." He moved to the couch, across from his father. "As for Ferrer, it was a mistake that he let him slip through. Maybe you should start thinking about succession planning."

His thin smile when he said that was returned by a broader one from his father. It was a private joke between them that they liked to inject 'corporate speak' into their discussions. After all, theirs was a highly profitable operation with a cash-flow that certainly qualified it as big business.

"Why don't you make that your project," said his father. "Josep has been with me from the beginning and it is fitting that when the time comes, we retire together. And you are right that you will need you own, younger assistant, someone that you trust. It's logical that you should be the one to find that person."

They both sat back, enjoying the expensive liquor and slipping into their own thoughts. Andre quietly studied his son. He looked a younger version of himself – average height, slim, blonde hair, angular features - except that Lukas seemed to have a much harder edge to him. His son's eyes could actually look cruel when he was angry and that worried him. Andre had found that perseverance and money could resolve almost any problem and he rarely resorted to violence to get what he wanted. His experience was that violence resulted in unpredictable consequences and usually stirred up undesirable attention. He knew that patience was not a trait that Lukas had inherited and he couldn't shake the feeling that Lukas would be too quick to turn to aggression when his plans were thwarted.

CHAPTER 1

"yes...Yes...YES! Get over the line you good thing."

He was on the rails at the finish line; close enough to feel the thud of hooves on the ground as the horses thundered past, kicking up clods of turf and dirt. The air smelt of new mown grass and sweating thoroughbreds. As he walked away from the fence, he looked at the betting slip, not for the first time, as if the name and number of the horse printed there might change if he didn't keep a watchful eye on it.

"Thank Christ for that," he muttered to himself; closely followed with a self-reproaching, "God I'm an idiot. Fancy trying to get ahead on the last race of the day."

It was known disparagingly as the 'get out stakes' - a reference to the fools and the desperate gamblers trying to dig themselves out of the mess that they had gotten into with their losses for the day. But today he had done it. Fifty quid at 10 to 1; money in the hand and the past eight losing picks erased.

He surveyed his surroundings. Spring was trying hard to give winter the shove but thus far having only partial success. Today, the early drizzle had gone and the weather was mild – or at least mild in comparison to what Dublin could produce. With the pressure off, he was able to appreciate what a lovely race course it was. The Curragh is one of Ireland's oldest tracks and the most famous when it came to flat races. It is home to a number of classics including the Irish Derby. There were no feature races today and so there were only a few hundred patrons, mostly hard-core punters who'd be there if Armageddon was scheduled for the following day; and would probably try to get a bet on the outcome. Later in the season from May through July, the big events are run and it's a much different story. That's when the Curragh takes on a carnival-like appearance and atmosphere.

He thought back to the when he came to the races just to be part of those special occasions. He and a dozen of his University friends would scrub up and dress up, trying to attain that look of sophistication and money that none of them actually possessed. The course is located in County Kildaire about 40 kilometers from Dublin and to get there, they'd join with the throng at Heuston Station boarding one of the special race-days trains that ran to the track. The short rail journey added to the anticipation and excitement of the day. Back then it was about the theatre of a good race day. The smell of the grass, the beauty of the horses and the thrill of a winning bet, albeit for a very small wager. And of course, the beauty of the young ladies, dressed to impress, looking a picture at the start of the day and maybe even better when the drinks kicked in and they were a little disheveled and a little careless with their skimpy outfits.

He used to think of himself as an astute reader of horses. He always went around to the stable area and checked out the horse in the stalls and those doing circuits in the walking ring. Then he watched them in the mounting yard. He felt he could pick the horses that were fit, keen and wanted to run, compared to those that were dull in the coat and still carrying extra conditioning. And equally, those that were really not interested in being there – that were too fractious or were breaking out into a sweat. There was nothing better than seeing that the boom two-year-old hot favorite looked out of sorts and then choosing to back something to beat it with a good payout.

In truth, while he was wholehearted in his love for the drama, he didn't really know horses in any depth and losing bets mostly offset any jackpot selections.

He smiled to himself as he recalled the reaction of his best mate Dylan to these outings. Dylan was very down to earth, hated dressing up and didn't share his love of horse-racing. He'd look him up and down, raise his eyes to the heavens and utter his favorite old saw that was trotted out whenever anyone was dressed in a suit. "God man, you're done up like a pox doctor's clerk." Most of the time this would be closely followed by; "Anyway, have fun – me, I'm off to the boozer to watch football."

His thoughts returned to the present as he lined up in the payout queue and waited for the jockeys to weigh-in. When the siren sounded to signify 'correct weight' and winnings could be collected, he forcefully expelled the air in his lungs. Unconsciously he'd been holding his breath. It was very rare for a winner to be disqualified because the jockey had weighed in light but it could happen. And after all, he had been having a bad day, and everybody knows it's on days like that when the 'once in a blue moon' sort of thing happens. "Enough of the negativity," he told himself. "You've come out a winner, it's Saturday and it's time to meet your mates at the pub. What more could a young guy want?" *Well maybe a hot date, rather than a night out with the boys,* was his next wry thought.

He felt a little surge of elation as he pocketed his winnings. *Hell, I might even shout Dylan a pint.*

CHAPTER 2

His mood upbeat, Aiden left the track and returned to his house. It was a smallish two-bedroom semi-detached brick of the Victorian era. The house had belonged to his grandparents on his mother's side. When they had passed on, she inherited the property. She'd very much wanted to keep the home in the family so she had held on to it and rented it out. After Aiden had graduated and found work, he put it to his mother that it was time he left the nest and proposed that he could rent the house. At first she tried to insist that she wouldn't take his money and he should live there rent-free. Attractive as that offer was, he knew his parents could not really afford for an asset like that to be generating no income, so after a sit-down family meeting they had settled on an amount that they were all happy with. He could afford it and it was well under market rates so his mother was content that she was giving him a help along.

The house was located right on the edge of the city-proper and the area had gone through a cycle typical of such suburbs - degenerating during some tough economic times but now going through a revival as young professionals began to buy into the area to take advantage of the proximity to the city. He liked his home enormously. Whilst it was not the chic bachelor pad that some might have preferred, it was comfortable and radiated that aura of welcome that sometimes can be felt in old family homes – almost as if the happy times had permeated the foundations.

After the previous tenants had moved out, he and his father spent several weekends sprucing it up ready for him to take up residence. Not a renovation, more of an updating. Although he was no handyman he could handle patching and painting. But the real bonus for a footloose young man was its location. He was within walking distance to most of what he needed and his usual hang-outs were easy to reach. As a bonus, the commute by motorbike to the research clinic where he worked was about as straightforward as it could be in a busy city.

A quick shower and shave freshened him up. He dressed casually in jeans, tee-shirt, sport-style loafers and linen jacket. Like most guys, he would swear that getting ready to go out amounted to nothing more than throwing on the first things that came to hand, but in truth, an observer might adjudge that his preening would make a metrosexual proud. He fooled with his hair, looking for that neatish but slightly tousled hair that he preferred; or more importantly, that the girls seemed to prefer. According to a couple of girls that he had dated, having his dark hair styled this way softened the strong line of his nose and his high cheekbones and gave him an appealing look of vulnerability, while highlighting his green-hazel eyes. One lover impishly referred to it as the JFL. He found out later that it meant the 'just fucked look'. He ran a hint of product through his hair and thought "Geez, it takes a lot of messing with your hair to make it look like you haven't been messing with it."

Satisfied, he splashed on a little Armani aftershave (he refused to use the word cologne) and checked himself in the mirror. "That's not half bad Aiden," he said to the guy looking back at him. "There I go again," he said to the mirror, "Thinking aloud." Talking to himself was something that he did quite a lot. Then again, he reasoned the habit is probably not too unusual for someone living alone.

His parents had named him Aodhán, a Celtic name meaning little fire; perhaps with great expectations of what their only son might achieve. In his rebellious teen years, he thought that the name was pretentious and smacked of delusions of grandeur. He adopted the anglicized version of his name, Aiden. Aiden James Donnelly. His middle name was after his uncle on his father's side. Uncle Jimmy was also his god father. He was an only child – uncommon in Ireland – as a result of problems his mother encountered giving birth.

Aiden always described himself as 'average, plus a little bit'. He was 6'2" in height; average plus a little bit. He had played a number of sports across his school life including tennis, rugby, a bit of swimming and those fine Irish games, Hurling and Gallic football. He also went to martial arts sessions a couple of times a week; not really for the self-defense but more because of the all-over workout that it provided and because he had a fascination with Asia and Asian philosophy. As a result of all this, he had developed a well muscled, athletic build. He was lean but not skinny and had broad shoulders; average plus a little bit. In the second half of his twenties, he still played football to keep fit and for the mateship. He was quite a handy player, not the best on the team, just average plus a little bit.

He was quite contented with whom he was and he liked his values. He saw himself as honest with a strong sense of fair play and a loyal friend. Not without fault of course; he could have too long a memory when he felt that he had been wronged, had a tendency toward pessimism and suffered an occasional bout of mild depression. Because he recognized and wrestled with these short-comings, he felt that this should give him some extra karma points

He was meeting the guys at their preferred pub in Temple Bar, an old part of town that to some had become a little too self-conscious in its role as a tourist magnet. But he liked it and besides, where there were tourists, there were female tourists. What's more, his experience was that the young, modern members of that gender were rather aggressive in their pursuit of fun and they seemed to find the Irish accent irresistible.

He was running early and it was a mild night, so he decided to take the bus to the city center and walk the rest of the way. As he strolled through the shopping precinct to Temple Bar, he took in how much the streetscape had changed. In recent years Dublin had been going through a boom. Not long ago, it was becoming run-down, suffered from high unemployment and a serious 'brain-drain' as young professionals left in droves to pursue careers elsewhere in the world. Dublin was on the ropes but it was not down. It's that kind of town. It has always had spirit and it knew how to hold on and continue the fight. Eventually the money started to come. A score of big companies decided that England had become too expensive and had moved their operations to Ireland, mostly Dublin. With the inflow of investment came a new sense of vigor, new opportunities and a sharp rise in general prosperity. Before long, the young turks were choosing to remain in Ireland and many who had left, began to return.

Most of the change had been positive and there was no doubt that the upbeat vibe was infectious. Aiden was less pleased that the streets lost some of their local charm and identity when the high-end fashion stores moved in. Now when you walked around the Grafton Street area, it felt like you could be walking through a hundred other towns in Europe. He felt the same way about the encroachment into the pubs of that homogenized style of food known as 'international cuisine'. As he complained to his friends, it was getting nigh on impossible to find simple pub food, like stews and Guinness pies. Another issue was that in common with virtually all cities that have gone through rapid growth, infrastructure improvements had not kept pace and the traffic had become horrendous. He was thankful that he owned a motorbike rather than having to negotiate peak-hour in a car.

It was strange to think of the town as a 'happening' place but that is what it had become. Just last weekend, Dublin had hosted a U2 concert, a European Cup match against the Netherlands, the Hurling final and as icing on the cake, Billy Connelly was in town. On Friday night before the football game, the streets were full of hulking Dutchmen sporting their national colors of green and orange. They were more than matched by smaller but equally patriotic Irishmen decked out in green and white. The next day, as he rode past Landsdowne Road Stadium with the match in progress, the roar of the crowd buffeted him like a physical force. His budget dictated that he had to choose between this spectacle and U2's first concert on home soil in 12 or 13 years. He went for the U2 option but felt a tinge of regret when he became caught up in the crowd noise. The feeling intensified when he learned that Ireland had won the game. But it was completely washed away that night at the concert as soon as the first chords were struck and he along with thousands of other fans were transported to music Valhalla.

Sunday was the Hurling final and the streets were again awash with color. This time the blue and yellow of Tipperary versus the maroon of Galway. It seemed that the entire populations of both cities had come to Dublin to cheer on their boys on at Croke Park.

His thoughts returned to the present as he entered Capel Street and crossed over the River Liffey. Cutting through the side streets of Temple Bar to reach Westmoreland, he could hear the by the sounds spilling from the pubs along the cobble-stone street that the precinct was starting to liven up. He went through the open doors of the hotel and could see Dylan was already there along with two more of their pals, Michael and Shannon.

"Yo Aiden, over here" yelled Dylan, waving from where he was propping up the bar in their favorite corner. It was their sought after spot because it had a good view of the large screen TV on the wall. It also had a good view of the door so that they could indulge in that other favorite spectator sport of young men - 'babe spotting'.

Dylan Byrne stood around 5'9" and had a wiry but athletic build, sort of like a whippet to Aiden's greyhound. The metaphor stayed true in that their hair and eye coloring was almost a match. After the second Austin Powers movie, Dylan had to endure a truck-load of 'mini-me' jibes until the lads eventually tired of the joke and moved on.

"Ah my man," he continued, "I can tell from that dopey grin on your face that you had a good day with the nags, so it must be your buy. We're just about empty here." Just to emphasize his point, Michael picked up his glass and sloshed around the inch of beer that remained in the bottom.

Michael Gallagher was all around Mr. Average, a little shy of 6 ft in height, reddish-blonde hair, blue eyes and a physique that was just right for buying clothing straight off the rack.

They were all motionless for an instant, looking at him expectantly. Aiden laughed at the image that came to him. "You lot look like an installation put together for Madam Tussauds."

"Yeah, well the title would be 'Three Thirsty Men Awaiting," retorted Shannon.

With a height sitting between the other two, Shannon Doyle was stocky, broad and barrel-chested – a bear of a man. His shaved bullet-like head and a bull-neck were ideal for rugby, a game he loved. He had a darker complexion than the others - something that his friends jokingly put down to a having a passing Roman Centurion in his ancestry. Despite his intimidating look, he was quick to laugh and slow to anger but just the same, was someone that you wanted on your side if things got ugly.

They had all been friends since they were thrown together in their first year of high-school. Despite this, their careers had taken different paths. Each was successful in his own way, due in some part to their friendship. Attitudes were changing in the revitalized Ireland but it was not long ago that there was a part of the Irish psyche that viewed the pursuit of academic or career excellence by anyone in your peer group with derision or even a degree of suspicion. Striving to be the best ought to be confined to the sports arena. Else you risked being labeled a try-hard or a nerd, or heaven forbid a management wannabe. Much better to be one of the lads.

Not so with their clique. Right through their schooling they had competed amongst themselves to see who scored the best results. As a result they were all doing well in the commercial world. Aiden worked as a research technician, Shannon was an electronics wizard working for a large security firm, Michael was inching up the ladder in corporate law and Dylan was the IT guru of the gang.

Aiden reached the bar and duly stood pints all around. Their preferred tipple was Harp larger when the weather was mild or Murphy's when the cold wind called for the warming richness of a stout. Not that there was anything wrong with Dublin's most famous product, Guinness. It was just that they got into Murphy's in their student days, probably just to be different and had stayed with it.

As the evening unfolded, it became clear that it was to be a barren night in the female tourist stakes.

"It looks like we've picked the wrong pub lads." Shannon observed, "What about we throw a few darts and sink a few pints instead then. We've got a football match on tomorrow, so an early night probably won't hurt. Well, not too much."

Throwing a few darts was Shannon's prescription any time that things got a little slow – mainly because he was by far the best player of the group. He almost always won even when half-drunk and they had long since given up having a bet on the outcome. Instead they had recently started playing a game that they had been introduced to by a couple of big South-African lads that involved drinking penalties – much more fun. They called the game Rhodesian Killer Rules and its scoring system introduced an element of luck that meant that Shannon was not totally invincible and sometimes one of the others was able to steal a win from him.

They played a couple of games but no-one's heart was really in it and it was only around 11 p.m. when they called it quits and went their separate ways home. Aiden was tucked up by mid-night and asleep within minutes.

Ever since adolescence, Aiden had awoken each day with a popular song rattling around in his head. Sometimes the song seemed appropriate to something going on in his life but mostly it seemed to be simply a random tune; or if it did have some sort of relevance, he'd not found the key to the cipher. Lately they were invariably classic hits by Irish bands. Today it was Thin Lizzy's 'The Boys are Back in Town'. That was an easy one to figure out. He had a football match today and the song was their unofficial anthem – probably in common with half the other teams in Ireland.

Sunday flew by as Sundays often do. After a sleep-in, he set about the chores that he had to get done before the working week began again. Those mundane things that he put off until the week-end like a trip to the supermarket, catching up with his laundry and a giving the place a rudimentary clean.

Then it was off to the game. It a tight contest and after letting a couple of scoring opportunities slip away, they lost by two points. It was one they probably should have won - but a couple of pints after the game eased the disappointment. That's one good thing about amateur sport – once the game is over, it doesn't really matter if you win or lose, you can either have a drink in celebration or in consolation.

There was nothing else going on that night so Aiden was home in time to watch the second half of a Sunday Night movie on TV. It was an inane, B-grade action movie featuring a couple of fading stars who should have known better. Aiden stuck it out through to the end for want of something else to do, and then headed for his bed muttering "I want that hour of my life back."

CHAPTER 3

The working week dawned under a grey, threatening sky. Just another typical Dublin morning thought Aiden as he set off for work, accompanied in his head by this morning's melody - U2's 'Angel of Harlem' – perhaps because he'd recently been thinking about their concert or maybe not.

He parked his bike in the 'Staff Only' section of the car park at the clinic. The good news was that the weather man had promised that the clouds would clear by midday and the outlook was for a fine and clear afternoon. He checked his watch and was pleased to see that he had ample time before work for a coffee in the café across the road. A good thing - Aiden didn't like being late. He appreciated punctuality in others and tried hard to demonstrate the same virtue. On the other hand, the brown mud that passed for coffee in the kitchen at the center was very much a last resort.

He enjoyed his job as a technician at the facility. The overall program covered a broad spectrum of research across biomolecular and biomedical sciences. Facilities were world class and Dublin was developing an international reputation for cutting edge advances in diagnosis and treatment of a number of disorders. The group of researchers was drawn from a raft of scientific disciplines but perhaps surprisingly, the cooperation between the diverse teams was excellent on the whole and egoism was minimal. Often the discoveries made led to new avenues of enquiries and in turn spawned new ventures.

The specific project that Aiden worked on began as a study of brain patterns and the biomolecular changes that occurred during the sleep cycle. Over time it had evolved into experiments that used neuroimaging and neurological feedback as a means of training individuals to invoke sleep patterns at will when in a resting state. The aim was to develop a drug-free approach to helping people with sleep disorders - insomniacs and the like.

Aiden made his way to the wing that housed his project. As he walked down the hall past the analysis laboratories to his domain in the ward area, he exchanged the usual Monday-morning greetings with his work colleagues – how was your weekend, how did your team go – the normal pleasantries that every worker is familiar with. Not that anyone really pays much attention to what's said. By and large, the people that he directly worked with were a good group. Of course, there were a few PHD's who were 'up' themselves and looked down on him because he only held a degree and not a doctorate. But that didn't bother him. He was much more a hands-on type rather than a theoretician and was happy with his role. At University, he had not set out to achieve Honors, let alone going on to post-graduate studies. He was a solid B or B+ student, nothing more. Just average plus a little bit.

The only person that actually irked him was the director of the project. Until he had met Dr Simon O'Mara, he hadn't truly understood the meaning of prissy. O'Mara was a pursed lipped, tut-tutting type who looked like he found the very air he breathed to fall short of his standards. Aiden suspected that his real problem was that he was being left behind by the new young guns and was using his position and seniority to prop up a sagging ego.

O'Mara was tall, thin and slightly stooped. His gait as he moved around the facility was better described as skulking rather than walking. When Aiden had first joined, one of his new colleagues had summed up O'Mara as one who 'could get a job haunting houses'. Aiden fully understood the reference the first time he was on the receiving end of O'Mara suddenly seeming to materialize beside him. Another wag had put it even better when he nick-named him 'Monty Burns'. Fortunately, O'Mara spent most of his day to day time shut away in the laboratory or at conferences and so Aiden only had to put up with him when a made a rare visit to the wards.

Aiden was looking forward to the day ahead. A new group was coming in to be put under observation and embarking on a new study was always a buzz. His role as the liaison point was to settle them in, run through the aims of the project, explain the processes that they would be part of and to supervise the procedure of hooking them to the monitoring equipment.

When seeking new subjects, the program advertised in the local newspapers and tried to attract people who fell into as many categories as possible in terms of sex, age and sleep habits; from sound sleepers to those exhibiting symptoms of sleep apnea to those who declared themselves to be full insomniacs. During the testing, some of the group would be housed in a shared ward and some segregated in a room by themselves. This was done to add yet another dimension to the data being collected. After testing and benchmarking had been completed, a sample sub-set of the group would be asked to remain for additional testing and to become part of the new experimental approach of neuro-feedback training that they were now employing.

Aiden entered a conference room to greet the new group. His eyes swept casually around the room and then did a little double-take when he registered a familiar face. Induction was not scheduled to start for a few minutes, so he took the opportunity to approach the lanky, slightly unkempt, middle-aged man sitting a little apart from the rest of the group, in the corner of the room.

"Uncle Jimmy," he said, keeping his voice low so as not to be overheard by those nearby. "What on earth are you doing here?"

"Top of the morning to you too Aiden," he came back. Then with a familiar grin he went on. "You boys are offering 50 quid a day for me to do nothing and you're throwing in free food and a bed. Besides, I wanted to see what you got up to during the day."

Aiden couldn't help but return the smile. "Okay, but remember, we're serious about our research and I like my job, so none of your usual shenanigans, alright?"

Jimmy did his best to look wounded – like that could be achieved with anything short of an axe. "Boyo, I'm cut to the quick. How could you even think that?" Another grin shattered any pretense of his having taken offense. "The little I know about what happens here seems fascinating. Believe it or not, I am very interested in studies involving brain functions. And I promise I'll behave, so you can do away with 'Uncle', okay. I know you only use that honorific when you're trying to be all stern and serious."

That brought forth a chuckle from Aiden. "You know a little too much, you old scoundrel," he replied, affection clear in his voice.

It's really not so surprising that Jimmy would turn up at some time, thought Aiden. There's not much that he hasn't turned his hand to if there was a little money attached. Jimmy was a bit of a rogue but he was well liked by everyone who knew him – he was what the Irish called 'a good aul skin'. At the same time, he was a man of complex layers; he could surprise with his depth of knowledge on a multitude of subjects. These days his hair was turning silvery-white and he wore it tied back in a sort of pony-tail. Coupled with his open face and kindly-looking eyes, he looked like an aging hippy. Aiden could not recall him ever having a full-time job but he always got by. In fact, Aiden suspected that he had a lot more money behind him than he ever let on. He'd always been someone that Aiden could talk to about anything. Jimmy's upbeat nature was a perfect counter-weight when the blues started to get a hold on Aiden. His fondness for his uncle was deep and it was a feeling that Jimmy was returned to him with interest.

They had just started the induction session when the door burst open and Dr O'Mara swept into the room, full of self-importance and trailing a couple of arse-licking sycophants. It was completely true to form. When he chose to grace them with his eminent presence in the wards, it was always without the courtesy of any pre-arrangement. It was as if he didn't trust his staff and thought that by sneaking up on them he might catch someone out.

It was also his habit to arrive after a session had commenced. He would rudely interrupt and take over center stage – just another demonstration of who was in charge. It was a custom that impressed no-one but himself and possibly his lackeys. He proceeded to regale the mostly glazed-eyed inductees with the history of the program and all of the successes that he had overseen within his many individual projects. Maybe annual funding bids were coming up and he had deluded himself into thinking that this would somehow help his case.

All through the lecture, Aiden stood off to the side with his fingers literally crossed and his eyes fixed on Jimmy. O'Mara was just the sort of over-blown twerp that got under Jimmy's skin and Aiden waited for the heckling to begin. But true to his word, Jimmy behaved. Apart from a nearly inaudible muttering of 'what a fuck wit', that elicited a few snickers from those nearest him, Jimmy held his tongue.

O'Mara finally finished with the seemingly mandatory, "Are there any questions?" After a fruitless and drawn-out minute, punctuated only by the sounds of a few coughs and the scraping of chairs being shuffled about, he turned on his heel and left as abruptly as he came.

Aiden went over and closed the door. *Bastard always leaves the door open.* He returned his focus to the group. A part of him was disappointed that Jimmy didn't fire a few darts at the pompous prick.

"Sorry about that folks," he apologized. "Let's get back to why you are all here."

After the induction session was completed, his colleagues set about separating the group in line with the statistical samples that they wanted to establish. Jimmy had listed himself as an insomniac which thought Aiden was a gross exaggeration, if not a down-right lie. Without letting on about their relationship, he arranged to get Jimmy into a private room. Why not use your influence to give your uncle a little extra comfort, he thought. Besides it will be easier for us to have a bit of a chin-wag. *And I can keep a bit of an eye on him.* When Jimmy got bored, he became what teachers called 'a disruptive influence'.

The days passed without incident. He enjoyed having Jimmy around and when things were a bit slow in the ward, he often found himself in Jimmy's room, just chatting about old times. A few twinges of guilt were stirred up when Jimmy mentioned his folks. He'd been totally slack about phoning, let alone visiting them in the last couple of months. After he had moved out of home, his parents has sold up their house in Dublin and now owned a small pub in near Wicklow a popular sea-side town to the south of Dublin. He mentally ran through all of the lame excuses - they could have phoned him; he had been busy and time had just slipped by; it's been so long now, he'd be embarrassed to contact them so he should wait for a birthday or something similar as an excuse. In the end he gave himself a figurative slap across the back of the head and promised himself he would call them at the weekend. If their initial reaction was a little cool that was okay, he had earned some discomfort. Anyway, he knew that they would come around quickly and all would be well.

The benchmarking was now finished. Aiden called the group together and advised them that it would take another day to finalize collating the data. It would then be time to select the sub-group who would stay on for another two weeks and undertake more detailed testing and observation. After the briefing finished, Jimmy signaled for Aiden to accompany him. They crossed the ward to Jimmy's room. He closed the door and said in a hushed tone. "Can you arrange for me to stay on?"

"I guess so. But why would you want to? I thought you'd be bored shitless by now."

"It just happens to be a good time for me to be out of the way for a little while."

The remark started Aiden's mind going in a dozen different directions. *What trouble has he gotten himself into this time?* "Stop being evasive. What have you been up to?" And he added pointedly "Uncle Jimmy?"

"No, no it's nothing like that. If you must know, it's Maureen. She's been putting a lot of pressure on me lately about it being high time I married her."

The look on his uncle's face coupled with his own feeling of relief made Aiden laugh out loud. "You're hiding out from Maureen? You old coward. Well I'm on her side. You've been together for what, ten years? She'll leave you, you know and then where will you be; Lord knows no-one else will have you."

"I know all that and I do love her. It's just that I can't see myself as married."

"Uncle Jimmy, it's time to pay the piper. Get over it."

Jimmy sighed, "Yeah, I guess you're right. Just let me stay a while and get my head around it."

"Okay, but one condition. You're going to call her and tell her where you are and I'm going to listen-in. I had no idea she doesn't know where you are; she's probably frantic."

"No, no... it's not like that. She knows where I am but not for how long. And I wouldn't worry too much about her fretting. We had a wee barney and she showed me the door. Told me to bugger off and not come back unless I was carrying a ring."

More laughter from Aiden. "She threw you out? I'm liking that woman more and more", he teased.

It was easy enough for Aiden to include Jimmy in the group that stayed on and he managed it so that he stayed in his private room. He left Jimmy by himself and spent the rest of the day getting set up for the next phase and settling in the other subjects who were staying on.

CHAPTER 4

The next day, as part of his rounds, he was back with Jimmy, connecting him up for further observation. In this phase, it wasn't just about mapping brain-wave patterns. The procedure also involved a graphic view of the brain that indicated areas of the brain that were activated during various scenarios. From there, some of the subjects would be involved in learning to use feedback techniques to train themselves to re-produce this certain brain states at will.

Aiden had finished connecting Jimmy to the monitors and had confirmed that the data was feeding through. Jimmy was sitting up, relaxed and studying the racing form guide for the day's meeting at Fairyhouse - an odd name but a pretty course situated not far from Dublin. He knew Aiden shared his love for a bet and they often discussed the chances of a horse that one or other fancied. "Hey Aiden, I've found a good one. I'm going to be stuck here all day hooked up to this machine, can you be a good lad and put a bet on for me."

"Sure can. What's its name?"

"It's called Danehill's Pride. It's in the last. Put a hundred on it straight out will you."

Aiden took the form guide and had a look at the field. "Hang on Jimmy, you're losing it. That's an old stager of a hurdler having a warm up on the flat before taking on the jumps in a couple of weeks. It'll go round at 50-1. Don't you want to have it each way or better yet, save your dough?"

"Nah, I was just lying here looking at the form guide, thinking about having a bet and I got a good feeling about this one."

Aiden caught the monitor out of the corner of his eye and what he saw made him take a closer look. "Well one thing's for sure, you've definitely got some sort of a feeling about something."

He could see that the area around the pineal gland was lit up like a Christmas tree. "Funny," he murmured "This is new. I've never seen that sort of effect before." He peered at the monitor lost in his own thoughts. *Very weird...one for the specialists, I guess. I'm just a technician...not here to interpret the output. Bullshit Aiden, you know a damn sight more than the PHD's give you credit for. And that's way outside any known effect.*

Jimmy grabbed his arm, hard, interrupting his musings. He spoke quickly and intently. "Aiden, I need you to do something for me. Don't ask me why - I'm not even sure myself - but I don't want anyone else looking at this. Can you just shut down that thing? Right now. And can you scrap whatever has been recorded by that machine?"

Seeing the look of alarm on Jimmy's suddenly ashen face, he disconnected the apparatus immediately. He tried to sound reassuring. "No problems, okay? Whatever it is showing up there doesn't look like it's got anything to do with any of the studies we're doing here. So if you want it gone, you got it. It'll just take a couple of minutes. If anyone notices a gap, I'll tell them that the monitor went down for a while – it happens."

He had sufficient permissions on the system to easily accomplish the task and set about removing any trace of what had just transpired. But before he erased it from the system, he backed up a copy to his USB flash drive. Just as his uncle could not explain why he wanted the record deleted, Aiden could not say what drove him. Mere curiosity? Maybe that was it. All he knew was that he needed to keep a record of the phenomenon.

By the time that his lunch break had come around, he had pushed the mornings' events to the back of his mind. Not forgotten, just put it aside for now because he had work to do with the other members of the study group. He knew that he would get back to it. He and Jimmy needed to talk. Even if his uncle did not know exactly why had wanted the record erased, he must have some idea as to what scared him and what he didn't want anyone to see.

During his break, as promised, he went down to the betting shop with Jimmy's hundred in hand. Standing in the queue, waiting to place the bet, Aiden mentally debated whether he should follow Jimmy in on the wager with some of his own money. *Jimmy's always been a lucky bugger, especially when he needs some cash. Oh why not...I'll risk twenty...go for the win bet? No...ten each way. Maybe the thing can run a place and I'll have something to show for it. It's not unheard of for a jumper to do well on the flat when fresh back from a spell in the paddock. At least the distance of 3000 meters should suit.*

Back at the clinic, it was mid-afternoon when Aiden heard the rain begin to beat steadily on the windows of the ward. The noise level increased as the shower became a real down-pour. *Wow that was not in this morning's weather forecast. But then again this is Dublin.*

He glanced at his watch. It was an hour before the race was due to be run. He smiled because he knew that Danehill's Pride was a known mud-runner and the more it rained, the more the horse's chances improved. In racing parlance, the horse 'grew another leg' when the track was wet. *Silly turn of*

*phrase when you think about it. But then again, most old
expressions that we toss around don't stand up to too much
analysis. More to the point, if this weather keeps up it will
really shorten the old boy's price. Good thing I got on early at
fixed odds and not starting price odds.*

The rain continued to fall heavily and the track
continued to soften. By the time the horses jumped, the track
was a bog. Jimmy had a radio is his room, so Aiden had joined
him there to listen to the race. Aiden kept one eye on the door
at all times. *This is exactly the sort of time that O'Mara would
pick to come barging in.* The radio's volume was low so as not
to be overheard by those out in the ward and he had to strain to
hear the race-call. It was no surprise that their horse was
toward the tail of the field after the first thousand meters – he
did not have the early speed of some of the other runners. But
as the race unfolded, his stamina began to tell and after two
thousand meters he was mid-field and closing on the leaders.
From then on it was a foregone conclusion. Danehill's Pride hit
the front with 200 meters to go and went on to win by three
lengths. Both men were glad that it had not been a close-run
thing. As it was, it had been hard to stifle a roar of triumph. If
the race had been in the balance up to the finish line, it would
have been impossible to suppress the urge to cheer their horse
home.

As soon as he finished work for the day, Aiden headed
off to the betting shop and collected their winnings. From
there, he rushed straight home and shoved the wad of notes
right to the bottom of his sock drawer. It was a little unnerving
having so much money lying around. For a second time he
made sure his door was locked and the security bolt was firmly
in place. He felt himself becoming almost jittery, like when he'd
had too much coffee. *Jeez, you'll be hyper-ventilating next –*

calm down. He needed to give himself something else to think about and so he set about putting together a meal. Most nights he cooked for himself. He enjoyed it and fancied himself as having a bit of natural flair in the kitchen. And cooking as therapy always worked for him. Tonight though, he kept it very simple – bangers and mash served with packet onion gravy and mushy peas, washed down with a beer.

The distraction worked for a time but after he finished eating, he could not resist any longer. He went into his bedroom, retrieved the cash and spread it out on the bed. It was the most cash he had seen at one time. *Pity I don't have a girlfriend - we could both roll around in it naked*. That not being a viable option, he instead settled for counting and stacking it in little piles. Even though most of it was not his money, he couldn't keep the smile from his face. Eventually, he returned the notes to his sock drawer and went to bed. He couldn't wait to give the money to Jimmy and share in his joy.

He made sure that he arrived early to work next morning and immediately went to Jimmy's room. "There you go Jimmy, five grand," he said handing over the wad of notes. "Not a bad day's pay for lying on your back." He couldn't resist adding a little jibe, "You could buy a nice ring with that and still have change."

"Oh, very funny boyo. As a matter of fact, I might just do that. Here have a hundred – your commission for doing the running around," he offered, waving a note at Aiden.

"No you keep it. I had a bet on it as well – just a little nibble but I'm happy."

"Okay, just so you know that I appreciate you doing the leg-work for me and I'm happy to share a little with you."

Aiden was quiet for a moment and then his eyes held Jimmy's. "What I need you to tell with me is what was on your mind yesterday. You know when you had me erase that recording. I'm going to be busy with the other subjects through to lunch but I'll be back after that and I'd like you to tell me what had you so fired up."

"Alright Aiden, I'll try – not sure it'll make much sense to you, though. Not even sure that it makes sense to me."

CHAPTER 5

The morning rushed by, his lunch break came and went and it was closer to 3 p.m. when he was finally able to get away. Jimmy was wired up and a quick check of the monitor showed that there was no unusual brain activity. He disconnected the apparatus and sat down on the end of the bed.

Without prompting, Jimmy started to speak. "Since you left this morning, I've been thinking about the best way to explain. I'm not sure if you will understand but here goes." He paused, gathering his thoughts and then went on, "You know how people call me lucky – well truth is there's a lot more to it than that. Sometimes, like yesterday, I get a feeling – I can't describe it - I just call it 'that lucky feeling'. It's not something I control really, it just happens. And when I get it, I know I'm going to win. You understand? It's not like maybe I'll win, I know it. And then I win."

Aiden opened his mouth but Jimmy held up his hand to indicate that he hadn't finished. "Trouble is it can be hard to know when it's the real thing – sometimes when I think it's happening, it's just wishful thinking – and then I lose big time. I've gotten better over the years at picking the genuine thing but I can still get it wrong."

Jimmy stopped and Aiden jumped in. "So yesterday you thought that the brain activity was caused by what you were feeling."

Jimmy nodded and waited for Aiden's questions. For a time Aiden just sat, staring out the window but seeing nothing. Had anyone else made a claim like this, he might have laughed out loud. But this wasn't anyone, this was Jimmy. This was a man that he had known all his life, that he trusted, that he loved. None the less, his thoughts raced. *Do I believe him? Could it be true? Luck's not a thing, it's not tangible, it's just luck. Do I even believe in luck? Hell, sometimes I feel like I'm onto a good thing when I have a bet – statistically you're going to be right now and then. But I saw his brain light up – something was going on. Maybe it is real. Could it be?*

He realized that he was getting nowhere. Finally he said, "I'm going to need some time to think about this. I'm not saying I don't believe it. I know you believe it. It's just that the whole thing seems so weird."

"I know, I still think it's weird and I've been living with it for a long time."

As he was about to leave the room, another thought struck him. "Jimmy, yesterday you looked like it was more than just not wanting anyone to see the record of your brain activity, you looked almost scared."

His uncle sat silently for a time and then half nodded to himself as if reaching a decision. "Okay Aiden, I know you and I know that you can't resist a puzzle. Ever since you were a wee lad, you always had to pull things apart to understand how they worked. Soon you're going to decide that you need to pull this thing of mine apart. So I'm going to tell you why I want you to leave it be. I'm going to tell you a story that I've never told anyone." He stopped for a moment, his eyes looking inward as though reading his own thoughts. "You might remember years back when I worked for a time on freighters, shipping cargo out of Galway to ports around Europe. Well, this one trip - it turned out to be my last stint - we docked at Marseilles for a 4-day layover while waiting for a return cargo. I'd just been paid so I was out on the town looking for fun. Marseilles is a place where you could get anything you wanted if you had the dough, so me and the rest of the boys spent the first couple of days getting up to the sort of mischief that you might expect. And no, I'm not about to tell you about it - except to say that those French gals do have something about them."

Again he stopped but this time, Aiden could see from his half-smile that Jimmy's thoughts had slipped off down some pleasant side-alley. Aiden gave him a look and pulled himself back on track with an almost physical effort. "Anyway, back then I liked to gamble on cards more than the horses and after a while, I decided that it would be a bit of a lark to go and get in on a game. I'd heard about an illegal gaming house down near the docks that was supposed to be okay. By that I mean that if you had a win, you could actually get out with your money and all of you bodily parts intact. So I went to this joint and got a seat in a poker game. There were five of us playing, three Frenchmen, a German and me and a few others were hanging around, watching the action. When I joined in the game, I could see that one of the Frenchies was doing pretty well. I wasn't a particularly good player but I liked the game – things like the betting tactics, the bluff, trying to read other players. You know, kind of like it was the challenge not the money. I'd have been happy just to hold my own but half-a-dozen hands in I got the feeling. I really felt good about my hand. I'd had a few drinks and was half pissed so I went in pretty hard. And I won. A few hands later, I felt it again and I won again. That's how it went all night. People came and went from the table and the only ones who did any good were me and the same Frenchie that had been winning when I first sat down. It was dawn when I left the table and I had three grand in my pocket and back then that was worth a lot more than it is now."

At that moment they both heard beyond the door the rattling and clinking heralding the imminent arrival of the tea-trolley in the ward outside their door.

"I'd kill for a cuppa," announced Jimmy, hanging his tongue out for emphasis.

Aiden wanted him to finish the story but put aside his impatience. Slave driver. Let the poor man have a drink. This is hard enough for him as it is. Besides, Mrs. Callahan will barge into the room in any event. He glanced at his watch. She's running late today, so at least she won't want to hang around for a gossip. As if on cue, there was a quick rap on the door and without waiting for an invitation, Mrs. Callahan, the tea-lady, popped her head around the door and announced, "No time to stay for a chat today boys – two will it be then?" They both nodded and her head withdrew from the doorway. They could hear her humming to herself as she bustled about pouring their cups of tea. They did not have to tell her how they took it. She had a quite unusual ability; she was able to remember everyone's preferences after being told just once.

They drank their tea in silence. Finally, Jimmy put down his cup and resumed his story. "Okay, let me backtrack to the game and I want you to pay attention – this part is important. I told you that there were a few guys watching the game; well one of them, he looked Spanish or Italian stayed there the whole night. Everyone else sort of drifted in and out but not him. I noticed him because he was watching the French guy who was winning – sort of studying him like. At first I thought that they might be together and might have some sort of a scam going but then after I win a couple of hands, he starts focusing on me as well. About half-way through the night, we all took a break to get a drink and take a leak and he left the room for five minutes. I think he made a phone call because twenty minutes later, another fella joins him and they're both watching us. This second fella looks right out of place in this sort of a joint. He's sort of distinguished looking and his clothes look seriously expensive - you know, seems more like a banker than a gambler. So there we are me and the Frenchman sort of taking it in turns with the big pots. The others were winning a few hands but hardly ever the big hands. Most of the time the way the cards are playing either me or the Frenchman were throwing in our hands when the other one was winning. But then there were two hands with pretty big pots where we both stayed in. I won them both and I can see that the Frenchman can't believe it. He's looking at me with this really puzzled look on his face. At the time I didn't understand why. Anyway, after about an hour I see the banker type getting up to leave. He gives the other guy a little nod and goes out the door without saying a word. It was weird – a bit creepy too. So then later when I get up to leave, this guy who'd been watching comes up to me and he hands me a business card. All the card has on it is the name 'Josep' and a phone number. He tells me that he represents some rich businessmen who are looking to hire a bunch of expert card players - that they want to stake these players and take them to casinos around Europe to play. He says that I should call the number on the card and talk some more with them – that there was a lot of money to be made. He was pretty smooth but I didn't like it. He got a look in his eyes when he talked about 'expert card players'. It all felt wrong. So I told him, yeah that sounds great, just to get him off me." Jimmy stopped and went to the window. Aiden was hooked. He wanted his uncle to finish his story but forced himself to be patient and wait.

Jimmy rested his hands on the sill and without turning from the window, started up again. "Like I said I'm not that much of a player and the way he was watching us, he should have seen that. It should have been obvious to him that I'd been lucky not skillful, if he was really out recruiting top-line players and all. Then I started thinking that Frenchie was not that good either – he was pretty blessed too that night. That got me wondering that maybe I'm not the only one who gets 'that lucky feeling' – maybe the Frenchie get's it too. Next thing I see is that this Josep guy has gone over to the Frenchman and is handing him a card as well. That made up my mind. I definitely wasn't the only one with the gift and somebody was out there trying to find us."

Jimmy turned back to face Aiden. He was nearing the end of his account. "As soon as I could, I got out of there. I decided it was time to do a runner. I didn't even go back to the ship. I found a driver who was taking a truck up to Paris and hitched a ride. From there, I made my way back to Dublin."

He walked over to where Aiden sat, put his hands on his nephews shoulders as if he wanted the physical contact to underline what he was about to say. "So, Aiden, that's the whole of it. Do you get it? I have this peculiar thing going on and it looks like some others do as well. And on top of that there's someone out there looking for us. I don't know what they really want and I don't care to find out."

"But you've avoided them all these years then?"

"Yeah. For my part, I've never needed much, so I've been careful not to get greedy. I win a little here and there and I keep my head pulled in. There's another thing I want you to understand. You used the word 'scared' earlier but you're wrong with that. It's not fear at all, it's like I just don't want any part of someone poking around my business and my loved ones. No-one's going to own me - that's against my nature. I do what I do when I want and I answer to no-one. Except maybe Maureen," he added with a small grin, trying to lighten things a little.

Before Aiden could speak, his uncle became serious again. "I don't want you to say anything more right now. Don't want you to ask me any questions. It's your knock-off time, so I just want you to go home and mull all this over. We can talk tomorrow."

He knew his uncle was right, so he simply got up from the end of the bed, gave Jimmy a reassuring pat on the arm and left the room, closing the door behind him. He could not face dealing with anyone in the ward right now, so he slipped out the back door, walked quickly to the parking lot and was away into the evening traffic before anyone could corner him. But not entirely unobserved; Simon O'Mara, lurking in the shadows, watched him depart.

CHAPTER 6

Aiden picked up a pizza and a couple of beers on the way home. Tonight was not one for cooking therapy - he just wanted to start picking apart the bizarre events of the past couple of days. The first beer disappeared in no time. *God I needed that - maybe I should have gone for a shot of Jameson's. So now, how do I make any sense out of all this?* He opened another beer, put the pizza box on his coffee table, threw back the lid and took a slice of pizza. He sat back, eating slowly and let his thoughts roam free. He liked to think of himself as being practical and was uncomfortable with where this thought process was taking him.

"I'm not superstitious. This is nonsense", he declared adamantly to the walls around him. Yeah right Aiden, he came back at himself – scratch an Irishman and find someone who is at least a little bit of a believer. It's cultural and there's no getting away from it. Reluctantly but with an increasing degree of acceptance, he recognized that this was especially true when it came to the concept of luck. There was so much that was considered as the essence of being Irish that was tightly bound to the idea of luck. And the notion that luck was something that you could possess or acquire. It started with 'the luck of the Irish' and went on from there – lucky four leaf clover, lucky leprechauns. Okay, so I draw the line at believing in the 'little people' but there are other things that I don't entirely discount and if I'm honest with myself, the idea that someone can be lucky or unlucky is something that I can't bring myself to dismiss. I've known people like that – everyone has – they win lucky dips and even lotteries, they get the right card at the right time. And it's not just Jimmy, I've known others – everybody knows somebody like that. Some people even reckon that I'm a bit of a lucky type myself. Yeah, right! Okay so if it is true, what does it mean? Where do I go with it?

He'd unconsciously gotten up from the couch and was pacing around the room. His thoughts were jumbled and could almost feel his mental wheels starting to spin in the dirt. *This is going nowhere; I need to get my mind off it for a while.*

He turned on the TV and watched the evening news broadcast, trying to focus on finishing his pizza. The news was the usual run of tragedy, interspersed with politicians talking a lot but saying very little. Listening to the talking heads worked for a short while but then started to annoy him. He shut off the TV and put on some music instead. He closed his eyes and tried to clear out all thoughts. When he had calmed himself, he felt ready to return to the conundrum. Aloud he told himself, "Alright, first things first. Let's try to do this in at least a half-arsed scientific way."

He opened another beer, picked up a notebook and pen and installed himself back on the couch ready to take notes. He often found that jotting down his thoughts helped him straighten things out. *Let's begin with the theory that this ability is real. So what is it? Okay, it began with that weird brain activity that was centered on the pineal gland.* He knew it was only a dozen or so years ago that it was established that the pineal is the source of production of melatonin. With that thought, he had a momentary twinge of professional guilt. Melatonin was thought to have a function in balancing circadian rhythms and he might have been a bit hasty when he said that Jimmy's reaction was outside of anything that they were working on. He quickly dismissed the feeling. What he saw had nothing to do with production or secretion of a hormone. *So one of its functions in known but is that all it* does. *There might be more to its purpose than just that. Going back in history they thought so anyway. In completely different parts of the world and in completely different cultures, they were fascinated by the pineal. It was seen as highly mysterious and mystical. Descartes studied it extensively and he believed that it could be where the soul was located – he thought that it was the link between the mind and the body. In yoga, it has been called the third eye. And strangely, the pineal has been found to be similar to retinal cells in lower animals. Believers of the third eye concept held that the pineal was dormant but with meditation, it could become the means to unlocking the power of extrasensory perception.*

He might be a skeptic when it came to the supernatural but he'd always been of the opinion that there might be something to ESP. *Maybe it's like that – not reading thoughts but reading the future. Some sought of prescience.* "Yeah, nicely dressed up with pseudo-science - sounds much better than fortune-telling or soothsaying," he told himself a trifle ruefully. "And way better than clairvoyant – always saw that is a synonym of charlatan." He was letting his attention drift along aimlessly and admonished himself with terse thought. *Back on task Aiden.*

As the night wore on he continued alternating between thinking to himself and thinking aloud. That was fine by him – he worked better that way. *Okay then, let's go with prescience. Like when Jimmy's horse won after the rains came. His uncle didn't know what was at work but maybe he unconsciously 'saw' it was going to rain. Once the track became a bog, it was no great surprise that Danehill's Pride saluted.* "Yeah, I like that."

It gave him comfort that he could bring an element of logic to the outcome, if not its precursor. Aiden never ceased to marvel at the wonder that is the human brain. They were beginning to understand so much more about the brain but with every advance, it seemed that there was even more that was still unknown. To him, it was like the exploration of the ocean depths or even the exploration of the universe. When you work in the business of studying the brain, no matter your role, you hear and read so many amazing stories about this magnificent organ; things that made the saying 'mind over matter' so apt but at the same time so inadequate a description. He didn't go around espousing the notion but deep down he believed that its potential was unlimited. When in the midst of their experiments he was passionate about his work and felt blessed to be part of a leading-edge program. But right at this moment, he felt he might be out of his depth. He was struggling to accept that the brain activity he observed was directly connected to the onset of Jimmy's lucky feeling. It was daunting and he knew what he baulked at. If he took that mental step, the logical progression forced him to acknowledge that he might have recorded an event as outlandish as prescience in action.

He shook his head as if he could physically eject the negative thoughts and again gave himself a mental dressing-down. You're at it again Aiden – doubting yourself, seeing all the reasons why things can't be – ever the pessimist. But why sell yourself short? So what if you're a technician and not a scientist or a neurologist. You're a professional with plenty of expertise in the field. And you're the one that's spends day in day out with the groups, seeing the action first hand. If anyone is going to be first to see an unusual event, then it's going to be you. This is Practical Science 101. You tested the hypothesis against available empirical evidence. And it looks to support it. He ticked off the events as they had unfolded:

Jimmy says he's feeling good about the chances of a longshot and wants to bet on it;

When he gets the feeling, the monitor shows very strange brain activity;

The 'prediction' turns out to be accurate;

Jimmy describes his hunch as the result of 'that lucky feeling' and says it's something that happens every now and then.

He says that when he gets the true feeling, he always wins – no exception.

Okay so let's say this prescience is some sought of innate ability. And from what Jimmy has seen, he's not unique – there are others with the talent. Then it might be somehow genetic – it might be extremely rare but still something natural that can be inherited. But now what? I'm back to square one – back to the same question that I started with. What do I do about all this?

He was starting to feel the effects the beer and fresh thoughts would not come. "Give it away, Aiden", he told himself. "Time to sleep on it."

He expected that sleep would not come quickly and anticipated a night of tossing and turning. But the beer buzz did its work and he was asleep in minutes. As sometimes happens when he slept on a problem, he woke at 4 a.m. with a plan forming and a new feeling of resolve. He knew how he wanted to proceed. Now he just had to convince his uncle and that was not going to be at all easy.

He decided to get an early start on the day, so he reset his alarm for 6 a.m. rather than the usual 7 a.m., rolled over and dozed until the alarm sounded. He wanted to be as calm and relaxed as possible when he faced his uncle so he started by taking a long leisurely shower, humming the Corr's cover of Fleetwood Mac's 'Dreams'. Then he put together a favorite breakfast; lightly poached eggs – they had to be a little runny in the middle – served with buttered toast. Normally this was a meal restricted to a weekend when he had more time. He accompanied by a pot of leaf tea – he preferred it to coffee first thing in the day. And it had to be leaf tea, not a tea-bag. He took it black without sugar and made enough for at least two cups.

As he ate, he planned his approach. He decided that he should treat this as a cross between a debate and a sales pitch. He would need to show the benefits of what he proposed. As well, he needed to anticipate all of Jimmy's worries and arguments and be able to counter them. He made notes and read them through several times, rehearsing aloud.

The minutes raced by too quickly and he was feeling under-prepared when a glance at his watch told him it was time to head to work. His ride to the clinic passed a blur. All the way in, he continued to concentrate on his spiel and gave scant attention to the traffic around him. *Not very smart. Bit lucky to get here in one piece.* He parked his bike and entered the complex. A quick check of the wall clock told him that as per plan, he was early. He stopped for a moment in the foyer looking about him but no-one else was around. *Typical, here I am putting in extra time and nobody's here to notice. Expected to earn a few brownie points for the next pay review. Oh yeah, like that's likely. That old prick, O'Mara, can always be relied on to notice any screw-ups but he's blind to anything positive that might go on.* His thoughts moved on. *No point standing around out here wasting time – win or lose, it's showtime with Jimmy.*

He went through the ward, rapped on the door, took a deep breath and with a perfunctory "Hope you're decent," barged into Jimmy's room. He wasted no time on pleasantries and started in on his speech as he closed the door behind him.

"Uncle Jimmy, you need to hear what I have to say. And I you need to keep an open mind, okay. I've been thinking this though most of the night. Now, this thing you have, we just have to find out more about it. We're in the perfect place here to do it - we have the equipment and the time. I can help you recognize it – to know when it's happening for real. And what's more, we might be able to train you to get more control over it – surely that would be a good thing for you, wouldn't it? Look, I know you said you wanted to stay unnoticed but just finding out more won't change that. It doesn't mean you have to go out winning big-time or anything. Besides, you don't even know if anyone would even care – if 'they' still exist, they must have given up on you by now. So if you wanted to use it more then, well I think..."

His eager justification trailed off, the rest of his pitch forgotten. It had finally registered with him that Jimmy's face had borne a look of resignation when he entered the room. Now his uncle wore a small smirk.

"My turn now Aiden, you don't have to go on. You know what they say – when you make the sale, it's time to shut up. You're not the only one who's been trying to think this through. I already told you that I know what you're like - that I know you need to work out what makes things tick. So I knew before you got here that this was coming – that you'd want to pull it apart and try to see its innards."

Aiden was stunned to silence by the direction that events were taking.

Jimmy went on. "But I worked out something else last night – I want to know as well. I'm ready, you see. I've had this gift for a long time now and I thought that just having it was enough; that it wouldn't be right if I looked at it too closely. Sort of like testing fate. Maybe by questioning it, I'd lose it - it might somehow go away. Probably my doubts were mostly a case of good old Irish superstition. So now I've made up my mind. I've decided that I'd like to find out what I have and how far it can go." Then with a wink and a smile. "And if all hell breaks loose, well then, it'll be for the devil to take the hindmost."

CHAPTER 7

Lukas Muller sat in a high-backed leather chair leaning forward with his forearms resting on the dark wood of the polished walnut desk. He had tired of constantly travelling around and for the time being had made Brussels his base. His residence was a suite at a high class hotel. Like his father, he shied away from the overly ostentatious. But on the other hand, more so than his father, he enjoyed the creature comforts that wealth could buy. So whilst it might not be considered the absolute best accommodation in the city, it was not far short.

Brussels suited him nicely. He was fluent in French, German and English, so language was no problem. The location meant that when necessary, he could reach other parts of Europe with ease. He enjoyed the mix of its historical culture and its growing cosmopolitan feel. And best of all, these days there were so many politicians and lobbyists around with lavish expense accounts that he could live very well and still easily maintain his anonymity. The staff at the hotel was top of the line – they knew that he was a stickler for privacy and thus far their conduct had been faultless. Another bonus was that the hotel provided its guests with the use of a boardroom style meeting room and today his lieutenants were coming in for their regular monthly meeting.

He had finished scanning the summary reports of the state of his unique and extraordinary gambling empire that his executive assistant Philippe Durand had brought to him. As was customary, he showed no emotion as he pushed the papers across the desk to where his assistant sat. "Thank you Philippe. Is everything in readiness for the meeting?"

"All is arranged. The team will be assembled and ready to present to you in an hour."

"Good, then I will see you there in one hour," said Muller dismissing him.

"Yes, very good sir," Durand responded, rising and taking his leave.

As the door closed Muller sat back in his chair and crossed his arms. Alone now, he allowed himself a small smile of satisfaction at the progress he had made as head of the organization. He would wait for each man to present his formal report but based on the summaries, he knew that things were running as expected. With all in readiness, he let his thoughts drift back to the day when his time had finally come.

It was five years ago. His father, Andre, summonsed his gambling team to his inner sanctum and declared that he was handing over the day to day running of the business to Lukas. Consistent with his penchant for treating the operation as a corporate entity he informed the group that Lukas was to be CEO and assume all power and authority that had previously resided with him. Then with tongue firmly in cheek, he announced that had just created a new role of Executive Chairman and as he adjudged that he was the sole qualified candidate, had promoted himself to the position. Henceforth, he would be involved purely in an advisory capacity.

After announcing the changes, he had dismissed the others and then set out to explain his reasons in more depth to Lukas.

"I know that you surprised, but I've given this a lot of thought", he said. "The world has changed." A pause, then, "I've seen too many men stay on too long in positions of power - to a point where they become a hindrance. I don't want that to happen to what I have built. You are ready and I judge it to be time for a generational change." Another pause, longer and his look reflective, "Besides, with Josep gone, it is not the same – it does not give me the same satisfaction."

Lukas could see that his father had drifted off, deep into his memories and so quietly rose and slipped out of the room, leaving him to his reverie.

As Lukas left his father's room, he let the feeling of elation wash over him. He respected his father but it was inescapable that his father's heart had not been in the business for some time now. More importantly, whilst he acknowledged the wealth that had been generated, he firmly believed that his father's methods were slow, ponderous and outmoded. A good example in his eyes was father's reluctance to move Ferrer on as soon as his usefulness began to wane. His father seemed to have a near devotion to the man. At the very least he treated him far too much like an equal, not an employee.

For his own part, he was certain that he could drive the business to heights that were far beyond anything his father could envision. He had ideas, innovations that he was keen to implement – things that his father had not been interested in trying. Moreover, he believed that his father was not hardnosed enough. In the modern world, you had to be tough to win and only winners are rewarded.

Lukas had no way of knowing that some of what was running through his father's mind was in stark contrast to his own thoughts. Having mentioned his name, Andre thoughts had turned to Josep. He had never told his son the full story regarding Josep – perhaps that had been a mistake – not that it mattered any longer. His loyal accomplice had retired a rich man 18 months earlier and had purchased a villa on the coast just outside of Barcelona. There he spent his time happily tending his small patch of vegetables, olive trees and grape vines.

Andre knew that for his son, this choice of lifestyle only served to confirm Lukas' view that Ferrer had always lacked ambition and vision. "You can take the man out of Catalonia but you can't take Catalonia out of the man" was a favorite line that his son used when referring to Josep. To Andre on the other hand, being able to recognize and follow a path that brought you happiness was a sign of wisdom and he sometimes envied the man that had been his subordinate but also his friend over many years.

He sighed, thinking that this was yet another example, perhaps, of generational change. He hoped he was wrong about Lukas' ruthless streak when it came to money but in his heart of hearts, knew that it was a deep flaw in his son. It represented another clear difference between them - Lukas had not understood that to Andre, it had never been just about money.

CHAPTER 8

Soon after taking control, Lukas began overhauling the business. He decided that he needed be released from day to day drudgery to focus matters of strategy. And so as his first action he had begun his search for an assistant. His requirements were quite specific – whilst the appropriate skills were important, what was paramount was finding someone with absolute discretion. Hiring Philippe Durand had proven to be as inspired a choice as it had been serendipitous.

Muller had been reviewing candidates for weeks and was beginning to despair of finding the right person when Durand had come to his attention. His name was mentioned in the morning newspaper as an unresponsive witness in a Courts Marshall of a French Army Colonel. The Colonel was on trial for misappropriating army supplies and selling them on the black market and Durand had been the Colonel's staff sergeant. The army investigators were convinced that he had been a willing participant in the racket but in truth, the Army was really only interested in taking down the officer. The prosecutors believed that corroborating testimony from Durand would make absolutely watertight an already strong case. They subjected Durand to enormous pressure through a variety of threats to get him to turn on the Colonel. What impressed Muller was that the army was able neither to implicate Durand nor get him to testify against his commanding officer. In the wash-up, the Colonel was jailed and Durand was encouraged to accept a discharge.

The thing that clinched it for Muller was that Durand was known to him. They had been at boarding school together and even back then, Durand had a bit of a reputation as someone who worked the angles. Not that they had ever been more the fellow students but that was of no consequence. He could not think of anyone, male or female that he felt particularly close to. Not that this ever bothered him; he had never wanted for company - or gratification - whenever he felt the need.

Muller succeeded in locating Durand in Paris. He gave him only the vaguest outline of the business but the man was happy to accept the position based solely on the hefty pay on offer. Over the next six months, as he continued to demonstrate his capability and prudence, Muller gradually brought him across more and more of the operation until finally he was fully across the true nature of the organization.

His next step was to expand his support group. He needed expert help to realize his vision. His father thought small and was able to get away with a very small team. In those days Andre himself looked after most of the 'housekeeping' and handled the financials of the business with the help of an accountant and a lawyer, both kept on retainer. Ferrer ran the 'stable' of gamblers. This included being the 'spotter' and recruiter of possible new talent. It was also his responsibility to confirm that new recruits genuinely possessed the gift before finally bringing them on board and putting them through training. Lukas himself served his apprenticeship by helping out in all facets of the business.

Under his regime things were now very different. In addition to Durand he had brought on board four full-time managers. They were the men who would report to him today. The only function that remained on an 'as needed' retainer basis was that of his legal advisors. Even here he had made changes. He had moved his business to a firm that had a reputation on the street of having a number of clients of dubious character.

Muller's thoughts returned to the present as he checked the time on his wristwatch. It was a high end Swiss classic and another example of his liking for fine things. Its quality and workmanship gave him pleasure every time he looked at it. The meeting was due to commence shortly, so he left his suite and caught the elevator to the 12th level where the executive business center was located. The conference room was at the rear of the floor.

As was only appropriate, Durand and the other four lieutenants were already gathered around the board-room table. Muller liked punctuality or to be more accurate, tardiness displeased him greatly – a trait that was well known to all in the room. He took his place in the seat of power, at the head of the table and surveyed his team with a feeling that bordered on smugness. He had assembled a highly competent group and basked in the glow of his own shrewdness. After a perfunctory "Good morning gentlemen," he nodded to signal that the meeting should commence.

The first to report was his accountant - a Swiss-German named Thomas Weber. Although Muller was trained in finance, he did not share his father's passion for numbers and so had brought on Weber to handle the chore. His was a high cash flow business and Weber had proved to be particularly astute in managing investments in the short-term money market as well as handling the longer term strategies.

The remuneration structure that his father had set up was well thought through and Lukas had retained it. The business bore the cost of staking the stable of players and they retained 30% of their monthly winnings. The remainder was then applied to cover all expenses, including the very generous salaries paid to four of the men assembled here. The profit after these outlays was shared in diminishing proportions between himself, his father and Nick Kelly, the man who now ran the stable of gamblers. Kelly earned more than the others. He was critical to the success of growing the operation. Not only did possess the gift but it was his role also to find and vet new talent.

Weber would communicate only a very high level view to this forum – the more granular view was reserved for Muller only. Indeed, this was true for all presentations. Muller accepted that to do their jobs properly his men needed to know something about what was happening within the business but his natural reticence meant that he preferred to share as little as possible.

He used the same jargon as Muller – those with the gift were known as 'players' or 'talent' and as a group they were the 'stable'. As expected, the report indicated that the business was in good health; all performance indicators were solid there was nothing material that was unfavorable. In summary, since his father's days, costs had increased by 60% but the rise had been more than offset by extra income from a larger stable and an increase in average winnings. Muller could see that the overall position meant that his monthly share of profits would to continuing to be at least €400,000 each month. When added to the gains from his portfolio of personal investments – also managed for him by Weber – he had become quite wealthy. Better yet, his affluence was still growing.

Muller then turned to Nick Kelly. Ferrer had originally discovered Kelly in a casino in Denmark. It emerged that he was an American of Irish ancestry who had spent the greater portion of his adult life in Europe. He had left the US hurriedly after learning that he had worn out his welcome with a pair of connected casino bosses in Las Vegas. He was recruited to the team and quickly came to Lukas' notice. Although an unrepentant scoundrel, he had a natural charm about him and carried that indefinable aura that marked a leader. When Muller was seeking a replacement for Josep, Kelly was an obvious choice. In Muller's opinion, in a short time he had developed into far a superior operator to his predecessor.

Kelly rose to speak. As usual his narrative was concise. "There are no material issues at present and the players are happy with their lot. You might have got wind of a few grumbles a couple of weeks ago, when there was some talk about an extra bonus for very high wins but I've put that to rest – they know that they are already very well off."

He glanced at his notes and continued. "Our diversification into other forms of gambling is evolving. In addition to as our main staple of poker, we now have players involved in roulette, black jack, baccarat and horse racing. I'm confident that the future looks bright in all these areas."

There were nods of support around the table.

"Moving on to the matter of finding and qualifying new recruits. Of the three recent prospects, I have established that two do not come up to the mark. If they possess the gift at all, it is limited and far too erratic for our needs. They have been paid off for their trouble and I've let them go. The remaining candidate – his best performances are with roulette - is undergoing further testing but at this point I'm confident that he will come through and join the stable. This will bring the stable size to eighteen."

Muller noted with satisfaction that this represented an increase of six since he had taken over. Kelly went on to add that he had two more people under observation but that it was very early in the process and he would update progress at the next meeting. He concluded his presentation by saying, "Our experiment with George and picking winning stocks is going well. Not surprising, I guess. Many would agree that the stock market is really another form of gambling - just that it involves people who think it's a business pursuit," he said with a wry smile. Kelly was the only one of the group who seemed to be able to get away with a little levity around Muller.

For his part, Muller was pleased with this new direction. He had formed a view from his own observations that people with the gift seemed to do better in the form of gaming that interested them the most. A further observation is that the players tended to specialize - it was rare for them to be effective in more than one variety of gambling. In this case they'd gone a step further with an experiment with the stock market.

This foray into stocks was a fortuitous accident. George Marlow was previously a stock broker who had lost his license when caught out being involved in insider trading. He'd been spotted by Kelly playing roulette and brought on board. But when being taken through the induction process he performed poorly. Kelly was convinced Marlow truly had the gift and was nonplussed at his below par results. It was during a break when he noticed Marlow going through the business section of the newspaper that he had an inspiration.

He took his idea to Muller. "I know that this will sound a little strange but I think I've found out why George is not living up to expectation. I'm sure his ability is real but he's been using it on the wrong game. You might think I'm crazy but I think that his natural forte is the stock market."

Kelly waited for the expected rebuke. It didn't come. Muller might be a cold-blooded fish but his self-held belief that he was an innovator was actually close to the mark. He embraced the idea immediately and instructed Kelly to find a way to confirm his hunch. Over the next month, Kelly had assigned Marlow the task of targeting stocks, looking for big winners and to his relief the gift began to manifest itself with regularity.

The new direction was now starting to pay off with solid earnings flowing through. The ultimate vote of confidence was when Muller instructed Weber to follow Marlow's tips with some of his private funds. Beyond the profits, it amused Muller that they had moved into 'legitimate' business and he took great pride in sharing this new direction with his father. Right now Muller did not have sufficient resources to do more in the area but he was convinced that this was an avenue worth exploring further. He had earmarked for the future the need to expand their spotting activities into some of the world's major bourses.

Next to report was David Lawson, who held the entirely new role of Training and Research. This activity was a recent innovation that Muller had introduced some six months earlier. The position had two main aims and both were entirely pragmatic. Muller was not particularly interested in the how and why of the gift. It was there to be exploited. What he wanted was to grow his stable and to improve its per capita earnings. So Lawson's core task consisted of developing and implementing better training methods; better methods to drive the stable to improve control of their talent. The secondary focus was to find a more reliable way to identify those with the gift.

Muller believed the program would result in increased effectiveness and therefore profit growth. When he set up the role he understood that this was a new field and it would take time to make genuine headway but nonetheless, he was starting to become impatient. He was eager to hear whether Lawson was making any concrete progress and unconsciously, leaned forward slightly in his chair in anticipation. This month's summary implied some advancement but the report was sketchy; he wanted detail.

The report did not begin auspiciously. "Let me start with training. I'm working with Nick Kelly and together we are conducting an intensive review of the approach that we use at present. Right now we are really still in the analysis phase and no conclusions had been reached as yet."

Seeing Muller's mouth tighten Lawson added, somewhat lamely. "But we are getting close to the end of the review and I'm sure that we will produce a number of excellent recommendations." When this failed to move Muller, he changed tack and hurried on. "On a more positive note, I'm getting good traction in researching the genealogy of those with the gift. Even though it is early days, I have gone back five generation thus far and I've already found that two of our men that have the gift have a common ancestor. This is very encouraging support to our supposition that the gift might be an inherited ability. My next step will..." He trailed off as Muller made a cutting gesture with his hand. In his eagerness to please, Lawson had started to reveal too much detail.

"Very good David. Enough for now. You and I will pick this up later."

From Muller's tone, Lawson knew that things were a long way short of being 'very good'.

The final member of his team did not report to the group. Renzo Olivadi was his head of security and any matters that might need to be discussed were for Muller's ears only. One reason for this was that unbeknown to the group, part of Olivadi's job was to investigate everyone who was part of his operation. The purpose was to find those hidden secrets that each would desperately like to keep buried. Muller felt much more comfortable if he had some final leverage over his people. Olivadi was ex-Interpol. Nothing was ever proven but suggestions of corruption and connections to organized crime saw him forced out of Interpol under a cloud. Nonetheless, he had been able to maintain links to a number of Interpol operatives particularly those who were like he had been - open to providing information for a fee. With his connections Olivadi had proved to be very, very effective at uncovering the kind of information that Muller sought. As well, his contacts into the criminal underworld turned out to be extremely helpful on occasions when Muller required the services of less than savory characters.

They moved on to talk briefly about general business. There was nothing of any importance that anyone wanted to raise, so Lukas wound up the meeting.

"Gentlemen, you are performing to my satisfaction, but I want you to exceed my expectations – I want to be delighted."

Everyone around the table knew of Muller's penchant for injecting snippets of corporate-speak into their meetings but they also knew that Muller was serious about his message – utterly serious.

CHAPTER 9

End of shift had finally arrived. The other researchers had gone for the day and all was quiet. Aiden could start his investigation in earnest. His approach would be to try to reproduce the effect by mirroring as much as possible of the circumstances of the previous episode.

Aiden wired Jimmy up to the monitor and handed him the sports section from the Irish Independent newspaper. It contained a form guide for an upcoming race meeting.

"Okay Jimmy, I want you to go through the paper, just like you normally would and tell me if you start to feel anything."

"You know I'm happy to give it a try," he replied lying back on the bed and wriggling his shoulders into the pillows, trying to more comfortable. "But like I told you, it's not something that I can control very well. I can't just turn on when I want to. Mostly it just happens."

Aiden gestured toward the newspaper. "Understood. But we have to start somewhere."

Jimmy got the message and began to studiously read through the racing guide, horse by horse, event by event; his brow creased in concentration as if willing something to happen. He reached the end of the paper and looked across to Aiden more in hope than expectation.

Aiden shook his head. "Nothing out of the ordinary showing up on the monitor."

"Alright, I'll run through again," offered Jimmy. "I thought there might have been a little twinge like the start of something with a horse in the third race."

He returned his focus to the paper. Minutes later he looked up excitedly. "Yeah I think I'm starting to get the feeling – it is in the third. I'm getting really keen on number 7. Can you see anything?"

Another head shake from Aiden. "Sorry Jimmy – there's nothing at all."

"There must be. You must've hooked it up wrong."

"I haven't made any mistakes. I do this all the time and I can see from the display that it's working as it should. Just keep trying."

"I bloody have been trying and it feels to me like I'm getting it. Maybe it just can't be seen on your equipment. Maybe the other day was just some sort of a coincidence - like something else was showing up in my head – but not what we thought – not the feeling."

The same discouraging thought had occurred to Aiden. But hearing it said aloud prodded his stubborn streak into action. He refused to accept it. "No Jimmy, it couldn't be a fluke. You having the feeling and me seeing a reaction that I've never seen before right at the same time. It couldn't be a coincidence."

Aiden had a very quick and analytical brain and even as he was speaking, he was weighing things up in his mind. By the end of his declaration his bullish stance was ebbing fast. "Surely it couldn't," he appealed a trifle lamely to no-one in particular.

Jimmy was well aware that Aiden's earlier conviction was waning. He had seen it happen before. Aiden could be a real terrier when a puzzle captured his imagination. But he possessed an unhelpful and unfounded tendency toward self-doubt. And when his optimism fled, pessimism was waiting eagerly in the wings. He needed to rescue the situation before it deteriorated any further. "Hey buck up boyo. If it was easy, somebody else would have figured it all out by now. I was just getting a little frustrated, you know. Of course what you saw on the machine was me getting the lucky feeling in all its glory. So let's get back to it before we talk ourselves out of getting a handle on the sweetest little gift that I can think of."

As usual, Aiden found his uncle's enthusiasm infectious and he found himself smiling. Jimmy was one of the few people who could bring him out of a blue funk. "Okay. Thanks. I'm sorry I started to lose it but I'm back and I know we'll crack this thing."

"Look Aiden, I think I know part of the problem. You said you wanted to mirror the last time but like I told you, the feeling mostly comes on when I'm relaxed – and right now we're both wound up tight. I'm trying too hard and that's causing me to have a bad case of wishful thinking. Now I know a good way to unwind a bit – just like I'd do at home when looking at the race form. Why don't you nip down to the nearest pub and bring me back a half-bottle of the hard stuff. We'll both have a dram and then I'll try to pretend you're not even here. On second thoughts, if it's for both of us, you'd better make it a proper bottle – no point taking short-cuts."

Jimmy said it with a wink but Aiden knew it was a good plan. He certainly would not say no to a drink and it might just do the trick. Still, he wanted to let his uncle know that he was really back on track and the best way to demonstrate was to indulge in a bit of the banter that was always the hallmark of their conversations. "You old reprobate. Is there nothing you wouldn't do for a drink? You've probably just been faking it up till now, so that you could wangle a whiskey out of it."

Jimmy joined in the repartee. "I'm deeply wounded. As if I could be so conniving with my favorite nephew. Well, maybe I would have if I'd thought of it earlier."

Aiden returned 20 minutes later clutching the bottle of Bushmills – his uncle's favorite - and two tumblers that he had commandeered from the kitchen. He poured them each a solid nip and simultaneously, they took a long pull of the smooth amber liquid. The "aahh" that followed was also in sync and the slap-stick nature of the moment drew a laugh from them.

"That's better."

"Much"

"You've not told me yet what you think the lucky feeling is all about," said Jimmy while pouring another shot into their glasses.

Aiden started tentatively, choosing his words carefully. "I've been trying to think my way through it – trying to come up an explanation that's not altogether half-arsed. And obviously, I don't know anything for sure - right now it's only speculation." He saw Jimmy's look of exasperation, eyes raised to the ceiling and stopped. He gestured with hands raised, palms outward, took a breath and started over. "Sorry. Enough of the disclaimers. I'm working on the theory that it is a natural phenomenon. The brain is an extraordinary thing and there is so much that we don't know about it. But I'm thinking that it might be like prescience – you know, like you get to know something that's in the future that makes the odds of winning a certainty."

As he went on Jimmy was pleased to see Aiden's confidence growing with each word he uttered. "From the little we know it seems to fit. I believe that your brain has a faculty or an extra sense that only a very small number of people have. And even if someone has it, they might not ever know it. Maybe like other senses, it can be stronger for some more than others."

"Okay, you know much more about this brain stuff than I do but answer this for me. When you say that it's natural, how does it come about?" asked Jimmy.

"If you mean how does one person have it and not another, I think it must be genetic. My supposition is that it's all to do with a very rare or recessive gene that doesn't come to the fore very often. Everyone knows that there are plenty of disabilities that work like that. So why couldn't it also result in an extra ability?"

Jimmy nodded to signify that he was still following Aiden's proposition and then said, "I've been trying to think of anything I haven't told you about it from my end. You know, with living with it for so long and all. But there really isn't anything. It's just been a part of me for years. No, hang on a minute. That's something right there. I haven't had it all my life. It only started, that I know of, when I was in my twenties. Do you think that could mean anything?"

"I guess it could mean that it only kicks in when you mature or stop growing or some such. There are studies that show that the brain goes through changes when a child is around thirteen or fourteen years old. It sort of reorganizes itself. Maybe with this ability, there's another change that happens when you get a bit older. Lots of other things work like that in our make-up – puberty being an obvious example. So in itself, it's not very unusual in nature."

With that, the conversation waned and they got back to the task at hand. Again they tried to elicit a positive brain response. But once more their efforts proved fruitless. Finally, Aiden said, "Time to call it a night Jimmy. Plainly it's just not going to happen right now. We'll try again same time tomorrow."

Seeing a look in his uncle's eye he said, "Don't worry, I'm not about to drop my bundle again. I'm still feeling good with this – we'll make it happen."

Jimmy did not appear convinced that he remained positive, so Aiden tried to lighten the mood with a little levity. "I'm beginning to think it might have something to do with the tides or maybe the phases of the moon," he said with a smile. Then as an afterthought he chuckled and said, "If all else fails we might have to fall back on reading tea-leaves, eh?"

That comment had the desired effect and his uncle responded. "I'm more of a steaming entrails man myself. But you're right about giving it a rest. I for one have had enough for now. I think I might just lay back now and read the newspaper – mind you I'll be sticking with the front section and leaving anything to do with racing well alone." Then he added, "Don't worry about tomorrow. Most people call me a lucky old bastard but nearly as many call me a stubborn old bastard. Of course I prefer to see myself as having a quiet determination – but whatever. When you come back tomorrow boyo, you'll find me ready and raring to go."

They said their goodnights and Aiden left his uncle with the remains of the Bushmills for company and headed home. Traffic was light and it was a pleasant ride. *At least that's one bonus from staying back late at work.* He had only just gotten out of his riding leathers when there was a rap on the door. It was Dylan with a six-pack under his arm. Aiden let him in and they both walked into the kitchen to put the beers in the fridge.

"We missed you at football training tonight" said Dylan with a hint of censure in his voice. "You'd best call the coach with some sort of excuse or he might leave you out of the side this weekend. And we wouldn't want that now, would we. Specially since we're playing St Barts and that's always a bit of a hoot." St Barts was a heavy-weight club and had been the

Dublin league Champions several times. They all enjoyed the challenge of trying to match it with them. Win or lose - the more likely outcome - it was a good gauge as to how well they themselves were playing.

"Oh shite, I forgot all about it. Damn, something came up at work and I only just got home, myself."

"I sort of assumed that you weren't here holed up with a pretty wench or some such. But I thought I'd call round and check to make sure. I brought my camera just in case."

"Very funny, smart-arse. You open a couple of beers and I'll phone Frank."

Their coach, Frank Ahern, liked to try to come off as a no-nonsense, hard-nosed tyrant. Possibly the result of watching one too many movie about competitive sports. The truth was that beneath the gruff exterior, Frank was just like the men he coached – competitive when the game was being played, sure - but what really drew him to football was the social side after they left the field. The chance to have a drink, have a laugh, tell some lies. All the guys on the team could see through the façade but when they weren't in the pub, by unspoken agreement, everyone went along with the pretense.

Aiden made the phone call. The conversation went through all of the ritual stages. Outrage and deep hurt at Frank's end and supplication and penitence from Aiden. Eventually, the coach allowed himself to be convinced that his prodigal player would accord the game due reverence in future and all sins were absolved. When he returned to the kitchen, it was clear from Dylan's smirk that he had listened in on the call.

"What?"

"Oh nothing. I was just thinking that there can't be any race that can match the Irish with the gab. You laid it on so thick, I'm just hoping Frank was wearing a snorkel or he might suffocate before he digs himself out."

"Well it did the trick and that's what counts. All is forgiven and he says I'm in the team on Sunday. So now you don't have to worry about my absence showing up how much I have to carry you during a game."

"You wish. So what's going on with the clinic? It's not like you to be putting in extra hours. Are you hoping Monty Burn's will come up with a pay rise?"

He'd told Dylan about O'Mara's latest nick-name and Dylan liked it a lot. They'd spent an hour trying to decide which of O'Mara's hangers-on made the best fit as Smithers. The discussion then quickly lapsed when Dylan suggested that Aiden was hapless enough to fill the bill as Homer.

"Oh yeah, he's full of that sort of largesse. No, it's just that there's a lot going on with the group that we have in at the moment. Actually, I expect that I'll be staying back most nights for the next little while." He thought about telling Dylan what he was trying to do with his uncle but it was too early. If the experiment led somewhere, with Jimmy's agreement, he'd bring his friend into his confidence – there was not much they didn't share with each other. But right now, there was nothing concrete and if it all came to naught, it would be best if only he and Jimmy knew anything. He suddenly decided that at the moment he was fed up with it and wanted to put the whole thing aside for a while.

"Tell you what; I'm sick of thinking of work right now. Why don't you hang around? I'll whip up something to eat and we'll have a drink or three and talk about anything other than my job."

"Sounds like a plan. Matter of fact, I was hoping to con a meal out of you. My cupboard's a bit bare right now and I'm sick of eating Greasy-Joe's of any and all persuasions."

And so by mutual agreement, they put on some music and spent the evening talking, in no particular order, about women, sport, their mates and the odd foray into politics. The conversation was punctuated with comfortable periods of silence that can only happen with good friends – when no one feels obliged to fill the void with prattle.

CHAPTER 10

The alarm clock sounded the start of another day. Today Aiden awoke relaxed and alert with a Sinéad O'Connor song featuring as his wake up number. The evening with Dylan had allowed him a respite from deep thinking and was just the therapy that he had needed. Now he couldn't wait to get back to it. Today, he had a new approach that he wanted to try. The tactic meant that he would have to tell his uncle about his earlier transgression but that was fine. He'd been feeling guilty about it in any event and coming clean would be good for his soul.

His day was spent forcing himself to concentrate on his tasks with his usual diligence but he couldn't stop himself glancing at the wall-clock at regular intervals. Like the proverb warned about the watched pot, all that he achieved was to make time flow like traffic on O'Connell Street at peak hour. Finally the work-day drew to a close and his colleagues drifted off to pursue their various after-hours plans. When he got to Jimmy's room, he could see that the time had dragged just as much for his uncle.

Jimmy literally rubbed his hands together as he said "It's about time you got here, I've been bored shitless all day. I don't know about your day but for me it's been like waiting for the froth to settle on a Murphy's when you're standing at the bar with a monster of a thirst."

Aiden was delighted with the intensity of his uncle's enthusiasm. It made it easier to be completely honest with him. When Jimmy was fully committed to anything, you couldn't move him from his path with anything short of heavy armory.

"Uncle Jimmy, I want to come at this thing from another direction but before we get into it, I need to tell you something. You won't like it but I hope you will forgive me."

"Let's have it then – spit it out and we'll see how bad it looks."

Aiden realized that he had his head down like a naughty schoolboy. That was not the way he wanted to do this, so he straightened up and looked his uncle in the eye. "Okay then – I should have told you this at the time but I didn't and I'm sorry. The other day when I erased the record of your brain patterns from the main system, I kept a copy."

He took the tiny pen drive from his pocket and held it up. "I don't know why I did it exactly. It was like I didn't understand what I was seeing but sort of knew that what was happening was important and I didn't want to lose it. You're probably mad at me but I have to tell you that now I understand a little more about what was going on, well part of me is still ashamed of what I did of course, but part of me is glad that I have the copy. I firmly believe that it's the key."

Jimmy simply sat for a time and then in a quiet voice speaking slowly like he was still assessing his feelings he said.

"I don't like that you did this behind my back and I have no doubt that if I had have known about that little thing in your hand a couple of days ago, I would have smashed it. But now I think that maybe I'm okay with it." After a couple of seconds he continued, his voice more assured. "No scratch that, I'm more than okay with it. I'm glad too that we have it. So now, what do you mean that you reckon it's the key?"

"You haven't been part of it but one of the things that we do here is to work with some of the subjects using a technique called Cognitive Behavioral Therapy. Basically, it starts with the idea that what we think has a bearing on how we feel and how we react physiologically to what going on around us. Then what we do is to train people to be able to produce certain brain patterns at will and also to be able to avoid other brain patterns."

Jimmy blinked slowly and deliberately a couple of times. It was a habit he had when he was absorbing facts. The he said, "I thought of two phrases while you were explaining – 'mind over matter' and 'think positive'. Is it like that?"

"Good enough as a rough analogy," Aiden replied.

"Okay – so let's get to it then."

"I've got to set up some additional equipment first. Come on and give me a hand; it'll be a lot quicker."

Aiden led them to a storage area at the back of the ward. There was always someone shunting equipment around so it was unlikely that anyone would take much notice of them. With Aiden giving instructions and both of them doing the lifting, they soon had a trolley loaded up. They wheeled it back to Jimmy's room and Aiden began to assemble the kit while he explained his plan.

"We're going to start off by using EEG monitoring and feedback. Like I said, I want to try to use the sequence that I recorded to teach you to put your brain in the same state again. I know you've not done anything like this before and it can take a bit to get the hang of it but I've got an idea that might speed things up. I've done a lot of training myself using this method and I'm pretty good at influencing my own brain patterns. So I'm going to hook me up as well and I'm hoping that maybe I can walk you through the process by getting you to copy me on the basic stuff. That said you'll be on your own when we get to the nub of it, where you're going to try to turn on the feeling."

He finished hooking both of them up and inspected his handiwork. The room had enough gear to impress a veteran of a Cape Canaveral launch. "What I want to do is to replay the event on one monitor and have both of us try to match the four basic wave patterns. As well as being able to see what's going on, I've set it up so that when we get closer to a wave pattern, we'll hear a pleasant sounding humming noise. If we diverge from it, we'll hear a more jarring noise. Sort of like the old game of 'getting warmer/getting colder'."

"Alright, I get it. So what about the other screens. The ones with colored pictures of brains"

"Those are our brains. The monitors display a picture of what's going on in different parts of them. It's actually a simulation but it's very clever really. It uses a sophisticated and very complex piece of software to produce this view. But it's quite accurate and it's what you're going to use to stimulate a lucky feeling episode. See that pea-like thing at the base of the brain? That's the pineal gland and that's what you're going to light up."

They began – watching the replay monitor and their own displays. Aiden led talking Jimmy through each step and Jimmy did his best to follow. First the alpha wave, next the gamma, followed by the beta and finally the delta. There were numerous restarts. Most of the time, intense concentration on one wave caused disruption to another. Eventually they had what they wanted and were able to hold the patterns steadily. Aiden signaled a break and they both fell back. They looked at one another with satisfied smiles. They both nodded and their shared look said 'I want to whoop and jump up for a high-five but I'm just too damn tired'.

Aiden spoke first. "That was sooo good. But we need to rest a minute; then we get serious. When we do it again, we should get to the right place a little more easily. That's when it's down to you. You need to visualize the lucky feeling and try to make it happen. Keep thinking about what the effect looks like and where it occurs and bring it on."

Jimmy's expression said it all for Aiden. "Right now though, do you have any of that Bushmill's left? We've earned one and there can't be any harm in just the one, eh?"

Fortified, they got back to it. As hoped, it was easier this time. They reached the point where they had emulated the desired brainwave pattern and Aiden nodded that his uncle should now try the next step. He doubted that the exercises they had undergone up to now were really required as a precursor. They were more an aid to train his uncle and to help him build confidence in the process. Now they had reached the critical stage of this approach – this was the point of success or failure.

Aiden turned his attention to Jimmy's screen. He was with him all the way; going through the same visualization; concentrating as hard as Jimmy. It was as if by force of his own will, he could make it happen for his uncle. And then they both saw it. The pineal and immediate area was showing activity. It was like the sputtering of a damp match, rather than the fierce flare that they had seen last time but it was clearly visible – it was actually happening. He glanced at his uncle and saw that his face had relaxed and a half smile had touched his lips. His attention returned to the screen and they both watched, fascinated. The effect had stabilized a little but still it remained subdued, like a bud that was not yet ready to fully bloom.

Suddenly the color drained from Aiden face and he let out an audible gasp. The instant effect was to break their concentration and all activity on the screen ceased.

What had shaken him so deeply was that while engrossed in watching Jimmy's monitor, a strange feeling had started to seep over him. By reflex his eyes had flicked across to his own monitor and he was confronted by the image of a brain - his brain - and it was also showing activity around the pineal gland – embryonic certainly, but nonetheless clearly visible.

This was beyond surreal, it was totally unreal. His world contracted to a single point, his breathing became shallow and he could feel a sense of panic threatening to engulf him. He shook himself and tried to relax. Bringing to bear his martial arts training, he sought to clear his head of all thoughts and to concentrate solely on breathing. He sucked in air, in deep, measured draughts and held it for a time before releasing it slowly. Gradually, he began to regain control and allowed awareness of his surroundings to return.

His uncle was watching him, studying him closely. "I know that look. You felt something too."

"But...but..." Aiden stammered.

"No 'buts' about it. Don't you believe your own theory? You said it was probably a rare ability and it was possibly genetic. You're my nephew, my blood – why couldn't it show up in you?"

"But the odds seem so long – that it should happen now. I'm struggling, really struggling with the whole thing."

"What are you saying? It was okay when I was the guinea pig but when things get a bit close to home, it's a different story? So what do you want to do? Give it away because it's got a little weird? That's not you, Aiden. We both know that. Start acting like the man I know and start thinking like the scientist that you are."

Jimmy began ticking off on his fingers. "Like I said, the heritage is right. You're about the same age as I was when it happened for me. We've been using equipment that's designed to help people bring about brain states. And while you've been training me, you've been training yourself as well. We were doing the whole thing in tandem and I think it's entirely feasible that what we have been doing has triggered the gift in you."

Aiden's thoughts raced. *He's right – well at least in the fact that I can't just dismiss it as impossible. We need to keep going and explore this more. The big difference is that now I'm part of the experiment.* When he spoke, his voice was quiet and his tone was introspective more as if he was thinking aloud. "Okay, let's say that I accept all that. But at the moment it's a side-show to what we are trying to do. Your brain activity was certainly visible but it didn't have the same strength, the same vibrancy as before. I wonder why that was."

The question was rhetorical and Jimmy remained silent. He had nothing to contribute and he knew that the best way forward was to let Aiden work his way through the problem. It did not take long. "Wait! I think I know." Aiden was clearly excited, the words spilled out quickly. "We were concentrating on producing the effect and we were starting to get results. But the essence of what we are trying to do is to invoke an ability that can be used to reach an outcome. *God that's a fine piece of mumbo-jumbo.* What I'm trying to say is that the action needs to have a target – something to work on."

Surprisingly, Jimmy nodded. "I get it – and it makes sense to me. So let's give it a go"

He went to the desk and returned with the form guide for a meeting scheduled for the following day. They went through the sequence again together – this time with Jimmy dividing his attention between the screen and the guide. When the glow began to manifest itself on Jimmy's monitor, Aiden shut down his machine and focused on his uncle. The glow spread and brightened until it had fully blossomed. His uncle's face took on a beatific look that was a mixture of satisfaction and relief. Rudely, Aiden saw a likeness to the one that a baby gets upon filling a nappy.

His uncle pointed to a horse. "That's the one," he said. "It will win and there's not a shadow of a doubt. What I just had was a true feeling, not wishful thinking."

Then with a grin, he handed the guide to his nephew. "Your turn boyo."

"What? No, no – I'm not ready yet."

"You won't know if you don't have a go, now will you. But just remember this. If you start off with a defeatist attitude, it'll never work. I believe in you. So get your head in the right place and let's make it happen."

A short while later after a barrage of his uncle's deft combination of encouragement and cajolement, Aiden was hooked up and trying to summons the glow. His uncle stood behind him, a hand on his shoulder.

"Jimmy, I know you're trying to help but ever since school days, I've always had trouble doing my best with someone hanging over me. It's like taking a piss with someone watching."

"Very subtle Aiden," said Jimmy wryly. "But I don't need a 'ton of bricks' to fall. You go about it. I'll not even here. And if I was here I'd just be looking out the window for a while."

It took minutes, long minutes but then it began – it actually began. Aiden let his eyes drift over the form guide, flicking back to the screen every few seconds. He came to a name that he fancied felt right. He concentrated on the horse and on the screen image. Almost hesitantly at first, the flicker on the screen began to solidify and then it spread until it covered the entire region of the pineal. Simultaneously, a feeling of 'rightness', of 'certainty' – he had no other words that seemed to fit – flowed through him.

"That'll be the one for Race 2," he said, pointing to the number 7 horse and trying to sound more assured than he felt.

He could see that the ember-like radiance that he had managed was a pale imitation of his uncle's effort. Jimmy had noticed it too and sought to re-assure him in the usual way –

with a bit of gentle ribbing. "Maybe your horse will only sneak into a place, eh." Then he slapped him on the back. "Just kidding. Remember, I've had this gift for a long time – you're still wearing your learner's plates."

"Cheeky bugger – just wait till I get some more practice. Then you'll see. I'll glow like Mount Etna on a dark night."

"You know what? I think you might just be right with that prediction. But for now, it's getting pretty late, so we should make some plans about what we do next."

They were mindful of the fact that this iteration of the institute's project had only a little over a week to run. At that time the current intake of lab rats, including Jimmy would return to the outside world. At this time of the year in Ireland, race meetings were not held every day. So they had to make good use of all events across the remaining days.

The plan was to continue as they had begun. They would each attempt to find one winner per meeting. They would make only small wagers so as not to attract attention. As a further precaution, they would also place some bets that they expected to lose – what they were doing was more about practice and learning, not profit. To begin with Aiden would back the two horses that they had selected for the following day's race meeting. As a gesture that was part tongue in cheek and part Irish practicality, they decided that the bet on Aiden's selection would be for the win and a saver for the place.

CHAPTER 11

The next morning, as he was leaving the house to go to work, Aiden caught himself whistling – yes actually whistling. It had succeeded in displacing his morning tune and that in itself made him laugh out loud. *Could we be just a little bit excited then, Mr. Cool?* He decided that it was entirely justified. Today was momentous. But what really puzzled him and at the same time pleased him greatly, was how positive he felt. Normally, when he looked forward to something, he could not stop his thoughts from drifting to what might go wrong, trying to find the down-side – real or imagined. *Maybe I'm different now. I guess my brain might have altered with the advent of the gift, so it could be that it has also changed how I think? Maybe I'll be a bit more like Jimmy and from now on, when things happen, I'll just meet them head-on.*

He arrived at the facility and set about trying to appear normal as he went about his duties. Despite the fact that this phase of the project was coming towards an end, there was no shortage of tasks to be done. Aiden was thankful that he was fully occupied and was not dwelling on the afternoon's racing. That was true, at least, until after he had placed the bets during his lunch break. It was only an hour until the second race – Aiden's race – but it was one of the slowest hours that he had endured. As the second hand dragged itself through the last five minutes, he joined his uncle and they tuned his radio to the race broadcast. They both feigned complete composure muttering phrases like 'it's a certainty' and 'it's already across the line' but when the moment came and the horse won, the facade was blown away. The celebration was reminiscent of the aftermath of a World Cup goal. They managed to keep it together a little better when Jimmy's horse saluted later in the day. As the day wrapped up Aiden brought up something that he had experienced when his race was on.

"One thing I didn't realize from our talks is that the feeling comes again when the event is actually happening. It kicked in just before the horse jumped."

"Didn't I tell you that? Sorry...yes that is always the way it is when it's a real episode."

"I bet if I wired us up today, we would have seen the same brain activity. Interesting even if I have no idea what it means. Anyway time I was going. I'm spent - it's been a big day. It'll be early to bed for me tonight."

Aiden floated home that night. The euphoric feeling was unlike anything he had ever experienced.

CHAPTER 12

Over the next days, they put their strategy into effect, placing small bets and mixing winners and losers at every meeting available. That made full use of the facility's feedback equipment at their disposal to hone their talent. Almost before they realized it, the end of the working week was upon them and that meant that a big day of racing would be coming up the following day. On Saturday, race meetings were to be held at three tracks around Ireland, so with plenty of options to work with, it would be a good yardstick to measure their progress.

They approached the test full of confidence. With the training they had put in, the strength of Aiden's 'aura' now looked to be the equal of his uncle's, while Jimmy was now pretty much able to invoke the effect without needing visual feedback at all. Their belief in their ability was unshakable and they each set about with gusto the challenge of finding a winner at all three meetings. They completed the process and sat down together to review the chosen bets. They quickly realized that they had both taken a horse in the same race – but they had selected different horses as the winner. Aiden could almost feel the crack start to appear in his self-assuredness. He went through a procession of emotions – surprise, puzzlement and finally dismay. Judging by the bemused expression on his uncle's face, Jimmy was grappling with similar feelings.

Aidan spoke first. "I don't understand what's happened here. Clearly something is wrong. I must have gotten ahead of myself and screwed up. It looked right on the screen but it must have been some sort of false positive – like you said has happened to you sometimes. Just forget about it – we'll go with your choice."

"No, that's not what we agreed. We said that while the experiment was on, we would go with whatever we chose. So we put money on both of them, simple as that. Besides, I watched the way your screen lit up and for mine that was a real episode."

Aiden didn't look convinced so Jimmy continued. "Still have doubt, do you? Look, do you remember what I told you about when I came up against the Frenchman? We both have the ability but on two hands when we went head to head, I came out on top. I've thought about it since and the only way I can make sense out of it is that I figure that in some way I was stronger than the Frenchie. My gift I mean. So I reckon this is actually a good thing. I can't believe how quickly you've seemed to have developed and this test will likely tell us more about how good all this feedback training has been for you."

Aiden mulled over the words. It took about five seconds for his analytical side to be hooked and another ten seconds for his competitive bent to kick in. His eyes shone with anticipation.

"It's not right how well you know how to play me," he said but his tone showed amusement not angst. "So it's not just a test, it's also a contest, eh." Then he added with a chuckle "Okay, you old bugger – bring it on."

With a slap on the back, his uncle pushed him toward the door. "It's Friday", he said "Time for you to get out of here. Go and have a beer with your mates and relax. You can get the bets on in the morning."

Aiden made no argument. He could see the wisdom of his uncle's suggestion. He had been under a lot of pressure and he could do with a diversion – at least until tomorrow. So with a nod and a promise to call in to see him late the next day, Aiden left.

CHAPTER 13

As soon as he got outside, he put in a call to Dylan and arranged to meet at their pub for a few ales during the traditional Friday night 'happy hour'. He had no way of knowing but his simple decision to have a night off from the pressure cooker that his life had become turned out to be as momentous, in its own way, as anything that he'd been doing with Jimmy.

They were onto their second pint when a trio of young ladies came into the pub and fronted the bar. The two lads both put into play their best attempt at the 'nonchalant appraisal' – that's the one where men think they are being totally clandestine and women immediately perceive what's happening but pretend they haven't noticed. But, with their 'spidey-sense' aroused, the women complete their own much more thorough evaluation – usually unnoticed by the male 'hunters'. Aiden and Dylan glanced at each other and gave the universal sign –a small nod with bottom lip pushed out and accompanied by raised eyebrows – signaling that the females in question were definitely of interest.

Why is it that when faced with trying to strike up a conversation with attractive women, most normally confident males seem to come out with a line that is totally lame or more often, can only manage something insulting? It's as if they can't help but regress to the level of a six year old in the playground.

Aiden's own effort did nothing to raise the standard. One of the girls fronted the bar and after carefully confirming that wine was included in happy hour pricing, ordered a round of the house red. Her accent was clearly Scottish, and Aiden opened with an inane remark to the effect that it was good to see a Scot upholding the national reputation for having a canny approach to money.

The response was immediate and cutting. Still facing the bar, she called over her shoulder to her girlfriends, "And here we have a fine example of the common Irish twit." Then she turned to him, looked him straight in the eye and added, "To be sure, to be sure!" With that came a dismissive flick of her luxurious shoulder length hair, black as pitch and gleaming in the light of the bar.

She was physically quite petit but when she faced him, Aiden almost took a pace back. He had no inkling of course but it was at that moment, the moment when she put him in his place, with green eyes flashing, that the hook was planted. He was caught.

The colleens took their drinks to a nearby table and fell into their own conversation. As the evening went on, Dylan decided to try to engage them. Banter had always come easily to Dylan and soon he was happily ensconced at their table. A chastened Aiden hung back for a time but finally made his way over to the lass that he had insulted.

"I'm sorry for my woeful attempt at humor. I really am much nicer than that. Can I have a chance to start over?" He held out his hand. "My name is Aiden."

Again her eyes pinned his. After a few moments, they softened and a half-smile flickered across her lips. Aiden's stomach did a small somersault.

"Okay, apology accepted – I'm on a holiday after all, so I should be relaxed and easy-going."

She took his hand briefly. Her skin was soft, fingers long, fine, well manicured but her grip was surprisingly strong for someone who looked delicate. Aiden's stomach did a small somersault.

"I'm Sharni. My friends are Jennifer – Jen - and Kate."

"Hi all," said Aiden with a small wave of his hand. "By way of penance, let me get the next round, eh?"

There would be no protests of course, so Aiden went off and organized the drinks without waiting for a response. When he rejoined the group at the table, the mood was light and happy.

As the night wore on the conversation and the alcohol flowed easily. The visitors were from Glasgow and had taken a cheap Ryan Air flight across the Irish Sea for a long weekend in Dublin.

"It was my idea," said Sharni. "I have some holidays coming up and I thought I might spend them over here. So the plan was to have a small taste of the place before I made up my mind."

"So you have an interest in Ireland then?" asked Dylan and added, "Come to think of it, Sharni is an Irish name isn't it?"

"Yes and yes. I was named for my Great-grandmother on my mother's side. She was born near Dublin, so I think that I'll enjoy exploring it a little bit."

"Well I might be biased but I think for sure it's worth a longer visit than just a few days," replied Dylan.

With that they began to talk about what to see and what were the tourist traps to avoid. Kate announced that she was keen to attend a race meeting.

"You're in luck, then. Aiden here knows his way around all the tracks around Dublin."

Aiden tried to suppress the stricken look that passed across his face. Kate was not the one he was interested in.

Sharni came to his rescue declaring, "I'd be up for a day at the races as well. Count me in."

Again that half-smile touched her lips and he was both warmed and a little bemused. He couldn't help but feel that she could read him like a book. And nothing is quite as alluring as a woman who keeps a man feeling a little off balance. "Okay, it's settled then. They're racing at Leopardstown tomorrow. It's a pretty track and easy to get to. We'll have a great day, I'm sure."

Aiden was not really surprised when Dylan demurred. "Sorry folks, but the races are just not my thing. Why not give Michael and Shannon a call. They'd be keen I reckon."

Jen, who had been Dylan's main focus during the evening and clearly not someone to hang back chipped in. "Personally, I'd rather spend the day with Dylan as my tour guide around old Dublin. If he's free, that is."

Dylan declared that he was and so that was settled.

"Okay", said Aiden. "I'll go see if I can tee up the other guys. Be back in a minute."

Aiden slipped away to a quiet corner and made a couple of quick phone calls. He returned to the table with a mission accomplished look to him. "They're in. Now, the best way to get to the course is by bus and train so if you like we can come by at about eleven and pick you up. Where are you staying?"

It was Sharni who supplied the name of the hotel. "It's just around the corner. We're triple-sharing a room - makes it a bit more affordable."

This time, Aiden managed to bite back the first response that sprang to mind. Instead with a very straight face, he replied almost solemnly, "Great location and very sensible. Most of the places around Temple Bar are a bit of a rip-off. After all, it's only somewhere to lay one's head."

Land-mine avoided, he glanced at Sharni. The half-smile grew into a mischievous grin as she said, "Damn, I thought for sure, I could get us another penance round."

Heart soaring; *Wow all that and a sense of humor like mine;* he tried his best look of umbrage – fooling no-one. "Well I'm outraged! In the circumstances I believe it's now your buy."

It was at about this moment that Sharni's interest in Aiden went up several notches. She was strong willed and had no interest in men who could not hold their own with her. "I guess that's fair enough. But let's make this the last round. I'm ready for bed and I want to be in top form for tomorrow."

"Fine by me. The good news is that we don't have to rush in the morning. The first race is a juvenile maiden, so not worth worrying about. Let's say me and the other lads come round to your hotel at the civilized hour of eleven and we'll be at the course in plenty of time for the second race."

Sharni looked across to Kate, who signaled her agreement. "Done. Now let me get last drinks."

Around a half-hour later Aiden and Dylan walked the girls to their hotel. By some unspoken agreement, everyone knew it was not the time to try to take things further and they said there goodnights in the foyer.

Chapter 14

Aiden made his way to the checkout with a small trolley laden with artisan bread, cheeses, a selection of smoked meats a terrine and sweet tarts. And of course, several bottles of wine. He wanted to make an impression on Sharn and so he had risen early and after fifteen minutes of rummaging around to find his large picnic basket, had headed over to Andersons Food Hall. Now had the makings of a delectable al fresco feast.

Promptly at eleven o'clock, Aiden, armed with hamper and rug and with Shannon and Michael in tow, arrived at the hotel to find the girls already waiting and set to go, their faces aglow from a combination of the brisk morning air and anticipation about the day ahead. Sharni and Kate didn't make a big fuss, but their looks of appreciation when the saw that he had brought provisions made his early morning labor worthwhile.

An easy walk brought them to St Stephen's Green. From there a short journey by light rail followed by the race-day shuttle-bus had them at the track just after the first race. The paid their entrance fee, passed through the turnstile and chatting happily proceeded on to the course proper. The day was still cool but the sky was clear and the pale sun seemed to promise it would do its best to warm up the temperature over the coming hours.

The course looked a picture set against the backdrop of Killiny Hill - showing all the rich shades of green that typify Ireland. There was only a small crowd in so they were able to set up on the lawn, close to the winning post. As soon as they were settled in, Aiden excused himself from the group. "I've

promised my uncle to get a bet on for him," he explained. "I'm
going to take care of it now, so I can relax and enjoy the rest of
the day."

The bet was for Race 3. It was the race that he and
Jimmy had chosen different horses in the same event. As per
their plan, he took Jimmy's pick for the win and his selection
for the win and the place. On a whim he also took a wager that
they would come in first and second. When he rejoined his
friends, he found them happily debating the chances in the
second race. He tried to join in but he was too keyed up about
the race that would follow it. If he thought that it was tense
when he was listening to the radio with his uncle, being here at
the track took it to a whole new level.

His friends had finally settled on the horses they
fancied and had also decided that they wouldn't outlay any
money - this race would be for the glory of picking the winner.
When the race was run and won, Michael was triumphant with
Kate's horse running second a length further back. Reflecting
on the enthusiastic cheering as the horses came up the straight
neck and neck, Aiden was reminded that horse-racing wasn't
just about gambling - it was a noble and exciting spectacle. The
thought served to calm him as he waited for the next race.

They laid their blanket on the grass and broke out the
wine and food. The day was becoming warmer and the
conversation was easy and relaxed. Aiden had been reticent at
first but now made up his mind that he should let them in on a
chance to win with Jimmy's selection.

"I don't tend to give out tips because I feel guilty if they
don't come off," he told them. "But my uncle is a pretty shrewd
tipster and he fancies horse number five in the next race. It's up
to you if you want to put something on. It should be a good
price. It was 12 to 1 when I put a bet on earlier, so it should still
be at 10s."

"If Jimmy's giving it out, that's good enough for me," said Michael. "That man has more than his fair share of good old Irish luck."

"I'm with you Mick," Shannon chipped in.

The girls made it unanimous. "I think I risk €20. If it comes in it'll help pay for the trip. If it doesn't, there'll be no more betting today," said Kate with a grin. Sharni nodded that she would follow suit.

For the next 30 minutes, Aiden tried his best to appear as carefree as the others but as start-time drew closer, his nervousness grew. Finally a trumpet flourish sounded to call the horses onto the track. The group had taken up a position on the rails right at the finish post where they had a superb view up the straight. The horses were loaded without fuss and almost immediately the gates flew back and the race had begun.

This was a middle distance event of 2000 meters and Aiden could see that both of his horses had settled in good positions as they went down the back of the course. There was little change in order as the field swept round the turn. It was half-way up the straight when the jockeys began to make their moves. His friends began to cheer, their eyes on Jimmy's horse as it burst to the lead, looking strong. For his part, Aiden only had eyes for his pick as it emerged from the pack three lengths behind his uncle's horse. Jaw clenched with concentration, he began to will his horse to fight it out. Slowly, slowly it began to close the gap until it was within a head of the leader as the finish post loomed. 'Close but no cigar', looked the probable outcome when at the last moment the horse lunged, its neck fully extended as they crossed the line. It was a photo-finish. For several seconds Aiden stood gripping the rails with the elated voices around him sounding muffled and far off. Then as he began to return to normal, he felt his tension ebb, replaced not by excitement but by a profound sense of satisfaction. He knew without doubt what the result would be and it was confirmed two minutes later when the numbers went into the frame – a dead-heat.

His thoughts were running off down several paths simultaneously. He wanted to talk about it with Jimmy but that could wait until he saw him face to face. Besides, he wanted a chance to work through the implications of what had just happened on his own. He needed some time by himself. A small lie wouldn't hurt. "Hey gang, that was pretty good. A share of a win at the odds gets a nice payout. Listen, I told Jimmy I'd give him a call after the race, so I'll be back in a few minutes."

He made his way around to the back of the grandstand a found a quiet spot where he sat down on a bench. He slowed his breathing and let his thoughts flow. *Wow that was really something. Up till now, I've thought of this ability as a sort of foreseeing of what was going to happen. But it didn't seem passive at all during the race. It really felt like I influenced the result - like it was a force that I applied. Could it be that I can influence the future in a small way? I've read enough sci-fi about the possibility of multiple timelines. Maybe there really is something to it. The only thing to do is to see if I can do it again. But it needs to be a different experiment. So far the approach has been to invoke the feeling and then find a focus for it. This time I'm going to choose a horse and then try to bring the lucky feeling into play aimed at that horse. I'd best give myself a bit of time...need to work up to it. Yeah, and if I don't spend some time paying attention to Sharni, she'll wonder what she's been stuck with today and it will be one date and bye, bye Aiden. Okay, Race 6 it is.*

He took out the form guide and without looking, plonked his finger down, trying to make it a completely random pick. He looked down and saw that he had selected horse 4.

The race was a steeple chase and his horse was rated as one of the main chances at odds of 3 to 1. Aiden smiled to himself. *That's okay. It's a test after all and I don't want to have to try to carry a no-hoper over all those fences.*

Decision made, he went back to the lawn to re-unite with the group.

"Long phone call?" Sharni smiled in that way that he was starting to find familiar. Like it carried a message that said 'I think you're up to something but I won't push it'.

God, I've know her all of five minutes and it's like she can read my thoughts. He suppressed a twinge of guilt. "Yeah. Jimmy insisted on a blow by blow description of the race." He quickly changed the subject. "Have you all collected your winnings?"

Their answer was a range of the usual pantomimes signifying money in hand – patting thick wallets and purses, fanning invisible wads of notes.

Michael proffered a glass of red. "Here grab this. Now that you're back, you can join us in a celebratory toast. To Jimmy, thanks for sharing," he declared, glass aloft.

For the next hour, Aiden sat on the grass chatting and keeping his mind simply on a fine day out with a delightful group. The next two races were run and won without their money invested. Everyone was content to just to watch and cheer home the horses. He and Sharni continued to take it casually but the more they talked, the more they found that their views meshed on many subjects. A burst of afternoon sunshine warmed them and one by one they succumbed to its enchantment and lay back looking up at the sky. Talking subsided as each slipped contentedly into his or her thoughts.

Now was the ideal time for Aiden to concentrate on reaching a state where his lucky feeling was activated. Even without the benefit of feedback from monitoring equipment, the hours of practice enabled him to follow the process that he had devised with Jimmy. He was confident. No more than that; he felt potent. *It's happening.* He knew that if he was hooked up to the monitor, he would be seeing his brain lighting up. He was doubly pleased because he was making it happen when in an almost drowsy state. He had worried that it would only work for him if he was under extreme stress.

It was getting close to race time. He had toyed with the idea of not actually backing the horse – just see if he could bring home a winner without making it obvious to the group that he had a strong vested interest. But in the end, he decided that it would be a better test with the added pressure of his friends being part of the action. "I've got one I fancy in this next race," he announced to all. "The odds aren't brilliant and there are no promises but I'm putting something on number four."

"It's a steeple chase isn't it?" observed Michael. "I don't have much success with the jumps. Too much can go wrong. Still, I'm well in front so I guess I'll risk a tenner."

"I have faith in you Aiden," said Sharni. "I'll go twenty."

Kate who was a bit of a punter also went in for twenty. With a shrug of 'easy come, easy go', Shannon added ten Euro to the pool.

With Sharni in tow, Aiden went off to place the bet. On the way back they went via the parade ring as the horses were being prepared to come onto the track.

"There's ours," said Aiden pointing. "He looks a nice fellow. See if you can catch his eye and project positive thoughts at him."

Sharni laughed. "I'd like him to be ready to give his best without testing my powers of positive thinking. Still he does look sharp, the way his ears are up and he's looking around."

"Well, well. So I'm in the presence of an aficionado am I?" he said with a broad grin.

"I let everyone think that I'm just going along with Kate. But truth be told, I love racing. It scares me a little because I could easily become addicted."

Aiden understood immediately that this simple revelation was a large vote of trust. He had already noted that Sharni did not easily reveal personal things about herself. To be let this far into her inner circle warmed him immensely. Walking back to rejoin the others, Aiden took her by the hand. It was thus far the most intimate moment they had had. The way Sharni lightly squeezed his hand, told him his timing was right.

They took up their position with their friends, near the finishing post and in what seemed like no time, Aiden's moment had come –the race had begun. Being a steeplechase, it was a long distance event and he was content to let things unfold as they would for a while. In truth, he was in completely new territory now and had no idea when he should try to bring force to bear. He would leave it until late in the event and hope that he'd get it right. The race progressed and now the horses were turning into the long straight with three fences to jump. Two of the better runners made their move. His horse was caught flat footed and the leaders quickly established a sizable break. By the time they had negotiated two more fences his horse had moved to a clear third but was behind by too great a distance. Aiden knew it was time to try to influence things but was unsure of what he should do. *Have to try something – it's now or never.* He formed a mental picture of his fancy winning the race tried to project this thought at his horse. The gap between the horses was closing but not quickly enough. As they approached the final jump, his let his consciousness spread to embrace all three of the leading bunch and again sought to transmit the image of his desired result. Suddenly behind his eyes there was a burst of light like the popping of flash bulbs. It passed quickly leaving him with nothing more than a buzzing in his ears. The scene before him on the track took on a surreal quality. The action seemed to unfold in slow-motion as he watched. The leading horse jumped early and its forelegs brushed the fence. The impact was slight but enough to cause it to stumble and lurch sideways as it landed. The second horse was at its flank and the two collided; both almost when to ground, only the skill of the jockeys enabling them to regain their footing. But by then, the damage had been done. The near-fall had cost them several lengths and all of their momentum. Aiden's horse swept past them and hit the finish line a clear winner.

As he joined in the cheering and high-fives with the gang, part of his brain was busy processing what he had just witnessed. He felt sure this had been a breakthrough moment and that by virtue of the effort his strength had increased massively. *I did it, I actually did it...*Closely followed by another notion...*Weird how good luck for me was a result of bad luck for the two leading horses.* As he followed that thought thread, he sensed that he was on the verge of an important insight about his ability and how it might be used. *That feels right really. If the gift is a type of force then it's logical that it obeys the rules of physics and like any force it will cause an equal and opposite reaction.*

His reverie was interrupted and he was pulled back to the moment in a most pleasant way. In her excitement, Sharni had moved into his arms, wrapped her arms around his neck and pulled his head down to hers. Their lips met and the kiss lingered. For Aiden, the feeling was not unlike that which he had experienced during the race. Lights flashed inside his head and as they finally parted, he had the same buzzing in his ears.

"Wow," was the best he could manage. It might have been somewhat lame but it was enough to evoke *that* smile from Sharni.

"Clearly it's that gift of the Blarney that I'm attracted to," she said, her eyes sparkling with merriment as she spun out of the embrace. And then to further lighten the moment she gave him a playful dig in the ribs and declared, "Come on, it's time to celebrate. How about pouring me a glass of wine."

He understood her unspoken message. Their relationship was developing but here and now was not the time to take it further.

The remainder of the day at the races unfolded quietly and comfortably in the mild spring weather. They decided to stay for one more race and then leave before the last race to beat the small crush of the modest crowd all leaving after the last event. By the time they got back to Dublin, plans had been made for the rest of the day. They would go their separate ways to freshen-up and then meet at the pub at 7 p.m.

When they all got back together that evening, the unanimous vote was to stay for one round and then find a nice cozy restaurant in the area for dinner. Dylan and Jen had joined them after their day of sightseeing. Jen was full of praise for Dublin and adjudged the town as being almost as good as Glasgow – a high compliment from a Glaswegian; they can be a tad parochial about their home town. It soon became apparent that whilst Dylan and Jen had spent an enjoyable day together, they weren't looking to take the relationship any further. That was true also of Kate with either and either Michael or Shannon. They all got on well as a group but it was only Aiden and Sharni who looked likely to match up.

Temple Bar and the surrounding streets house an abundance of eateries from cafes to fine dining and they cover a variety of cuisines. They settled on a place that was stylish but casual and specialized in modern Japanese. The food was sublime and they put their winnings to good use with some quality wines to accompany the food. By the end of the meal, they were all 'feeling alright'. It had been a long day and the girls were not interested in going clubbing – much to the boys' relief. Instead they topped off the night by returning to their pub for a nightcap. As they walked back to the Arlington, Sharni took Aiden's hand and slowed her walking pace so that they fell back from the others. She spoke quietly to keep the conversation between the two of them. "Aiden, I'm really enjoying getting to know you and you must realize that I find you attractive. You could easily become very special to me. And because of that, I want us to take our time. I'm the type that takes a while to develop a relationship, but when I make up my mind, I give it my all."

"I can't believe how you can be so open, so easily. I wish I had your confidence. But I'm glad that's the way you are. It makes things much easier for someone like me who over-analyses and over-complicates most things. And I understand. And I'm happy to take things slowly."

Before saying their goodnights, they agreed to spend the next day with just the two of them wandering around the cultural centers, galleries and boutique stores dotted around the Temple Bar precinct. Sharni assured him that she would sort it out with Jen and Kate and that it wouldn't cause any friction with her friends.

CHAPTER 15

Aiden reached the hotel mid-morning to collect Sharni. Although it was Sunday, most attractions were open and they mingled with the throng of locals and tourists leisurely wandering the area looking through art galleries and bric-a-brak shops. They found themselves relaxed and comfortable in each others' company and as time passed, they chatted happily and found that their backgrounds were quite alike. Growing up in Glasgow sounded to Aiden, similar to growing up in Dublin. Both cities had been through hard times and had gone through something of a renaissance in recent years. Both cities had a strong youth culture and the youth of both cities generally refused to take life too seriously.

They stopped for lunch at a pleasant deli-cum-produce store. Sitting back after the meal, surrounded by foodstuff triggered an idea. "I know we've just now eaten so it's bad timing but this evening if it's okay, I'd like to cook dinner for you back at my place," Aiden suggested.

"Sounds a fine idea. I'd like to see where you live and I never knock back letting someone else do the cooking," Sharni replied.

"Excellent! Modesty aside, I'm not at all bad with Asian stir-fries or pasta dishes. So what's your fancy?"

"I do a pretty mean pasta, myself – that and curries are my specialties – so I think a stir-fry is the go. And I while I'm putting in my order, I just love noodles."

"I think I know just the thing. There's a Malaysian dish that I really like – Char Kway Teow. One of the main ingredients is flat noodles."

"You're on," declared Sharni.

"The Asian Market is not far from here and it will have everything we need. And it's a great place to explore – full of really interesting stuff. So after we finish browsing through here how about coming with me to pick up the ingredients for dinner?"

"That would be fun. I'm not big on supermarkets but I love poking around interesting food stores. In fact, let's go now – I think I'm galleried-out."

They flagged down a taxi for the short ride to Drury St and entered the immense basement complex. They joined the throng of shoppers maneuvering along narrow aisles packed with all nature of exotic goods, picking up the noodles and a variety of spices as they went. Then they fought their way to the fresh vegetables section and on to the meat and fish. Doing that task together was a simple thing but one that they both enjoyed immensely. As the afternoon drifted towards evening they emerged laden with supplies and hailed a taxi back to his digs.

After a quick tour of his home, he poured them both a glass of wine. They discovered another mutual preference – they both had a penchant for red wine and didn't give a tinker's cuss for the view that it should not accompany certain foods; like the noodle dish he was preparing tonight.

She stayed with him in the kitchen while he set about preparing dinner. He was a trifle embarrassed when he donned his apron but she put him at ease immediately. With a smile and with just a hint of satire she observed. "I do adore a man in an apron."

He tried to keep up the conversation but he tended to be somewhat single-minded when he cooked. So the next thirty minutes produced a flurry of peeling, chopping, stir-frying, seasoning and tossing.

If asked, she would have declared herself not yet hungry but when the smells from the wok hit her, she quickly reassessed her position. Sharni topped up their glasses as Aiden joined her at the table with two steaming bowls, brimming with seafood and noodles. Dining was punctuated with satisfied murmurings of 'mmm – hot', 'yum – good prawns' and 'oh yeah – chili hit' and the like. When Sharni finally sat back from her bowl, she raised her glass as a salute. "Even better than a man in an apron, I like a man who can cook."

"And I've always gone for a girl with a hearty appetite," he responded with a grin.

"Hey, that's enough about my appetite, mister," she came back in mock indignation. "I finished my bowl just to be polite."

Such was the level of ease between them that they did not even bother to leave the table as they continued to talk. The conversation moved to the subject of work. Aiden explained about his role at the clinic. Momentarily he even toyed with the idea of telling her about the discovery that he had made with his uncle but immediately realized that it would be a very bad idea on many levels. Apart from the need for it to remain a secret between him and Jimmy, it was a bit early in the relationship for Sharni to think she was in the company of a complete nutcase.

"It sounds like a really fascinating line of work, Aiden. I really enjoy what I do as well. I work with the police. Not as a member but as a research assistant with the intelligence arm. It's my job to help compile background checks on people and businesses when an investigation is going on."

"Wow. I'll think I can manage to put aside my innate Irish distrust of the authorities and not get all paranoid."

She laughed. "You're not alone in that. The Scots are every bit as skeptical about those in power as the Irish. So don't worry, I promise that I only use my powers for good. Seriously though, when I first started I used to be a bit concerned about how much information is out there about every one of us. But then I came to the conclusion that a transcript of my comings and goings would probably make for a top notch cure for insomnia. And yes, it's true that some coppers are bent but most are just ordinary people doing a tough job and trying to survive."

They continued to chat in that spirit for the rest of the evening. It seemed like only a short time had passed when they realized that it actually quite late. Sharni insisted on helping with cleaning up and they set about the task together, still talking happily, enjoying getting to know one another. Aiden put the last dish away and turned to find Sharni standing close to him, a look in her eyes that sent a tingle up his spine and simultaneously, down to his groin. Before he could speak, she moved fluidly into his arms and kissed him. The kiss deepened. As they parted finally, she looked at him languidly, her eyes half closed.

"I've changed my mind about waiting. Why don't you show me the master bedroom?"

He pulled her close and kissed her again. Long and passionate. Then he took her by the hand and led her to his bedroom. They came into each other's arms again, lips eagerly seeking lips, hands exploring each other with increasing fervor. Their clothes seem to fall from them. There was no awkwardness as they found the bed and began making love.

The next morning he awoke feeling as happy and contented as he could ever remember feeling. Sharni was still asleep so he slipped out quietly to the kitchen and set about making breakfast. She awoke to the smell of poached eggs.

When she stumbled into the kitchen he was plating Eggs Florentine. "Hmm, smells good. And looks even better."

He pulled out a chair for her and placed a good sized portion in front of her. She waited until he sat down as well and then started in with gusto. They'd already made reference to her fine appetite and again he was amused at how much she could put away for someone his mother would describe as 'a mere slip of a lass'.

After a few minutes, she looked over at him with her patented half-smile in evidence. "Aiden, this is delicious – and with just the right degree of decadence. The primordial creature who lives in a corner of my mind tells me I could easily get used to this." Then she added cheekily, "And I must confess, for some reason I'm feeling quite hungry this morning."

She put away another mouthful before adding, "I'm onto your game, you know - plying me with home cooking and good company. You might seem the trustworthy type on the surface but putting temptations like this in front of a simple Scottish girl – I'm beginning to think that under the surface lurks a lothario bent on seduction."

Aiden laughed. They hadn't known each other long but everything she did charmed him. She continually made him want to grab her and hold her. He was starting to care for her deeply. "Well that's your view of things but it's a different story from my side. Believe me; your enchantress leaves my playboy in its dust."

After breakfast they needed to take two showers. During the first shower, they decided to help each other wash some not very hard to get to places and unsurprisingly, they ended up back in the bedroom. When they eventually left the house, they took a bus into the city center and spent the remainder of the morning browsing the shopping precinct. The time for Sharni to leave was fast approaching. Aiden felt his buoyant mood begin to fade but she turned that around in a flash with a promise to return in a few months for a longer holiday and a declaration that she wanted to spend much of her time with him. She made it very clear that if Aiden didn't live up to his pledge to keep in contact via email and Skype, she knew where to find him and his punishment would swift and painful. They spent the final few minutes over coffee and then she stood up to go.

"I don't think it's a good idea for you to come to the airport. I might go all soppy and give far too much away. Can't have you getting a big head, can we? I'll just take a taxi back to the hotel and hook up with Kate and Jen."

They kissed deeply and with a wave and a smile she was gone.

Aiden sat alone for a few minutes, lost in thought. *Ah, Sharni McLaren you really are something.* Simply thinking her name gave him a warm feeling.

CHAPTER 16

With Sharni's departure, Aiden's thoughts returned to the momentous events that took place at the race-track. It was astounding that over the past two days he had hardly thought about it. But his time with Sharni had been just so meaningful and fulfilling; he had immersed himself completely in her company. But now it was time for him to sit down with Jimmy and tell him about his latest discovery. If he truly had been able to directly influence the result, the implications were huge. Short of a nuclear attack, he knew his uncle could be found at his favorite watering-hole on any evening at around 5 p.m. having a couple of pre-dinner pints – or as Jimmy referred to them, his appetizer of choice.

When he reached the pub there were only a handful of patrons but sure enough, his uncle was one of them. He was perched on a stool at the bar chatting happily with one of his old cronies; a man that Aiden only knew as Jack. Aiden made his way over and he and Jimmy shared a quick 'man-hug' – that's the one where it's a kind of half clinch and half back-slap. It involves about as much affection as two men are likely to display in an old-style Irish pub. He could see that their glasses were nearly empty, so Aiden waved to the barman to get his attention and signaled that he wanted a round for the three of them. Jack put his hand over his glass.

"Thanks for the offer son but I'm on my way home after this one. Don't want the missus to be waiting with the rolling-pin in hand."

They all smiled knowingly and nodded on cue. It's the sort of throwaway line that is muttered by men in bars all over the world. In truth, the spouse at home is probably quite happy to have some time to herself. The three talked sport until after Jack left and then at Aiden's prompting they took their beers to a quiet table at the end of the room, away from the other drinkers. Aiden proceeded to tell his uncle all about his experiment and apparent success with forcing the result he wanted in a race. By the time he had finished, Jimmy was looking decidedly uncomfortable.

"Hold up a bit Aiden. If you caused it - were actually able to do that - it makes me more than a bit nervous. It sounds like you're messing with fate or something. There's no telling where it might lead."

"Don't be daft. It's just another side to the ability. The result is the same. It's just a different way to do go about it."

Jimmy was far from re-assured. "We Irish are a superstitious lot – maybe not so much with you youngsters – but for me it seems a bit too much like hexing or witchcraft. I just don't feel right about it, so if it's all the same to you, I'll be sticking to what I know how to do."

"Fair enough. I wanted you to know about my discovery but I wasn't really suggesting that you should try the same approach. So let's leave it at that then."

A mollified Jimmy soon returned to his usual demeanor and mischievously gestured toward the dartboard on the other side of the pub. "As I recall you're a pretty ordinary darts player. Let's see if you can hit the bulls-eye. Here, I've got my darts with me. Should be a doddle for someone who can make an impact on 500 kilograms or so of horseflesh."

Aiden was highly doubtful but in the spirit of keeping things light, agreed to accept the challenge. They went across to the board and Aiden closed his eyes while he tried to clear his mind and concentrate on making the dart behave. Finally, feeling composed, and envisaging the result he wanted, Aiden threw. The missile flew towards the board, but in a complete anti-climax, hit the wireframe and bounced onto the floor. Jimmy roared with laughter and slapped him on the back. "I could almost see it trying to bend toward the bull but I guess that was just gravity," he spluttered. "Don't feel bad. Maybe it doesn't work with inanimate objects."

"More likely I need a lot more practice at getting my mind in the right space."

"Hey, you have a dartboard at your place. Maybe you can use a dart for practice at home."

"It's a thought but I don't think that it's entirely like training a muscle. Maybe it is partly about that but I think it's also to do with concentration and strength of will. When we used the feedback setup at the clinic, we made a lot of progress in a short period of time. The thing is we've gone about as far as we can with that as the tool. I know you're happy with where we are now but I want to go further – much further if I can. And if I want to develop, I need another approach."

"You mean a different machine?"

"No, I don't think so. And besides, I don't know of anything else out there that I could get hold of. I feel like it's more to do with training the mind or having better control over it...You know, just saying that aloud has given me an idea. Maybe meditation is the path I should follow. I know about it at a novice level. A couple of years ago, I got into it with my martial arts training. For a while, I often put aside an hour or so at night for meditating. Though compared to committed exponents, I was more of a dabbler. Yeah, the more I think about it, taking it up again might be exactly the way to go. But this time, I'm going to be more disciplined and take it up a notch."

The next day after he finished work, he went to his dojo. After putting up with an expected and warranted chiding from his master for being slack with his training in recent weeks, Aiden raised the subject of meditation. This thawed the mood in the room immediately. His master was an ardent advocate for the benefits to be derived from a dedicated regimen of meditation. He recommended a couple of books for him to buy and even said that he would be happy to work with him to fast-track Aiden's return to the path.

When he left the dojo, he went immediately to a bookstore known to stock a range of self-help style books and was able to find the volumes he sought. Over the next weeks he started to practice in earnest. He took up his teacher's offer and two nights a week, he received instruction from him. From the outset, he found it much easier than when he tried this previously. He concluded that this was likely to be a side-effect of the feedback training he had done with his uncle. Often when he meditated alone, his method was to try to clear his thoughts as quickly as possible and mentally go to the place in his brain that he thought of as the seat of his ability. Once he had reached the location he would envisage the area rousing and pulsating. Augmented by expert one-on-one coaching his progress was rapid. He even impressed his tutor – a man who by nature was slow to bestow accolades.

"I can hardly believe how quickly you have grown," he beamed. "If I hadn't known you for so long, I might even think of you as a prodigy and recommend you enter a temple to continue your studies. As it is, I'm wondering whether my coaching can take you much further. I suspect that you've reached a point where you need to study and practice alone and find your own path to continue your development."

"I think you are right. I couldn't have come this far without your guidance but it's now down to me."

With a promise to try to improve his discipline when it came to attending the physical training sessions, he left the dojo.

He continued to get together with Jimmy each week to find a winner or two using their well tried method. Lately, thanks to his regimen of meditation, Aiden sensed that he had greatly increased his power and improved his control over and his ability. He seemed to be able to invoke it more readily and consistently than previously. His uncle had commented on it as well. But Aiden was frustrated because in the end, it was merely a feeling and he could think of no way to measure objectively his advancement.

Thus far, he had been back to the track only once to attempt his newly discovered direct approach. He had been successful and was jubilant on the day. But now that a period of time had elapsed, a nagging doubt had taken hold; maybe he was kidding himself. In hindsight he knew he had made a mistake with the horse he had picked out as a test. He'd chosen the favorite for the race. The inescapable fact was that horse was expected to win and win it did. So it was possible that he had no influence whatsoever on the result. It annoyed him that he entertained even a shred of uncertainty. He had done it – he had felt it happen – he had forced the result that he wanted – twice. He should be completely confident in his ability. But the insidious, niggling little voice in his head would not be silenced. Clearly the only way to resolve the problem was to get out to a racetrack and prove it to himself once more.

CHAPTER 17

From nowhere, unpleasantness surfaced from an entirely different and unexpected direction. Aiden was at work putting the final touches to his report of observations stemming from the most recent intake of volunteers when he was summoned to O'Mara's office. He entered and found O'Mara behind his over-sized desk. He was leaning back in his chair, hand clasped behind his head, not trying very hard to mask the smug look that had replaced his usual haughty appearance. The office contained a meeting table but O'Mara rarely emerged from behind his desk when talking to his subordinates. Instead, he used his desk as a barricade, a position of power. At a gesture from O'Mara, he closed the door behind him and sat in a chair facing Fortress O'Mara.

"Donnelly, I have come across something very disturbing. I was checking the inventory records and it seems that some weeks ago, you were checking out equipment after hours. It's most irregular and I have to conclude that you have been conducting some line of research of your own."

He paused for effect, straightened his torso and tried to assume a stern aspect, aiming for intimidation. Unfortunately for him, he was not one who could look particularly threatening. If Aiden had even a modicum of respect for his boss, he might have been taken aback. But as it was, he was unfazed. He held his silence, waiting to see how this would unfold. Finally O'Mara got the message that Aiden was offering up nothing by way of confirmation or denial.

"As I'm sure you know, using the facility's resources for private investigations is forbidden and can be grounds for dismissal."

He stopped again, this time using the hiatus to don an unctuous smile, now trying to look conciliatory. Aiden suddenly felt the need to take a shower. "Of course, as Director, I have the authority to approve new directions of inquiry. You're a bright fellow. Perhaps you have come up with something innovative – something of sufficient importance that should be published. In those circumstances, I might see my way clear to approve this piece of work. Naturally, when we publish, I will be credited with leading the work and you will receive recognition as my assistant. Think about it. It's a generous offer – you have until the end of the day."

Aiden felt the heat rise as he absorbed the gist of what O'Mara had laid out. It was very close to blackmail. *You smarmy bastard.* Aiden took a moment to compose himself. *I won't give you the satisfaction of seeing me lose it but he can stick his job up his arse. I'm out of here.* "I don't need the time thanks. I'd like to tender my resignation."

"As you wish. I've tried to be accommodating but clearly you don't appreciate my generosity. Please remain where you are while I call security. They will accompany you to your desk while you gather your belongings and then escort you from the center."

As the seconds passed, Aiden's sudden rush of anger began to abate and now he was torn between disbelief and anxiousness, his thoughts jumping around. *He actually thinks he was doing me some sort of favor. He must be from another planet. Wow, this is all happening very fast. I like my job. I don't want to throw it away. Too late to change that. It would be impossible to work here now, anyway.*

Two security personnel arrived in a few minutes. He knew them enough to say hello when they crossed paths but here inside the office they were all business – saying nothing and almost standing to attention as the received their orders. Aiden got up and walked with out of the office. As he closed the door, O'Mara could not resist once more demonstrating how petty a man he was with a parting shot. "Oh and I'm afraid that I won't be in a position to provide you with a reference."

Once outside the office the demeanor of the security men softened. "God that man is a right prick," said one of them. "So lad, what's happened?"

"We decided on a divorce. Irreconcilable differences," was all he could manage.

No-one that he worked closely with was around at that moment and that suited him perfectly. He didn't want to have to try to explain to anybody. He just wanted to get out of there. It only took a short while to clean out his desk and pick-up his few things in the lunch room. In the car park, he handed his office keys to one of the guards, mounted his bike and left without another word.

As he rode home with a chance to reflect, his emotions churned. He went from anger to indignation and on to resentment. By the time he reached his house he had settled on righteous anger. He thought about calling Sharni or one of his friends so he could let fly about the injustice that had been done to him. But he shelved that idea as quickly as it came. He was not very good at the whole unburdening thing – he was more the mull-it-over type. And besides trying to explain the reason that he had to quit opened up a subject that he could not go into. Instead he poured himself a whiskey and brooded.

When the knot in his stomach finally gave way to hunger, he could not be bothered cooking so he ordered-in Chinese. He ate without tasting but it warmed him and filled the gap and made him feel a little better. He was about to pour another drink when he yawned deeply and suddenly felt very tired. The tension had exhausted him and he decided what he really wanted at that moment was the comfort of his bed.

He slept poorly and awoke at 4 am; the well known time of night for remorse. In the cold pre-dawn he was feeling very low worrying about his future. He enjoyed his line of work immensely but his career choice was in such a specialized field that his opportunities were very limited. What would he do if he could not find another similar position? He couldn't see himself happy in any other job. The more he worried, the more irrational his thoughts became. When he started to fret about money he abruptly snapped out of his funk. *You idiot,* he chided himself. *Money is the least of it. It's a very special talent and it translates into money. Whatever else might be going wrong, you'll not go broke.* This thought immediately spawned another. *Maybe it's time to make full use of my talent. Yes, for sure this is just the right time to stop fiddling around with small bets and ramp up the action for a bit.*

Decision made, he felt much more settled and with a raft of half-formed strategies wafting through his mind, he drifted back to sleep. When he awoke again mid-morning his ideas had crystallized and he was filled with enthusiasm. He was on a mission now and spent the rest of the day on the internet studying horse racing fixtures for all of the tracks that were within reasonable reach. His target group of venues was comprised of three in Dublin and four in the country. By evening he had worked out his schedule. With some overnight stops at more distant towns, he could attend four meetings per week – five if he really pushed it. When he called it a night he was well satisfied. Now he had a plan and at least in the short-term, it would keep him busy and give him purpose.

CHAPTER 18

So began a frenetic mix of travelling around the countryside on his motorcycle, staying in small inns and working hard at bringing home winners carrying sizable wagers. The first meeting he attended was a jumps only card at Kilbeggan in County Westmeath, a little over an hour from Dublin. The meeting was to be held in the evening and so Aiden had booked overnight accommodation in nearby Tullamore. It was an easy and pleasant ride from Dublin - much of the Irish countryside is green and lush and this part of the midlands is no exception. He had been quite tense when he began the journey but the scenery coupled with a warm day and a light breeze had a deep soothing effect on him. He always enjoyed getting out into the country and by the time he arrived the idyllic nature of the trip had put him in a holiday mood. He decided that he should try to get the business end of his attendance out of the way early and then reward himself with a couple of pints while he watched the remainder of the program. With that in mind he took a taxi to the track, leaving his motorcycle at the hotel.

He went directly to the mounting yard where the runners for the first race were being prepared and picked out his first horse. Next it was on to the betting ring where a handful of bookies operated. He spread his bets between three of them and then made his way to the Pavilion Bar, located right on the winning post. The mild weather had brought quite a few people out for the evening and the bar hummed with dozens of muted conversations, punctuated by the occasional sound of laughter. He wasn't planning to have a drink yet so instead he went through to the grandstand that fronted the bar to look for a suitable vantage point – one where he would not get too hemmed in but where he could still get a good sight of the race.

He found just the spot at in the far corner of the stand. It was at the front but was past the winning post and so would be less popular with the other punters. He sat down and took in the course. The track looked a picture and even as twilight approached, visibility was still excellent. It was not an especially expansive course and he would be able to see his horse clearly at all times as it went around the circuit. As start time approached, he felt like an actor sitting in the wings waiting to go on and so he occupied himself reading a magazine while the clock slowly ticked off the minutes. When his moment came, he was able to trigger his gift readily and tried to remain all business as he brought about the result he wanted. As before, it was a heady occasion but didn't want to get carried away and forced himself to damp down his emotions. *This is only the beginning...need to keep a lid on...not the time to get ahead of myself.* He tried to go with quiet elation but couldn't quite avoid a touch of smugness. After all, he had proven conclusively that his earlier forays using his new technique had been no fluke – that nagging voice of self-doubt had been silenced.

Aiden's plan was to restrict his attempts to two events and he let the next two races go and targeted the fourth race for his final sortie for the night. Again all went smoothly and he had his second winner. Well satisfied, he made his way to the bar and settled back with a celebratory pint. He let himself be drawn into a conversation with a pair of nice old codgers talking at the bar. They were locals and regulars at the course. And true to their stereotype they were not shy about airing their opinions on just about everything. But clearly their favorite topic for the night was a detailed analysis of what was right and what was wrong with the modernization of the venue that had taken place over recent years. Still they were quick with a joke and a laugh and Aiden enjoyed their company. He stayed with them until the last race, even following them in with a small outlay on a tip that they shared with him. They were good judges; their selection won and with no influence from Aiden. By the time he made his way back to his hotel, Aiden was more than a little under the influence and was asleep within minutes of reaching his room.

The morning was chilly and he felt as washed out as the sun shining weakly through the dining room window when he finally stumbled downstairs next day. But the hearty country-style breakfast that appeared in front of him when parked himself at a table by the fireplace was just the tonic he needed. By the time he was finished eating he was human again and ready to formulate his plan for the day. Over a second cup of tea he reviewed the racing guide in the newspaper. The third race had a considerable sized field of 15 runners and as a consequence the odds were open for all of the horses. He settled on his strategy. Today he'd have a single big wager and it would be on that race.

The day's races were at Leopardstown back in Dublin; a track Aiden had been to a number of times in the past. Being quite familiar with the layout, he could make this something of a flying visit – one race, in and out.

Having settled on a course of action, he went back upstairs to his room and packed his bag and then checked out. It was a leisurely ride and he arrived at the track in plenty of time for his race. All unfolded exactly as he wanted and so with mission accomplished, he headed back to his home to put his feet up in familiar surroundings. As it transpired he was not able to relax as much as he might have wished. The simple reality was that this was a very brief interlude and he'd soon be back on the road.

He was up not long after daybreak and on his way by mid-morning. This trip covered two meetings at tracks to the south of Dublin. The route meant that he would practically pass by the pub owned by his folks. Although he felt guilty about it, he had decided not to call in to see them. He had told them about quitting his job and while they were supportive, he knew that it worried them. He did not want to exacerbate matters by letting them know he was on his way to the races. Nor did he want to face the barrage of awkward questions that undoubtedly would come from his mother.

At the coastal Wexford track, he brought home two winners. He resisted the temptation for a quick pint at the quaintly named Bettyville Bar. He still had some travelling to do that evening. Leaving Wexford, he headed inland to Kilkenny City, the closest town to Gowran Park racecourse. This district is one of the most famous horses breeding and training areas in Ireland, probably only outranked by Kildare and on his infrequent visits to Kilkenny, Aiden had always enjoyed the ambiance generated by the reminders of its equestrian heritage. He arrived at his digs, a comfortable hotel in the heart of town and after unpacking his overnight bag, stretched his legs with a stroll around the compact town center. As he was admiring the medieval architecture on show, he was reminded that its status of 'city' owed more to an ancient charter than it did to the size of the township. His wandering took him along the river and up beyond St Francis Abbey Brewery before he circled back to his hotel past the many craft shops dotting High Street. He stopped in at a bookstore and bought himself a novel to read from the best-seller stand. By the time he reached his lodgings, he was ready for dinner and made straight for the cozy old-style front bar where he installed himself at a table that provided a view of the street through the side window. With a locally made ale in front of him, he sat back contentedly and gazed out the window watching the good citizens of Kilkenny promenade past. A gentle rumbling from his stomach refocused his attention on the business of eating. The bar served good honest pub food and after a quick perusal of the specials board, he settled on a hearty stew washed down with another pint of ale. He had intended to retire to his room and read after his meal but the bar had filled while he was eating and it was pleasant to simply sit back and absorb the bustling atmosphere. It was late by the time he called it a night and he finished only a few pages of his book before nodding off.

As he started out towards Gowran Park, the early morning clouds had already dissipated and the sun had cleared the haze from the high road he travelled. Now it was beginning to burn its way into the mist that clung on doggedly in the nooks and hollows of the surrounding valleys. The race card for the day comprised ten races and he set himself a challenge of trying to get three winners. The first two came easily and he gave himself a break for a couple of races before trying again. This time as he went through his routine, he had great difficulty clearing his mind. His mind wandered and the harder he tried, the fuzzier his brain became. He abandoned the attempt and began a sequence of deep-breathing and calming techniques before starting over. Still he was unable to function properly. This time all he achieved for his efforts was a thumping headache and blurred vision. Reluctantly he was forced to admit defeat. As soon as he broke off, his vision cleared and the headache subsided. Nonetheless it was quite a comedown – he had gone from a feeling of infallibility to one of inadequacy. Still a little dazed, he made his way from the seating area of the grandstand to the cafe at the rear. Over a strong coffee he sought to compose himself – indifferent to the race now being run.

By the time he'd finished his beverage, he had begun to re-gather himself. Overwhelmingly his sentiment was that he'd had enough of horses for the time being. The weekend beckoned and he craved his home and the company of his friends. Decision made, he made for the car park. As he walked along the lawn in front of the main grandstand he passed group of racing stewards. Not for the first time, he was struck by how much alike they all looked. And not simply because of their ubiquitous trilby-style hat. His impression was that they had a touch of the equine in their appearance - thin long faces, high cheek bones, tight all-business lips and prominent hawkish noses. Perhaps like their thoroughbred charges they were all distantly related; a product of a stud-farm somewhere where they were specially bred for their role.

His absurd musings made him feel much happier and by the time he had retrieved his bike and headed for the highway back to Dublin, he was almost back to normal. The ride through the country further cheered him and gave him time to put matters in perspective. *Toughen up Aiden,* he chided himself. *It's rubbish to let one setback knock you over. Look at the positives. One week and already you've pocketed the equivalent of two month's salary. And the money is tax free – how sweet is that. Okay there was a glitch today. Up to now, the gift had seemed to be sure-fire – so what happened? Is two results in a day is an absolute barrier or is it is more about how strong I am at the moment? Only way to find out is to keep pushing, keep challenging – crash through or crash.* Confidence restored he was ready to get back in the game – but not until he had a few days break. He spent the remainder of the ride admiring the scenery until he reached the outskirts of Dublin and had to turn his attention to navigating his way through the inevitable city traffic snarls.

Aiden spent the weekend happily pottering around and occupying his time on matters entirely unrelated to gambling or horses. The highlights were a lengthy, aimless and utterly delightful hour-long chat with Sharni via Skype and Saturday night with his mates listening to live music at a grungy but hip local pub. Sunday and Monday slid by quietly and by Tuesday morning, refreshed and recommitted, he was back on the beat. Over the following days he retraced a circuit similar to the previous week. The major difference was that he that he set himself to try for three winners at each meeting. His first two attempts were failures but he fancied that he almost made it happen on the second occasion. Or at the least, the effort did not leave him dizzy and completely drained.

He was back at the Wexford track when the breakthrough came – he brought home his third winner at a single meeting. It was a moment of immense satisfaction rather than jubilation. He had set himself a challenge and he had pulled it off. And even more importantly, it confirmed his hope that his ability was only limited by his strength of will and control over his mind. He repeated the feat at Gowan Park, the scene of his earlier failure. Happy with what he'd achieved, he reverted to his initial plan of confining himself to two winners per fixture. His reasoning was that he would be less likely to draw attention to himself. Already, he had begun to recognize several of the bookies; not particularly surprising because many of them made their living by travelling from meeting to meeting around the countryside much as he was doing. His concern naturally was that recognition might be reciprocal. As a precaution, he tried to avoid betting with anyone who looked familiar but that was not always feasible at smaller mid-week events where there were only a handful of bookies standing and the choice was limited.

By the fourth week, what had started as a jaunt was quickly becoming a chore. He was fine spending time alone – in fact he enjoyed it - but only up to a point. At heart he was a social animal and he needed to share his experiences with his friends. He now carried his netbook on the road with him so that he could communicate with his mates and Sharni when he stayed overnight somewhere. Although this helped greatly, he knew he was reaching the end of this cycle of his venture. The song in his head that morning was the Boomtown Rates number 'I don't like Mondays' and while he had no urge to climb a tower and start shooting people, the message to self was clear enough.

It was when he was back at Leopardstown that events took a turn that decided things for him. As he was collecting his winnings one of the bookies gave him a wave and called out to him. "Hey, young fella. You seem to be doing alright for yourself lately. I'm pleased that you didn't take any of mine. What's your name, son?"

This was the very situation that he wanted to avoid and warning bells went off in his head. It would appear very strange if he refused to answer – it was simply a friendly and innocent question - but he certainly did not want to give out his real name. He tried to quickly dredge one up. Earlier he had mulling over how much had changed in the short time since being forced to leave his job and by virtue of the quirky way our brains work sometimes, the first name that popped into its head was that of his ex-boss. "It's O'Mara, Simon O'Mara," he replied hoping that it came out sounding natural.

The man, O'Brien, according to the name stenciled on his bag, nodded and went on, "I think I've seen you at a few of the same tracks as I've been working the past couple of weeks and you've had some good collects if I'm not mistaken."

Shit, shit, think quick Aiden. "Yeah, I'm on holidays and just having a bit of fun. It's just about coming to an end. And you're right I got lucky once or twice but you haven't seen the betting slips that I've thrown away – and there were plenty of them."

That brought forth a smile from O'Brien. "That's what a struggling old bookie wants to hear. Can't have the punters doing too well, eh." With that O'Brien turned his attention to serving a patron who had arrived to place a wager.

Whew it looks like I got away with it. At least that bastard O'Mara has been good for something.

As soon as he was out of sight of O'Brien, he left the racecourse and headed straight home. He poured himself a beer and sat down at the kitchen table to think things through. *I got too carried away with myself. The adrenaline rush took over and I forgot the basics. When I work with Jimmy we're always careful. We keep our winnings quiet and sometimes deliberately lose so that we can make a song and dance about it. That way people tend to remember the losers not the winners. But here I am swanning around winning all the time. It's no wonder I'm being noticed. Now I need to go back and try to salvage the situation. If I'm just another loser, I'll quickly be forgotten. Then the smart thing would be to cool it.* And then his last thought on the subject brought forth a grin because after all, he had been very, very successful. *Well at least for a little while.*

    Two days later he put his scheme into play. He began the day by selecting his target horses in back to back races midway through the program. Next he went to a betting shop on the other side of town where he was a complete stranger and placed his bets. This was so that he was not out of pocket when he deliberately lost later in the day. Then he made his way to the track. He wanted to establish a pattern of increasingly desperate betting – the modus operandi of a mug punter. His first bet was a moderate amount on a no-hoper that performed as expected and finished down the track. Grumbling loudly about the injustice of the universe, he doubled his bet on another long-shot in the next race. It didn't win.

    The two following events were the ones that he intended to win through his off-course bets but here at the track, he would be backing more losers. He cautioned himself not to lay it on too thick. He wanted to be noticed but he also wanted to be believable; and without a doubt, he was no actor. He entered the bookmakers' ring shaking his head and trying to look dumbfounded that the gods had cruelly abandoned him. He doubled his bet again – it was now a sizable amount – and split it between two bookies. He made sure that one of them was with his new acquaintance, O'Brien. Apart from wanting him to notice that he was losing, he seemed a nice enough old bugger and so he might as well have a share of the spoils. Bets made, he went trackside and brought home the horse he really wanted to win. He didn't even bother to watch where the other one finished. He smothered a satisfied smile and tried to look suitably crestfallen as he slowly returned to the betting ring. One final time he went through the charade, doubling his bet and spreading half across several bookies and placing half with

O'Brien. This time the man looked at the amount being wagered and with an eyebrow cocked, he looked as if he was about to say something. It was that look of a father when he thinks his child is making a big mistake but then decides that maybe it's best to learn the harsh lesson. In the end he sighed knowingly and took the bet.

The race delivered the expected result – winner with the betting shop, loser with O'Brien and co. He felt quite pleased with himself – it was all a bit Machiavellian really and he was having fun. So much so that he was having difficulty trying to make himself look distraught. He wound up standing in front of a mirror in the gents toilet practicing facial expressions. Maybe I should have beer on my breath and come across a bit worse for wear, he thought and then quickly pulled himself back into line. *Getting carried away again Aiden. Just try to look shattered and leave it at that.* When he felt that he'd gotten his appearance about right, he once more walked slowly though the bookmakers ring. O'Brien saw him and waved him over.

"Looks like that winning streak of yours might have come to an end," observed O'Brien.

"Yes I think you're right. It was good fun for a while. I thought I couldn't lose but now I'm starting to give it all back."

"This may sound funny coming from someone in my business but if you want my opinion you should quit now and go home. Maybe buy yourself a nice present with what you have left – sort like a memento of a rare purple patch."

"I know you're right even if my ego wants to keep on going. Well my holidays are coming to an end anyway. So you know what – I'm going to take your advice and pack it in. And I might just treat myself with a nice new sound system I've had my eye on."

"Smart lad. Enjoy it and stay away from the punt okay," was the bookie's parting admonition.

"I'm not sure if I can promise that but we'll see, eh."

CHAPTER 19

Next morning Aiden arose happy that he'd put an end, at least for a time, to his punting roadshow. Hopefully in the wash-up, he had also managed to portray himself as someone who had been on a fling but whose luck had run out and he would slide quickly into obscurity in the minds of the bookmaking community. The venture overall, he decided, had been a great success. He checked his bank balance online and was gratified to find that although far from being wealthy he had certainly built up a nice savings nest-egg.

The only thing troubling him now was whether he should tell Jimmy about what he'd been doing. Or rather, he knew he should tell him but was embarrassed that despite the many warnings from Jimmy, it had not occurred to him at all that his actions might have had an element of risk. He hadn't ignored his uncle's apprehensions; they had simply not entered his thoughts. To that extent he had been selfish or at the very least, insensitive. He held out for two days of rampant procrastination before the nagging voice of conscience won out. He called Jimmy and arranged to catch up with him later in the day on the pretext that he wanted to buy him a beer or two – after all, it couldn't hurt to generate a few brownie points.

Maureen answered the door when Aiden knocked. She wasn't a tall woman and it was as if her 5 feet 2 inch frame was just too petit to contain her effervescent and generous spirit. It spilled over as she hugged him tightly and then held him at arm's length while she looked him over. "It's so lovely to see you Aiden," she said and dragged him into another embrace before stepping back and waggling a figure at him. "I should be scolding you for not calling round more often but as soon as I see you I can't help but forgive you."

Aiden's grin was as spontaneous as it was heartfelt. She had a way of making him feel special and he took pleasure in trying to do the same with her. "Hi Maureen – you're looking as fetching as always."

He fancied he saw just a hint of a blush color her cheeks and for sure she preened slightly. "You just keep that blarney to yourself young man. I suppose you're here to collect that old scoundrel of an uncle of yours. You're welcome to him – I'm always glad to get him out from under my feet." It was all said with an implied wink clearly coming through. She adored Jimmy and happily took him foibles and all.

At that moment he appeared in the doorway and interjected with a smirk, "Hope everyone's okay with me interrupting this mutual admiration society."

"To be sure, if I was 20 years younger, I'd be dropping you like a hot potato, you old goat. Now off you both go and don't you be rolling in drunk at all hours of the night."

They walked to Jimmy's current favorite watering-hole. It was an older style pub whose owners had resisted the urge to reinvent it as another of the increasing number of swish and expensive 'gastro-pubs' that were cropping up all across the city. They both felt that its slightly time-worn décor gave it a comfortable charm akin to that of a private club from days past. Much better than the results of some of the more pretentious revamps. There weren't many patrons in as yet and they quickly completed the mandatory greeting rituals before grabbing a table in the corner. As promised, Aiden lined up a round of drinks. Jimmy was a wily old fox and he suspected that Aiden had something to tell him but he had no clue as to what it might be. So he was happy to bide his time and wait for the youngster to enlighten him on the real purpose of their meeting up. They were into their second round when Aiden directed the conversation to the subject of horseracing. He tiptoed around the edges for a while and then with a deep breath, plunged into a detailed account of what he had been doing for the past few weeks. His explanation included the when and why he had realized that his excessive enthusiasm might have put them in jeopardy and what he had done about it. Finally he finished and waited nervously while his uncle processed everything he had heard. He had no idea how Jimmy would react but found himself surprised by the calm response.

"Don't be too hard on yourself boyo. I've actually been amazed at how well you've handled the gift up till now. You're young and it's a powerful temptation to cut loose. Don't think that I don't sometimes feel the same way. And what's more it was me, not you, who was approached in Marseilles way back when. So you should be proud that you've shown real maturity in not letting it go completely to your head. Even now when you did get a bit carried away, you had the wherewithal to try to rescue the situation."

"Thanks Jimmy. I really appreciate that you don't want to tear my head off. Anyway, I still mean what I say. I'm going to lay low for a while."

"I agree with you there. You should keep away from the track for a time. Let's you and me go back to the old approach and keep a lid on the size of our winnings."

"Count me in. I don't think that I could stop punting altogether – I'd go spare... Speaking of which, now that I'm not working and chasing horses around the countryside, I don't know quite what I should being doing with myself. I'm not one to lounge about day-in, day-out – any suggestions?"

"It's strange really. For a few lucky people, their work is their calling and they are completely satisfied - it defines who they are. But the majority of us get trapped in a job that we have to make the best of – some days are good, some bad and most days are somewhere in between. What about you, son? What did your career mean to you?"

"I enjoyed my job a lot but the funny thing is that I don't miss it nearly as much as I thought I would. For me now, it's more a case of what's next."

"Okay, well then I tell you my way and you can judge what might suit you," offered Jimmy. "As you know, I do a bit of work here and there when I choose to. People believe that I do odd jobs to get a bit of cash to get by on and that suits my purposes – less chance someone might wonder where the money comes from. But the truth is I don't do it for money. I take a job because there's something in the work that interests me. Like what I told about why I became part of that test group at your clinic; partly so that I could see what it was that you did and partly because the idea of studying the brain intrigued me. The rest of the time, I amuse myself in other ways. Over the years, I've tried my hand at all sorts of pursuits. Things like painting, sculpture, carpentry, welding. I even had a go at reading the works of some of our greatest western philosophers. My trouble is that I'm not very good at sticking at things. Not that I have any real regrets. It's often forgotten that acquiring knowledge and skills is a noble end in itself. You have a wonderful opportunity to explore things of your own choosing but as to what they might be, you're going to have to find that out yourself."

"Thanks Jimmy. All of that makes complete sense to me. You've got a knack for cutting through the fog and making things a whole lot clearer. I don't know yet what my grand pursuit will be but I'm confident I'll know it when I find it. Now for the next order of business – as I'm not in the shit with you, it must be your turn to get us last drinks."

Over the final round, they had a good laugh about some of Jimmy's ventures over the years, particularly the output from an ill-fated endeavor that combined his attempts to combine welding and sculpture.

The talk with his uncle inspired him to revive some activities that he had enjoyed previously but had let slide. He used to be a keen reader and the following morning found him at the library in the Eastern Philosophy section. He selected a number of books written by Thich Nhat Hanh a Buddhist monk and peace and human rights activist who left Vietnam in exile in the 1960's. From humble beginnings he went on to become a very highly regarded and influential teacher. He was also a prolific writer whose approach combined several Buddhist streams with elements of western philosophy that resulted in a more contemporary approach to meditation. Aiden had read one of his books previously and it had struck a chord with him both in terms of style and message. He had been intending to have a look at more of the monk's works but until now had not quite gotten around to it.

The next change he made was to get back into regular physical training at his dojo – much to the surprise his dojo master.

His interest in Buddhism and Asian martial arts traced back to a period spent backpacking in the Southern Hemisphere. He and Dylan had spent six months travelling together. They started by taking in New Zealand from end to end and then travelled up the east coast of Australia from Melbourne all the way north to the Great Barrier Reef. Next they flew to Thailand, covering Bangkok, Chiang Mai and Chiang Rai before following the well established trail overland to Sihanouk, Cambodia, up to the capital, Phnom Penh and on to Siem Reap; the base for exploring the astonishing Ankor complex of Wats and ruins. Siem Reap was also home to a surprising array of pubs. They finally dragged themselves away from Pub Street and crossed into Laos following the mighty Mekong River. There they embraced 'tubing' in Vang Vieng. This consisted of floating down the Nam Song River on an inflated rubber tube, starting with a Beer Lao in hand and stopping for a cheap liquid top up at any of the numerous wooden bars that have established themselves along the way. Their final stop was the historic and languid town of Luang Prabang; a place where it is easier to stay, drifting along happily than summon the energy to leave. But eventually the time came and then home via Hong Kong.

Everything about South East Asia enchanted him; the people and their humor in the face of poverty, the bustle, the sights, the food and even the exotic, sometimes overpowering aromas that were always in the air. Then there was the heady feeling of being on the edge. At no point was there any real danger but the foreignness of it all made every day something on an adventure. He understood why so many European pioneers had been drawn to the region, even beyond the obvious lure of a chance to make a fortune. They had wanted to continue on, keen to take in Vietnam, China, Malaysia, India and perhaps Nepal but they had run out of money and time. It was a profound experience for him; the region had gotten into his blood and he promised himself that one day he would finish the journey.

His love of cooking gave him another outlet. He set about improving and extending his repertoire, focusing on those South East Asian styles that he loved – particularly Thai and Vietnamese dishes. He enjoyed choosing a dish for the evening meal and then going out to source fresh ingredients. He had taken to having the lads around a couple of times each week and they had given his increased dedication in the kitchen a big 'thumbs up'. The final plank in his new lifestyle was his regular sessions with Jimmy, finding a winner or two.

Aiden's day to day life slipped into a pleasant routine and for a while he was content to drift along with it. But there was one thing that chafed. Aiden craved the challenge and the thrill of being at the track directly influencing race outcomes. He imagined that it was the same feeling that a dedicated jogger or gym-junkie experienced when they missed out on a steady fix of their chosen pursuit. For him, it had begun as a non-specific awareness that something was lacking and proceeded to grow by the day into a sensation of emptiness. He tried to stand firm but was losing the battle.

The upcoming Irish Derby, to be run the following Saturday proved to be too tempting. Aiden decided that he had to be there. What could be better than a big occasion and a big race? The next day when they were together he broached the notion with his uncle. "It's been a while now and seems like my on-course punting spree hasn't brought on any kind of backlash and I've gotta say, I'm really over not being able to be trackside. What about you and me go to Curragh to watch the Derby on Saturday?" Then he added cheekily, "You can pick one out and I'll bewitch it to make sure we get a winner."

"Ho bloody ho. I know it put the wind up me when you first told me about your method but I'm okay with it now – well anyway, I'm okay with you being the one doing it."

"Couldn't help myself. Got to get a little dig in when I can... So what do you say about Derby Day?"

"For sure, I'm up for a bet on one of our premier events – it would be unpatriotic not to, eh. (That said with a wink.) But as for going - no, sorry but it's not for me. It's been a very long time since I've been to racecourse and I plan to keep it that way. I'm not one for crowds and you know me and my low profile when it comes to the punt. I know too many people and

I don't want to be seen out there – especially when I make a collect from the bookies."

"Suit yourself. But I'll definitely go and I'll make sure we steer home the Derby winner."

"You'll be on your own with that as well, I'm afraid. I had a look at the form guide this morning and I couldn't raise a flicker when I studied the Derby. It was a strange sensation, like there was some sort of blockage or resistance when I tried to focus on the race."

"Weird. Well don't worry. You know how touchy these highly bred nags can be - I'll sort it out eyeball to eyeball with them on Saturday."

"Nice to see you so confident. As for my contribution, the good news is that I've got one in the 3rd and it should be at very nice odds."

Now that he was going to be at the course, Aiden was keen to bet bigger. He wanted to bring Jimmy along; at least as far as he was comfortable. "Excellent, I'll use that to stake me for the main event. On that subject, I think we should up the ante in the Derby. We can afford it. Even though we've stayed very cautious, we've still built up a nice bank behind us. And with the Derby being such a big event, there will be lots of big punters about and a huge betting pool. So I reckon we'd be safe enough with a bigger wager."

"I know my conservatism is a bit of a wet blanket but years of habit are hard to change. But having said that, there's logic to your argument and you probably deserve a reward for your patience. Okay, I'm game. How much do you have in mind?"

"Well, I'm thinking of having a thousand on your pick in the 3rd and then putting whatever I collect on my horse in the Derby."

"You're not messing around are you? I'm not ready to go that big. For mine, I'm happy to match you on the first bet but I'd like you to tuck away half of what I collect on my nag. The other half, you can put on your fancy."

"Fair enough - that's settled then. Now bring on race-day, I can't wait."

CHAPTER 20

The rest of the week crawled by until finally it was Saturday. Aiden figured that he would be far too edgy if he arrived at the track too early. He found ways to keep himself occupied and made it through the morning. He reached Curragh just after the 2nd race had been run, giving him plenty of time to place the bets on Jimmy's horse. All went according to plan and together their total collect amounted to €12,000. He was pleased that he had planned ahead by bringing with him three wallets and a money belt. The purpose was to spread the cash around on his person as at least some protection against pick-pockets.

With time to fill in until the main event, he made his way through to the warm-up area to have a look at the Derby contenders. The race was not until later in the day and the horses were still in their stalls. As he walked around the stalls he was taken by lovely big chestnut gelding whose coat gleamed like burnished copper. The horse was all the more distinctive in that he had four socks. But by far his most striking feature was that he was a bald face - his white blaze stretched across his forehead, his eye line and right down his nose. The name on the stall was 'Comanche Patch'; an appropriate moniker given that his markings evoked thoughts of an American Indian paint. Aiden checked his race book and found that the horse was reasonably well in the market. It was on the third line of early betting with odds of 7 to 1. *Perfect- not the favorite but not a donkey either.*

"You're the one for me aren't you boy," he said to the horse. The beast looked at him when he spoke and he fancied that he saw agreement in its eyes.

He returned to the betting ring to check the odds. His approach was to make a number of bets on the horse across the next couple of hours and spread around several bookies. His hope was that this tactic would keep the odds he received from shortening too much. After placing the first round of bets, something that should have been obvious finally dawned on him. *Shit, when my bloke wins, I'll be collecting over 50 grand.* He was already uncomfortable carrying around the cash he right now. *Whoa that's way too much dough to lug around on my own.* The solution came to him quickly. *That's it, the on-course tote – they pay out big wins by bank check. I'll put half of the money through them.*

After completing that task, he spent a pleasant hour strolling around the course, soaking up the festive atmosphere. The groups of young party-goers on the lawns were well into their bottles of bubbly and the noise level was rising – but it was a happy sound that spoke of good cheer and light-hearted banter. The dress code ran from casual to high fashion finery and on through to all sorts of costumes from fun to the outrageous and on to some that bordered on bizarre. There were those who marked the occasion fittingly dressed in jockey's silks or wore papier-mâché horse heads. Others looked as if they were getting an early start for Halloween or maybe still getting home from Walpurgis Night. Some perhaps had come straight from a bacchanalian feast. Aiden was particularly amused by the absurd look of a group of comely lasses who had dressed as the five food groups.

Twenty minutes before the Derby, he was back with the bookies making his final round of wagers. He was very pleased with himself as he reviewed his wad of betting slips but his euphoria evaporated to be replaced by dismay when he heard the sound of trumpets calling the horses to the starting stalls. He had become too absorbed in his mission with the bookies and had taken too long. Clutching his betting slips, in half panic, he ran towards the main grandstand. He inevitably found himself caught up in a throng of other stragglers. Pushing and shoving with the best of them, he fought his way up the stairs to the stand. He had been prudent in reserving a seat on the end of a row, high up in a back corner where he had an excellent view of the course but also where it was a little less crowded. The hitch now was that it was a long climb up to reach his spot. By the time he had clambered into his seat, he was gasping for breath and totally flustered.

As the gates flew back and the horses surged forward he forced himself to methodically work his way through his calming and focusing routine. By mid-race he was in control, primed and ready. His horse, Comanche Patch was well positioned as he began to set to work. At first it all proceeded in a way that was starting to become familiar. Almost immediately, everything slowed down and took on surreal air but when he pushed out his thoughts, circumstances changed quickly. The perspective was wrong. It was not like it had been when he had done this before. It was a little like he was seeing things through a fish-eye lens. And it felt different. It was as if he had come up against a barrier and now the barrier was pushing back. He mentally pushed harder, probing for a way through. When he looked at Comanche Patch, he could see that the horse was trying to accelerate but it too appeared to be meeting resistance. Aiden continued his silent struggle. Time seemed frozen. He had to find a way to penetrate. He concentrated hard, imagining he was shaping his thought into a tight ball. He compressed it more. Now it was a brilliant diamond-hard orb. He hurled it at the barrier. Resistance evaporated and he broke through. It was as if there had been a bubble around the entire field of horses and now his animal was free. With his influence it surged past the runners in front of it and went to the line to win by a length. During the tussle, Aiden had unconsciously risen to his feet. Now his knees buckled and slid back into his seat, his forehead gleaming with sweat and his breathing ragged.

As he composed himself, he reflected on what he had just experienced. He was quite sure that he knew what had happened. He had come up against another with the gift and he had triumphed. It was a heady feeling as his fatigue gave way to exhilaration.

When he went to collect, there was one more incident that worried him. As he accepted a wad of notes from one of the bookies, the man remarked on his success. That took the edge off his mood. *Shit, I've stood out more than I wanted to – not good.* "Others people's money. I'm just the gopher," he blurted out before hurrying away. It was not unusual for betting syndicates to use someone to make bets on their behalf. *Let's hope that throws him off.*

He got hold of the rest of his winnings as quickly as he could and immediately left the track. He was glad that half of it was in the form of a check but even so, he felt like his jacket bulged with bank notes and it was making him nervous. As a precaution he took a taxi home. He called Jimmy and arranged to pick him up on the way through to his house. The trip gave him time to reflect on all that had occurred and by the time the taxi reached Dublin, Aiden was feeling much less anxious. He had managed to rationalize his way through most of it. The comment from the bookie didn't worry him overly but the confrontation during the running of the race was a concern. Could it have repercussions? He couldn't see how they could be identified let alone be found. But still it was a complication that they could do without. He would have to tell Jimmy about it but he'd let him enjoy their success first before he filled him in on the details.

As usual, Jimmy's delight proved infectious and he readily joined in with the whooping and backslapping as they divided the booty. He bided his time and when celebrating had run its course, he recounted all of the circumstances surrounding the win. By the time he had finished, Jimmy had blanched visibly, so he added what they were both thinking. "I guess we've got to face it – it's highly likely that I've gone up against that lot that you told me about."

To his credit, Jimmy gathered himself and recovered quickly. The stricken look left his face and was replaced by one of grim determination. "Like I told you at the clinic, I'm in this all the way. I went with you on increasing our bet with my eyes open so as far as I'm concerned, we took a chance and now we'll see what comes of it. Besides, if it is them, it won't be easy for them to track us down. You said it yourself the other day – it's a big race and a lot of people were betting."

"I agree with you there. If they start asking around, the bookies at the track will probably remember me running around collecting the winnings but none of them know me by name."

"Yeah. Besides, how much time and trouble are they really likely to spend to find a needle in a haystack?"

The conversation went on that way into the evening with each reassuring the other. The discussion was washed down with plenty of beer and by the time they parted, they were feeling bullet-proof.

CHAPTER 21

Despite a slight hangover, Aiden was very, very pleased with himself. He ran his hands through his winnings, spreading the notes around and then stacking them again in a neat pile. He started to walk away but was drawn back to the stack and couldn't resist counting the cash for the umpteenth time. And for the umpteenth time it resulted in a Faganesque display; rubbing his hands together and chuckling maniacally. And to top off all being good with his world, Sharni was arriving tomorrow for a week's visit.

There was no football game on, so he planned to have a lazy, relaxing Sunday. He went out to his local store and returned with the oversized Sunday edition of the newspaper. After cooking his breakfast, he spread the newspaper across the table and settled in for an extended cover to cover read. The sports section put a slight dampener on his pleasant morning. The coverage of the Derby included a story about a sizeable betting plunge that had missed its mark. The amount involved was not mentioned but it was big enough to shorten the odds of the horse in question from second favorite to favorite. The distant alarm bells that sounded inside Aiden's head were quickly put down. But he did acknowledge the wry thought that out there somewhere, somebody would be royally pissed off.

In another part of Europe that somebody had summoned Nick Kelly to his office. When Kelly entered, Lukas Muller was behind his desk with Durand, his Executive

Assistant and Olivadi, his Head of Security occupying two of the visitor's chairs. Kelly took a seat and waited. It was a short wait. There was no preamble as Muller launched in. "What the hell happened? How did he fail," he hissed through clenched teeth.

Kelly sat, his face carefully composed – serious, brow furrowed, concerned – his usual ironic bearing fully suppressed. He knew he needed to tread carefully. When things went against Lukas, he could become vindictive and worse, he could be irrational in how he obtained satisfaction. Without waiting for an answer, Lukas continued.

"We lost €100,000 – you hear – 100,000. And that's not even contemplating what the winnings would have been. I want answers."

Kelly resolutely stifled the sudden urge to squirm in his seat. He felt like an errant schoolboy called to the Headmaster's Office. "I've had a long talk with our man and he's at a loss. He's positive that when he chose the horse, it was a true episode. The only thing that I can think of is that he came up against another player and he was outgunned."

"I wonder – could it be the Irishman – after all this time?" Muller muttered, thinking aloud. When he saw puzzled looks around him, he went on. "Years ago there was an Irishman that my father tried to recruit. But he vanished and has not resurfaced."

Muller gave them a brief summary of the incident and then turned his attention to Olivadi. "I think that Kelly may be correct. Whoever it is he is powerful. I want you to find this player. Start in Ireland. I don't care what it takes - I want to know who he is and where he is. And when you reach him, he must be made to join us."

Olivadi made knew it would be a waste of words to try to explain the complexity of the task that he had just been given. The way it worked with Muller was you received your orders and you carried them out. "I'll get a couple of men over there immediately. They can start with trying to uncover the money trail. We need to trace those who made money out of the result. It might be a long list, though."

"I don't care if you have to look into the entire male population. Find him and bring him on board."

"And if he won't join us?" returned Olivadi.

"Then that will be a decision he will live to regret. One more thing - bear in mind the profile of that Irishman I told you about. You have a rough description and approximate age. Talk to bookmakers, check out betting shops. He may have been prudent but somebody will know of a man who has just a little too much of the luck of the Irish."

Having taken positive action Lukas began to relax. Soon his whole posture exuded serenity. He concluded the summit with final instructions – his tone the epitome of amiable camaraderie. His men were well accustomed to these rapid personality changes. Much of the time, the term 'austere' was perfect in describing Muller, although there were times that he could cycle toward 'charming'. The disturbing fact was that he could just as easily tread uncomfortably close to 'psychotic'.

"Now let's get to it. Philippe, you work with Renzo on this. I want the best operators hired for the job – no shortcuts. We will not fail. Nick, no doubt the way the race turned out was traumatic for your player. Make sure he knows that he is not being blamed and has our full confidence. As for me, it's time that I visited with my father. I need to seek his advice and I do not like to discuss such matters over the telephone."

A week after handing over the business, his father had taken up permanent residency in a suite in a five star hotel in

Nice. By European standards, the suite was immense. It comprised two bedrooms, a marble bathroom with spa bath and double walk-in shower, separate toilet, a sitting room and a study. It was furnished to a standard that you would expect for a hotel of its class and the balconies off the bedroom and sitting room overlooked the Promenade des Anglais with the beach and beautiful Mediterranean Sea beyond. Andre had told Lukas that the sight of the lithe, tanned young things frolicking half-naked on the beach helped to keep him young. Lukas knew that his father was still an active and striking man and he had no doubt that more than one of these nymphets would have wound up gracing the king-sized bed in his father's suite.

CHAPTER 22

The flight from Glasgow arrived at 11 a.m. Aiden waited at the baggage collection carousel thinking about how close they had become keeping in touch through their cyber relationship. He was excited but now that the moment was at hand, he was also a little on edge. He had thought a lot about the time they would spend together. Could reality live up to the fantasy?

When he saw her approaching his beaming smile was spontaneous and he hoped that it would provide a solid cover for his nervousness. Sharni's happy expression almost outshone his own. They hugged and shared a gentle but tender kiss. Not much was said as they collected her large backpack and made their way to the taxi rank. Now that they were together in the flesh they were both just a bit coy – unconsciously waiting for affirmation that their feelings were mutual. Finally they verbally tripped over each other trying to get the conversation started and the chuckles that followed broke through the barrier. They chatted freely and easily and by the time they reached Aiden's house, they were completely comfortable in each other's company.

He had planned to demonstrate how sophisticated he was by letting events unfold slowly but as soon as they were inside, it took just one kiss and another part of his anatomy high-jacked all cognitive functions. Happily she was of a like mind. They renewed acquaintances frantically the first time and then later in a somewhat more unhurried manner.

Night was falling by the time hunger drove them back out into the world. They dined at a nearby eatery that specialized in southern Indian cuisine and then returned home to set about firming up the plans for what she had dubbed her grand tour of Eire. Aiden brought out a folder crammed with brochures and maps that he had assembled and dumped it on the table.

"Thanks for agreeing to calling in on my folks for an overnighter as our first stop," he said. "Their pub's got a nice country feel to it and the town's a pretty little place. I've already called my mother and she can't wait to meet you."

He left it unsaid that he couldn't wait to show her off.

"I'm looking forward to it as well – even though I'm a tad nervous about it."

"No need to be. I promise that Mary and Shaun are as easy-going a pair as you'll find and I know they will adore you. Besides, any heat will be on me. When I rang my mum she made sure she let me know in no uncertain terms that it was high time I paid them a visit."

"Mothers are the same the world over on that subject."

"That's for sure. Luckily I was prepared for a bit of scolding so I had my contrite voice ready and I think I charmed my way out of trouble."

"Hmm – sounds to me like errant sons might be the same the world over as well!"

"We have to be to survive against the way all women stick together."

She gave him a playful punch to the arm. "Oh the woes of the poor down trodden male of the species. Now let's get back on task. You were telling me about starting off with a visit with your parents."

"About that - I've also organized Uncle Jimmy and his partner Maureen to come down for a couple of days as well."

"That's great. You talk about him often. He's obviously a big part of your life – and I'm sure he's nothing like the rogue you make him out to be."

"You wait and see," he said laughing. "Now, I've got a few suggestions of where we might go but first things first. Any places that you've got in mind?"

"Well, I've done a bit more investigation into the Irish part of my ancestry and it turns out that it traces back to Killarney, not Dublin as I thought."

He couldn't stop himself from treading on thin ice. "You were only out by the entire width of the country."

"Ho, ho, very funny." She tried and failed in an attempt to sound miffed. "In point of fact, Mr. Smarty, the confusion came about because she did live for a time in Dublin before she sailed to Scotland with her new husband. My Great-grandfather was a Glaswegian who had found his Irish rose when on a trip to Ireland as a young man."

He decided that he had better not push it too far. "Ah, that explains it then. In any case, it works out well. Killarney and a circuit 'round the Ring of Kerry is on my list – great coastal run – you'll like it. So that gets a tick."

With that settled, they talked about other beauty spots that could go on the list. In the end they came up with a circuit that would take them west along the southern coast, up the west coast as high as the Cliffs of Moher and Galway Bay and then inland back to Dublin.

"I'm so happy that we're doing it on your bike. It'll be the perfect way to see the countryside. I'm much more interested in that and the small villages than the bigger cities."

That was the perfect segue for Aiden. Unbeknown to Sharni, the intention to travel by motorcycle had given him a notion of a surprise gift. He got in contact with her girlfriends to find out her various size statistics. Armed with that intelligence he had bought her a helmet and a complete set of leathers, riding boots and all. On the mannequin, they looked perfect. They offered the right amount of protection but were still feminine – figure hugging and stylish. The time was right to present her with the gear. He did the whole corny routine – making her cover her eyes while he laid out the items on the table, feeling like an excited child. When he finally allowed her to look, he was treated to a squeal of delight. She insisted on immediately trying on the entire outfit. The fit was perfect.

"So how do I look?"

"One word – Hot!"

"Good answer. I feel like Catwoman – and it's a really comfortable outfit. I might not take it off."

"Whoa, steady girl," he said, eyebrows raised in mock dismay. "Let's not get too carried away."

With a wink and a devilish grin, she replied, "Well it's possible I could slip out of it later."

Next day, they took the N11 highway out of Dublin, south to Bray and then the smaller coastal road through Bray Head and on to Wicklow township. Although it is officially the county seat, it ranks in size in the region behind Bray and Greystones. The town itself is set around a pleasant crescent bay and had become a popular tourist base for exploring the surrounding countryside. The steady growth in the number of visitors had resulted in new businesses opening, including a sprinkling of trendy restaurants and shops. Happily, despite the modernization, it retained its old-world feel.

The morning was pleasantly mild and the trip was easy. He loved riding but having a gorgeous woman behind him added a whole new dimension. Sharni took to it with assurance. She had a natural grace and seemed to know instinctively when and how to shift her weight to make the ride trouble-free.

He was looking forward to seeing everyone together. It had been a big thing when his folks took a chance to start a new venture at their time of life. Not many people have the drive to leave the city they grew up in and plunge into the unknown. What they lacked in experience was outweighed by the right mix of business nous and gregarious natures and they had made a fine fist of it. He was proud of their success and pleased with how happy they both were in this new life they had taken on.

They arrived in town midday and proceeded directly to his parents' place. It was a typical small country inn – stone walls, low ceiling complete with rough-hewn beams, floor of blonde wood. The timber of the bench tables, chairs and barstools were a dark walnut. At one end of the room a long polished rosewood-topped bar vied for dominance of the room with the huge bluestone open fireplace in the middle of one wall. Upstairs were six cozy bedrooms, decked out in period glory and two shared bathrooms. Jimmy and Maureen had come down the previous day and were first to see them enter from their table in the corner of the room and immediately came over to greet them. His father was tending bar – two barstools occupied by a couple of old snoozers who had probably been drinking there most of their adult lives. Didn't matter to them how many times the pub might change hands or change styles, it was their boozer and their preferred spot and that was that.

As soon as his father finished with his customer, he bellowed something in the direction of the kitchen and came round the bar. A moment later his mother emerged apron-clad from the kitchen. The sounds of welcome escalated to a cacophony as everyone spoke at once and for a moment Aiden and Sharni feared they might be swept away by a torrent of hugs and kisses. When the hubbub calmed, Aiden introduced

Sharni to all. He smiled when both his father and Jimmy gave him a covert nod of approval. He almost laughed out loud when his mother did the same.

Shaun had let the locals know he was closing the premises at 2 p.m. for a private function and as the time approached, the few old regulars still in the bar finished their drinks and with good natured remarks about the dangers inherent in lack of constant fluid, headed for the exit. He and Mary had spent the morning putting together the makings for a fine long lunch.

The family took their places and the mountain of food progressively came out. They all chatted happily between mouthfuls. Everybody was in fine form. Jimmy entertained with outrageous tall tales that caused Maureen to mutter more than once about 'silly old farts trying to impress a pretty young thing'. Shaun had them in stitches when he described the antics of some of the more eccentric characters from around the district who frequented his inn. Fortunately the subject of Aiden leaving his job didn't come up so he avoided any awkward questions on that matter. That said Aiden did hold his breath when Mary began to reminisce on his childhood. But on the whole he got off lightly with his Mary showing admirable restraint and only relating about half of the excruciatingly 'cute' things he had done as a baby, child and adolescent. His mother then moved on to what she would have judged to be very subtle enquiries about Sharni's background. Aiden thought that the depth of questioning would have brought a nostalgic tear to the eye of a member of the Spanish Inquisition. Somehow Sharni didn't seem to mind – another unknowable mystery of women.

They meal eventually came to an end late afternoon and Mary suggested that the youngsters might want to go upstairs and unpack. She announced that she had made up two rooms but stunned Aiden – doubly – by demurely by inferring that it was possible that they might only need one of the rooms.

Demure was not a word he usually associated with his mother and as for sharing a room with a women before wedlock, he could only conclude there was something in the sea air down here. With that they retired – waddled might be more accurate term - to their room.   They lazed around like a pair of anacondas letting the meal digest while downstairs the pub reopened and patrons began to drift in for their after-work tipple on the way home.

In the early evening, after freshening up Aiden and Sharni gathered up Jimmy and Maureen and took a stroll around the village center and through the docklands. The institution of an evening promenade is not as culturally entrenched in Ireland as it is in other parts of Europe but nonetheless there were plenty of people about and it was an ideal way to walk off the excesses of lunch. By the time they returned to the pub, Mary and Shaun were setting up for the evening dining session. They headed for the bar and Aiden organized a round of drinks. There were a dozen or so drinkers clustered around and he leaned over to make himself heard above the racket.

"Hey Da, we're all keen to help out – what can we do?"

"No real need. Your mum and me 'ave gotten it pretty well down pat these days – not like when we first took over. And it's the crowd size is about right; enough to make a good living but not too many to handle."

"Still, it doesn't feel right for us to sit on our bums all night while you two work. Besides it will be fun."

"If that's the way you want it. Tell Jimmy to come round behind the bar with me. It'll make a change for him to pour a few rather than just drink 'em. The rest of you can go out back and see what needs doin' there."

Jimmy didn't have to be asked twice – he practically vaulted the bar, grinning like an adolescent left alone in the

Adults Only section of a magazine store. He had a great time pulling beers while Shaun looked after the other drinks. Before long Jimmy was pretty much running the whole show. Shaun looked on from the wings smiling indulgently at his brother as he held court. He for one was not surprised that the man was a natural as a publican.

The others invaded the kitchen. Mary's cooking style was unpretentious but delicious. Not quite Gastro-pub fare but not far from it. As a result she and her assistant Linda had built a steady following in the township and beyond. The food leaned heavily towards locally sourced game and fish. The menu was emblazoned with the title 'The Duck 'n' Fish' – the name his father had chosen for the dining section. A loud guffaw or girlish whoop usually signaled that a customer had twigged to the sassy spoonerism. But most diners didn't catch on to it, above all the prim types who would likely be offended.

For a fleeting moment Aiden thought that it would be interesting to take over some of the cooking duties but he quickly realized he would be out of his depth. There's a vast difference between leisurely preparing dinner for a few friends and the pressure of a real commercial kitchen – even in a small tavern. So he busied himself with helping with the preparatory tasks of washing, peeling and chopping vegetables. He left the final plating to the experts – not his forte. Maureen and Sharni were content to pitch in with serving the meals and cleaning up tables. The extra help gave Mary more time 'front of house' mingling and chatting with patrons; a part of her role that she really enjoyed.

After the mealtime period finished and the kitchen was put back in order, the helpers assembled a large platter of food to share and joined Mary in the bar. They took up position at a table that had just been vacated near the hearth. A small fire was burning but more for atmosphere than a need for warmth as it was a mild night. Sharni noticed that Shaun was assembling several chairs on a small raised stage – more a dais really - that took up one corner of the room. Her curiosity grew as she watched him begin placing an assorted array of musical instruments on the chairs. She didn't have long to wait. Three middle-aged men came up from among those sitting around the room. From their build they looked like they could be dock-hands or fishermen - big-boned robust types - but they had a jovial cast to them. Each picked up an instrument; a fiddle, a frame drum and a concertina. After a moment spent tuning-up they went straight into a set of lively jigs and sea-shanties. Aiden explained that this was quite a common event in many traditional Irish pubs.

When the trio left the stage to a warm ovation of cheers and whistles, they were replaced by two couples who looked to be about the same age as Sharni and Aiden. They began playing covers of songs by the Coors. To the delight of all present they made a good fist of it as well. Sharni was delighted. This was music she had loved as a youngster and when she took up playing guitar she had learned to play most of their repertoire. Having consumed a few glasses of wine she suddenly found herself caught up in the moment. Without quite knowing why, she found herself joining the group on stage, picking up a guitar and participating in the show. Shyly at first but then with more and more enthusiasm she began to play along, egged on loudly by her companions. After several songs they tried to finish up but were forced back on stage for an encore by the cries of encouragement from the audience – led with gusto by Jimmy from behind the bar. Eventually the impromptu band pleaded exhaustion and was allowed to wind up. They returned to their tables through a gauntlet of high fiving and backslapping. No-one moved to replace them; sometimes the bar is set a bit high to be a follow-up act.

Shaun fired up the sound system and unobtrusive lounge music became a backdrop to the buzz of conversation. It was approaching closing time and customers began slowly drifting off. Shaun started doing the rounds calling last drinks to nudge the reluctant towards home and then came over to his family's table. He gave Sharni a broad wink. "That was a fine performance. Really got the room going. I should hire you and your new friends as our regular act."

Sharni blushed. She still hadn't quite worked out what had possessed her. But then her delight in the way it had gone overshadowed her misgivings. Her posture and the tone of her reply was a perfect parody of a self-proclaimed diva. "You know I'd like to accept - as a special favor to you of course - but after that reception, we'll be off getting an agent and going on tour right away."

Shaun glanced across at Aiden with a look that signaled approval. "She's very quick on the uptake son. She might just lead you a merry dance."

"Can't disagree Da. I may be daft but I can only say – bring it on."

As the room finally cleared out, Shaun set about closing up. With doors locked and all secured he disappeared behind the bar for a moment, returning to the table with six delicate crystal glasses and a bottle of Irish Mist – in his opinion, Dublin's finest liqueur. "Just a little nightcap," he declared. "I'm not one to get all formal but I want to have a toast." He looked around at all in turn, his eyes full of meaning. "Thank you all for coming down to visit. Here's to as nice a family day as I can remember – may there be many more."

They all nodded agreement and downed their drinks. The glasses had barely touched the table before they were topped up. Shaun assumed a defensive stance – palms and eyebrows raised. "What? We're Irish for God's sake. It's unnatural, not to mention unpatriotic to only have the one."

Aiden managed to negotiate their escape after the second drink, pleading weariness after a long day and they retired upstairs to their room. When they got into bed they found that they both felt a little inhibited. It might have been that they were under his parents' roof – or perhaps it was the sacred heart painting on one wall of their room. Whatever the reason they were content to go straight to sleep in each other's arms.

CHAPTER 23

The following morning they surrendered without a fight and worked their way through the mammoth breakfast that Mary laid in front of them. Their plan for the trip was that rather stay in the cities, they would seek out camping grounds and hire on-site caravans or cabins. They studied a camping guide and sorted out the options. After several phone calls they had secured digs for the next few days. It was time to move on and so they said their farewells and set off on the next stage of their Grand Tour.

Aiden took them on a circuitous route following a path not unlike the one he had travelled during his punting foray; inland through the hills, then south west back to the coast, at Wexford. There they took to the highway passing through Waterford before reaching Cork by mid-afternoon; their destination for the night. They needed to stretch their legs after the ride, so they parked the bike, grabbed a walking tour booklet and set off around the hilly streets seeking out the points of interest around the city. They took the opportunity to stock up on provisions – various delicacies as well as bread, cheese, wine and headed for the camping ground at Eagle Point. A flat boulder and two rocks on the pebbly beach provided their table for two as they dined al fresco watching the sun go down.

Day three found them starting out early heading to County Kerry. Coffee and a snack in Killarney fortified them for the run around the beautiful Ring of Kerry. The terrain juxtaposed fields and grasslands colored an impossible shade of green with rugged windswept cliffs. On return to Killarney, they strolled around the town center browsing the craft and souvenir shops that dotted the streets, frequently declining the many entreaties that they give a home to a leprechaun doll. One enterprising shopkeeper noting that were holding hands tried a different tack and insisted that Aiden would be doing his lady a severe disservice if he didn't buy her a Claddagh ring which features two hands holding a heart with a crown on top. She insisted on explaining the meaning of the ring was a heart for love, hands for friendship and a crown for loyalty. They managed to escape eventually and emerged from the store to find that a light rain was falling. This did not stop another local entrepreneur trying his luck. He was a Jaunting Car driver and he tried his best to persuade them to take a ride around town with him in his open horse drawn cart.

When Sharni pointed out that it was raining she was almost swayed by the driver's delightful and typically Irish reply. "No m'darlin', you have it wrong. That not be rain, that be liquid sunshine."

They left Killarney behind and headed north sticking to the Atlantic coast as much as possible, taking in the dramatic craggy outlook. In the late afternoon, their saunter through the main street of Tralee was interrupted when a short sharp downpour had them ducking for cover. The rain passed and they walked on, nearing a little corner bakery. The warm savory aroma of pies just out of the oven met the distinctive tang of evaporating dampness rising from the cobblestones. The evocative combination instantly transported Aiden to a dozen such moments when he was growing up. The wistful expression that came over Sharni, suggested that her childhood was not so different. On impulse, he grabbed her hand and pulled her into the store. They stocked up on steak and kidney pies and raced to their night's accommodation - a cabin in a little camping area beside a small picture-perfect fast-flowing brook. A quick reheat in the little camp oven and they settled down to a pastry-encased feast, accompanied with a can or two of Murphy's. Heaven.

On rising next morning they were greeted by the enchanting sight of a dozen fluffy tailed rabbits hopping around in the grass outside their cabin. But it was only moments before they were reduced to laughter as several of the rabbits began engaging in the activity for which they are renowned – a very quick change from a scene from Beatrix Potter to one from Fellini Satyricon.

Over the next few days they made their way up the coast, stopping at Limerick - sometimes disparagingly referred to as the knife capital of Ireland but they were charmed by the historic scenic walk around the Abbey River area - and Galway with its famous bay, before heading cross-country inland back to Dublin. Many little things made Sharni appreciate how similar were the Scots and the Irish. If anything the major difference was perhaps these folk took life a bit less seriously than her own people. Then again, maybe she was projecting and the observation had more to do with her own light-hearted holiday mood.

The tour had been punctuated by plenty of quirky moments. On one occasion when they arrived at their chosen camping ground the entrance gate was closed and locked. A large sign announced that the facility was closed for repairs and would not re-open for another week. As they stood around trying to come up with a 'Plan B', Sharni noticed a tiny wizened man working to repair a fence. The mere look of him brought a smile to her lips. She would not have taken much convincing to accept that she'd seen her first leprechaun. Another thing that amused her was a trait displayed by the locals that was repeated across numerous small country pubs they visited. When strangers such as themselves first entered, heads turned almost in unison to give the arrivals the once-over and the conversation became muted. Soon after you sat down with your drinks one of the patrons would come over and strike up a conversation that was invariably sprinkled with questions as to the who, what, where and why of you. Once that was established, the newcomers became accepted as part of the extended family, the volume went up and everyone went back to whatever they were up to before. Another milestone in the trip is that by the end, names of endearment had crept into their lexicon – words like sweetheart and honey. So far the L-word had not been uttered but it wasn't far away.

The final day on the road involved a long ride – they were keen to get home. They arrived in late in the evening and picked up a take-away meal on the way to Aiden's place. It was near midnight when they fell gratefully into bed. The let down from returning to reality left them feeling tired but happy and most of the next day was spent hiding under the duvet.

Dawn of the day of Sharni's departure back home came with an appropriately sky – every shade of grey from drab slate through charcoal with patches approaching a threatening black. The palette was complemented by a chill breeze and drizzle of rain. Again she was adamant that he shouldn't accompany her to the airport – finally confessing that she loved airport welcomes but just couldn't handle the goodbyes. As he saw her off in a taxi, his thought was of the cliché line - missing you already. It might be corny but it was also true.

CHAPTER 24

Surprise was Andre's foremost emotion when Lukas telephoned him to say that he was flying in to see him. They had not seen each other in several months. Their relationship was not as close as he would like and their times together tended to be somewhat awkward. It was not his son's aloofness alone - he recognized that his own shortcomings were partly to blame. He envied families who had an easy rapport but there was no escaping the truth - conviviality was not a strong suit for either of them. Nonetheless, he cared about his son and was not completely devoid of paternal feelings. So he was pleased that Lukas was coming.

From their brief conversation he had gleaned that the visit was more business than a social call. That was to be expected. Lukas might just be even more obsessed than he was in his early days starting up the operation. His musings about the past led his thoughts back to where it had all begun. Back then, he was a young and successful financier and as he was the first to acknowledge, a much nicer person. But that was before the tragedy – the event that diminished his humanity - that took away his heart and left in its place a shriveled prune.

In the second half of his twenties he had found his sole-mate. Annie Watson was not only stunning, she was also highly intelligent. Moreover, he was to learn over time that she was the embodiment of that rare phenomenon where a person's soul matched their outer beauty. She had swept into his life at a charity ball in Geneva. He had gone alone and told himself he was there because being seen at these events was good for business. In fact he attended many such events and in rare moments of self reflection he admitted that a large part of his motivation was an ill-defined sense of guilt – ill-defined but nonetheless real. He came from an affluent background with all of the privileges that flowed from prosperity. His parents had become wealthy during the war. It was never clear to him whether the money that flowed to him was untainted or if it had its roots in Nazi greed or Jewish desperation or perhaps a combination of both. In truth he'd never sought to find out – he'd not wanted the responsibility that came with knowing for certain the answer. Instead he used donations to fund-raisers as a balm for his conscience.

The moment he saw this vibrant, poised vision enter the ballroom, he had been captivated. She was also alone and he set about finding a way to meet her. Half-way through the evening, he saw her talking with a couple of women that he knew vaguely from some charitable foundation or other. Seizing his chance, he hurried over to them and greeted the women like long lost cousins. He was oblivious to their startled expressions as he inserted himself into the circle, made a couple trite conversational remarks and introduced himself to the object of his desire. Her name was Anne but she preferred, Annie. She was from the south of England originally but now spent most of her time between Brussels and Geneva working for a charity that targeted education for underprivileged children. They did not leave together, but at least he managed to arrange a luncheon meeting – a rendezvous for which he was quite prepared to part with a hefty donation.

The luncheon went well and led to another and then dinner. He did not need to feign interest because aside from his fascination with Annie, just being in her presence actually stirred in him nascent feelings of altruism. Her organization was called Reading Rights and he discovered that far from working for it, she ran it. Annie was an only child and her parents were close to middle-age when she was born. She giggled when she said, "I'm sure I was an accident. I suspect my father fell over one day, landed on my mother and sex took place inadvertently."

From an early age she had rejected most of the trappings that came with a privileged background and preferred to mix with, as she put it, 'real people'. Her parents had both passed on by the time she was twenty and when she found that she had been left a substantial inheritance, much more than she needed, she had started her foundation.

As they got to know each other, he found that there was nothing about her that he didn't like. He was relieved to find out that Annie did enjoy the high life; it was some of the people that moved in that orbit that she disliked. She hated pretentiousness and any form of snobbery. He began to enjoy seeing the reactions of people around her when Annie adopted a cockney accent and dropped a crude line into the midst of a posturing group. She was tall for those days, slim but with a woman's curvaceous figure. She would laughingly describe herself as 'all tits and arse'. Her eyes were smoky-blue in color and her hair was long, lustrous and blonde – but she had been quick to tell him that it was salon-blonde and in truth, her natural color was a bit of a mousey brown.

CHAPTER 25

They were on their honeymoon in the Canary Islands, when Annie sheepishly revealed that she 'had one vice that you don't know about'. She looked almost shamefaced as she confessed, "I love cards and I love to gamble. My poison of choice is Texas Hold 'em." Then her true persona resurfaced and with a cheeky grin she added, "The good news is that I'm damn good and I usually win."

With a laugh, Andre replied, "Well we better get to the casino. This place is costing a fortune and we could use some extra money."

How could he know that this small vice would ultimately prove fatal? In the years to come it was something he would ask himself countless times.

It was two years after Lukas was born that her life ended and with it a large piece of his. They were staying in Cannes and decided to leave Lukas in the capable hands of his nanny while they headed across to Monaco to spend the evening at the Casino de Monte-Carlo. Their hire car was a quite respectable BMW Series 5 but it looked a little down-at-heal as they parked it amongst the stable of Ferrari's that graced the plaza.

They had not been out much at all in quite a while without baby as a third wheel let alone to the most fabulous casino in the world. Annie could hardly contain her excitement. Her eyes shone and it was all she could do to walk sedately arm linked though Andre's up the stairs to the entrance. She wanted to run. Andre reached across with his other hand and lightly stroked her arm, as if calming a flighty filly.

They managed to keep their air of sophistication long enough to find a poker game. Annie sat down to play and Andre took a back seat as an observer. It was a high stakes table with five other players but neither of them was worried. The initial hands went well. She had some small wins and was modestly ahead after an hour of play. Then came a massive set-back. Annie held two aces in hand and was ready to attack. The flop was A7K. Everyone stayed in through some heavy betting. Clearly they each liked their pocket cards and the initial flop. It was likely that at least some of the other players were holding court cards. The turn card was a seven, giving Annie a full-house and putting her in an almost unassailable position. The pot was already large and she decided to bet all of her chips. If she scared them off, it would be an excellent win and if anyone matched her, so much the better. One by one they folded, until it was down to Annie and one other player. He was an unassuming type who seemed a little out of place in these opulent surroundings. He was perhaps a year or two older than Andre and based on his features and the few times that he had spoken, he was most likely Spanish.

They turned over their cards. She looked at his hole cards in amazement. He had stayed in with 2, 7 of different suits. Sure, he now had three of a kind but hoping to win consistently on cards like those would quickly send you broke. *Well I guess that's his problem. Still it's a shame. He seems like a nice enough fellow.* Her look of amazement turned to one of shock as the final card was turned. It was another seven, giving him four-of-a-kind and the winning hand. Annie sat unmoving, staring at the cards as the huge pile of chips were pushed across to the Spaniard. He had pulled off a long-shot of nearly astronomical odds. But there was no use bemoaning the outcome – it's called gambling because such things can happen.

His eyes were apologetic when he said, "Senora, I am sorry that it was you who was the victim of my good fortune. My name is Josep by the way."

She glanced over at her husband, who gave her a small nod before she replied, "Thank you for being gallant Josep, but I'm not done just yet. If you would kindly look after my place for a moment while I replenish my chips, I plan to stay in the game." With a smile that was a trifle forced she added, "And maybe I can have my revenge."

Andre's nod signified that he was quite happy for her to re-stake, even though she was now over the limit that they had agreed before leaving home. For his part, Andre new that the better player would triumph over time against the occasional bout of misfortune and he knew that she was a good player. Annie returned to the table and again proceeded to build her funds with regular solid wins. But then lightning struck a second time. Josep stayed in on 4, 8 and matched her when she went all in. The final three cards had filled in his required middle pins, giving a winning straight over her three kings.

This time when she looked across to Andre, he shook his head in response to her silent question. She excused herself from the table but asked that her place be temporarily reserved while she spoke to her husband. They went to a corner of the room where it was quiet. The conversation began amiably enough but deteriorated quickly.

"Looks as if it not going to be your night at the table," Andre observed. "Let's get a bottle of champagne and relax upstairs."

"No I can't quit now. I won't be decent company if I haven't had a chance to get one back. He can't possibly do it again."

"I don't think you're thinking straight. You're beginning to worry me. You have to know when to stop."

"Look Andre, I know what I'm doing and I'm going to get back in the game."

At times, tact was not one of Andre's virtues. He was far too accustomed to others obeying his instructions. "Annie, I forbid it."

His tone, his frown and his choice of words coalesced like components of an accelerant. Her disposition immediately went from a slow burn of frustration to a firestorm of infuriation. "You forbid it, you FORBID it," she said through clenched teeth. "You are my husband, Andre, not my keeper. Enough with the Swiss machismo. I can make my own decisions." And then she threw some fuel of her own onto the blaze. "Don't worry. I'll make sure that I transfer the money from my account to our joint account to make up for my losses."

Now it was Andre's turn to see red. "You know full well that it's got nothing to do with the money. You're being totally unreasonable. Go on then – back to your game. But I won't be staying here to watch. I'm leaving – you can hire a driver to bring you home when you come to your senses."

He turned and left the room without looking back. She stared after him but could not bring herself to call out. She was still too angry. As he pulled out of the car park, Andre could see that the night sky was as black and turbulent as his mood. By the time he had reached the road to home it was obvious that a nasty storm was closing in. He had calmed down somewhat and debated with himself about returning to the casino but stubbornness and pride would not release their tight grip.

Back at the tables, Annie had regained her composure and returned to the game. She had always had the ability to partition her emotions when required. This unpleasant episode was tucked away neatly in a drawer in her very ordered mind.

Make no mistake, she knew exactly where to find it and in the calm of the next day, it would be retrieved and laid before Andre. She was not being precious but firmly believed that it was important that Andre understood that whilst she adored him, she cherished her independence.

She turned her full attention to the game and played with aggression and skill, quickly increasing her stake. Twenty minutes later she faced another stiff test. This time it was Josep who bet a large portion of his chips. She held a very good hand but was seriously conflicted. On one side was a desire to try to win back a big hand, on the other was fear that she would fail a third time. Finally after a long pause, she looked across at Josep. She couldn't be sure but fancied that she saw him give his head an almost imperceptible shake. Whether it was real or imagined, it was enough to decide matters for her and she folded her hand. Two other players stayed in. It was their turn to experience what she had as the final cards again turned Josep's mediocre hole cards into the winning hand. She knew it was time to quit. She had begun to doubt her decisions and that was a recipe for failure when gambling.

She made her way from the table and cashed in her chips. Her mood was once more upbeat and now she would have enjoyed the champagne that Andre offered earlier. But she was not one to drink alone. Instead she arranged for a driver to take her home. Tragically, the fates had decreed that she would not arrive. Andre received a call from police two hours later. From what they had been able to piece together, it was purely an accident. When Annie and her driver left the casino, the storm was at its peak. The driver lost control on the wet, winding road and the car had hit a tree. Both occupants were killed instantly.

CHAPTER 26

Andre Muller's world fell apart. Of course he blamed himself. If he had stayed, Annie would still be by his side. Over the coming months, he went from inconsolable to morose to bitter. His business suffered and when he looked back, he could see that it was during this period that his son began to show the traits of the damaged personality that now caused him so much concern. It was as if his own demeanor during his worst periods had somehow infected Lukas.

As time passed he began to focus more and more on the events that led up to Annie's death. While the logical part of his brain recognized that he was being irrational, he could not shake the feeling that the Spaniard was to blame. How could this man who displayed a clear lack of skill, suddenly win big hands through pure luck. Not once but several times. It didn't make sense. Something was not right. And if it weren't for him, he and Annie wouldn't have argued and the tragic set of events would not have been put in train. The feeling reached the point of obsession. He recalled that the man's name was Josep and he decided to engage a private investigator to locate him. His plan or non-plan really was to confront the man. What he hoped to gain from this he could not say – he was driven by guilt and despair, not logic.

The investigator began by talking to dealers in the major casinos and finding Josep proved a simple task. Now they had the man's surname - Ferrer. At Andre's direction, the investigator kept his quarry under observation for several weeks. The report he compiled showed that Ferrer circulated between a small number of casinos in Spain, Monaco, France and Austria. He stayed at each place for one week and played only poker. The investigator noted that although the subject did not look to be a good player, he seemed to be able to win consistently - usually as a result of one or two very big hands. These remarks served to re-enforce Andre's impression that he was on to something. He needed to learn more. He needed to watch him first hand.

According to the investigator, Ferrer had just installed himself into a casino in Vienna. Observed habits meant that he would remain there for a while before moving on. Andre was on a flight to Vienna the next morning and by afternoon had installed himself in a suite at the casino. For the next three days Andre watched as the Spaniard played. The hands followed a pattern that was as Andre had expected. Ferrer would play conservatively for a time and then would come a game where he would seek to build the pot from the outset. His win ratio on these games was astounding. Even when he lost occasionally on a big hand, Andre speculated that this might have been a deliberate ploy to deflect attention. But what Andre found truly amazing was the number of times Ferrer won with poor hole cards being made good by extraordinarily lucky turn-ups.

He had observed for long enough. This would be the night that he would confront the man. He had booked a small conference room at the casino so they would not be disturbed. As the game broke up and Ferrer moved toward the exit, Andre stepped into his path. In a low voice he said, "We need to talk."

Josep was caught off-guard and allowed himself to be steered into the conference room. Andre stood very close to the bewildered Spaniard. "Do you remember me?" he asked; his blue eyes hard as gem stones.

"Yes, I think so. It was at Monte Carlo. You were with a delightful lady, watching her play. You argued when she lost and you left."

"Well my wife never returned home. Her driver ran off the road that night and she was killed. But it is you who I hold responsible."

The astringency of Andre's tone caused Josef to sway back to try to put some distance between them. "I did not know. I am so very sorry to hear this dreadful news. Your wife was charming and lovely lady."

Despite himself, Andre was moved by the man's sincerity. He was clearly distraught. Whatever else he might be this man had an air of old-world honesty about him. "You might not have directly caused the accident but you were the one who triggered the events that led up to it. I can't put it into words but I know that there is something not right about you and the hands you win."

Josep dropped into a chair, eyes down-cast. When finally he spoke, his voice sounded resigned. "Perhaps you are right. Perhaps I was the cause. It seems my gift might also be my curse. I have carried the burden alone for too long. I am going to tell you a secret that I have told no-one." Josep began haltingly but soon the floodgates opened and he told Andre everything that he knew and things he guessed about his ability. When he was done, he waited patiently for the other man to absorb his revelation. He wasn't sure what response he expected – disbelief, anger, perhaps derision.

He got none of these. Despite being a very practical type, Andre was surprised to find himself readily believing what he heard. The explanation fit with what he had seen. Indeed when he was starting to obsess about Ferrer, some of his more fanciful speculation was along these lines. Now as he mulled over Ferrer's admissions, something he had observed but not understood clicked into place and led Andre to an inspired thought. He had noted that on two occasions Ferrer had changed tables rather abruptly. The first time was when a young man with a British accent won a hand and the second time was the next day when that same young man joined the table where Ferrer was playing. His actions were inconsistent with his usual behavior and at the time had puzzled Andre. Now he thought he knew why and he put his suspicion to him. "You're not the only one are you? There are others, aren't there?"

"I think there are, yes. It is very rare but there are times at a table where I think that I have come up against another with the gift. When it happens, I fear possible discovery and I move away as soon as I can."

Andre realized that he had stumbled onto something momentous. But where he was usually quick to crystallize thoughts into plans and actions, here he found the implications to be mind-boggling. "I confess that I am a little overwhelmed with all of this. We were fated to meet, I think, but right now I need time to understand what to do with this knowledge. We will meet here tomorrow morning at 11 a.m. and talk further."

With that he left the room. That his demand was extremely presumptuous did not enter his mind. Both men seemed to know instinctively that their futures were now linked and that the hierarchy was set. For his part, Josep seemed relieved to have shared his secret and comfortable that his destiny was to be determined by another.

By morning Andre had settled on his plan. He had even managed to rationalize his actions as being done to honor the memory of Annie. When he met with Ferrer, he explained his vision. They would travel around casinos in Europe and it would be Josep's job to identify and then recruit others with the gift. Andre had put together an approach for him to use. The offer to become part of their group promised a plush lifestyle and generous rewards but also contained an implied threat. Josep was to portray the operation as already well established and having the means to put lone players out of business. Andre intended to stay in the background and only be referred to as a wealthy investor who funded the operation. New members only got to meet their backer after they had proven themselves trustworthy.

They immediately began to put the plan into action. Andre set to work establishing a company as a cover for the operation and arranging appropriate trappings to give the appearance of a going concern – bank account, post office box, business cards and the like. Josep pursued their first target. The obvious choice was the Englishman that Josep had identified there at the casino. Rather than avoid playing against him, Josep now sought him out and for the next three days spent long sessions at the same table. Gradually Josep began to establish a non-threatening dialogue. It was simple enough to learn that his name was Paul Mason and he had been playing on the casino circuit for less than a year. At the end of the sitting on the third day, he called Mason aside with the offer of a drink. He made his pitch and Mason proved an easy convert. When Josep revealed that he had the gift and could see that the other did too, Mason's response after a shocked silence was to suggest that they join forces. Josep explained that he was part of a larger organization and Mason was sold.

Over the next 12 months they found and recruited four more. They now had the core on which to grow. It was easier than expected. Commonly, the prospects were much like Josep. They feared discovery and were a little afraid of their ability. Finding that they were not alone was comforting and they welcomed the protection afforded by being part of a group. They seemed to enjoy direction and order being injected into their lives. Andre had also developed a technique for dealing with candidates who refused their approaches. Josef had discovered that it was possible for those with the gift to combine to nullify the ability in another. How this actually worked, they did not know. It was something that Josef had once tried as a whim and it had proved effective. Andre wondered if this facet of the gift had given rise to the notion of a Jonah; someone who brings ill-luck to those around him. In any case, it worked. And so whenever one of these recalcitrant hold-outs played, they would find one or two of Muller's men at their table ready to render the lone player's ability useless.

The few that still defied Muller were visited by hired thugs who let it be known that the casinos of Europe were now off-limits and if they wished to avoid a further and worse beating, the time had come to find a new home elsewhere in the world. With this as the business model, the stable continued to grow steadily and Andre's wealth accumulated quickly. He saw no reason to expand beyond Europe, nor did he seek to explore other gambling arenas. It was after he handed over the business to his son that such innovations became part of the plan.

Andre dragged himself back to the present. Lukas's flight arrived late morning and he reached his father's suite just after midday. Their greeting comprised a clumsy attempt at a hug accompanied by rhetorical declarations of 'good to see you; are you well'. Andre had ordered lunch to be served in his suite and it arrived soon after Lukas, sparing them from the need to labor through too much idle chatting. As expected from this class of hotel, it was a sumptuous meal featuring local seafood accompanied by a crisp and impeccably dressed salad.

As soon as they had pushed their plates aside, Lukas brought his father up to date with the progress being made on various fronts. Next he got to the crux of the reason for his visit, outlining the circumstances surrounding the failed wager on the Irish Derby. Then he asked, "You remember the Irishman that you ran across in Marseilles years ago? The one that disappeared after Ferrer approached him."

"Yes, of course. I remember it clearly. I was quite disappointed that we missed recruiting him. You think that he is involved in this?"

"I think it is likely but I'll leave that to our investigation to uncover. I'm more interested in something that you mentioned at the time. When you were discussing him you said that you thought that he might be very powerful. What did you mean by that?"

"It's something that Josep and I speculated about. With most abilities, practice can improve performance but there are those who seem blessed with an abundance of a talent even without training. In our business, sometimes we saw two gifted up against one another and one would triumph on a hand that both expected to win. That suggests that there are those who are stronger and those who are weaker. The Irishman did that with the Frenchman – on one big hand he beat him head to head."

"Your theory sounds like it could account for what happened with our player on the Derby bet. He came up against a more powerful exponent."

"What do you plan to do if you find this person?"

"If it turns out to be the old Irishman, he is past being useful to me and he'll be warned off strenuously. If it is a new player, I want him and I'll make sure I get him. He will join the team or he will pay dearly."

"You know that such talk bothers me. Be sure that you don't go too far to get what you want. Sometimes it is better to let it go."

"Father, you are too cautious. Only the strong are the winners."

Andre took his own advice and let it go. Lukas had satisfied his purpose in coming to Nice and announced that he did not plan to stay overnight – he was taking an evening flight out. Andre felt he should be disappointed but in truth it suited them both if their time together did not drag on.

"Thank you father. You have helped me. It was a good visit."

Andre agreed that it had been pleasant and he understood the simple reason. When they talked business, the conversation flowed and this had always been where they clicked. They could almost pretend they were engaged in a friendly family get-together. But if they strayed from that path, the interaction became stilted and the empathy evaporated. Still it was something by way of a bond and much better than no connection at all.

They made a better fist of their quick embrace as Lukas left the suite.

CHAPTER 27

Jimmy was leaving the pub to make his way home for dinner. He bid farewell to his mates and the publican and went out into the street. He had stayed on for an hour longer than he should have and the sky that had been cloudy all day was beginning to darken quickly. He hunched his way deeper into his padded jacket, thankful for the warmth and headed off. He noticed two beefy bruisers fall in behind him but didn't immediately think much of it. He was thinking of the Sheppard's pie that Maureen had promised for dinner. Being so late, he was hoping that he would get to eat it and not wear it.

It was when he was crossing a dimly lit laneway that they quickly closed the gap on him and together roughly man-handled him into the alley. Jimmy put up a struggle as best he could. "What the fuck is going on. If it's money you're wanting, you can take what I've got but it isn't much."

He could handle himself reasonably well in a scuffle but these two were professionals and gave him no chance to become balanced. He tried to get a better look at them as they shoved him hard into the brick wall but it was too dark to get more than a vague impression of them – broad, heavily muscled, no necks and bullet heads. He was sure that he had never seen them before. At first their features struck him as Germanic or maybe Slavic. Then when the smaller of the two spoke he fancied that the accent was more East London than anything else. "You got away once but you didn't hide well enough. You stuck your head out of the rabbit burrow and cost some important people a lot of money. And now we've got you."

His offsider underlined the statement by ramming Jimmy's head into the wall.

"I don't know what you're talking about," Jimmy managed to get out. His head spun and he felt blood begin to flow down his face from a split along his left eyebrow. But of course he was pretty sure that he did know what this was all about. He'd been half expecting something like it to happen for years now. His head was thumped into the wall again. He could not suppress a cry of pain as this was followed by a vicious punch to his kidney area.

"Don't waste your breath. The investigators have done their homework and they're very thorough. Our instructions are clear. They don't want you; you're of no interest to them. They reckon you're over the hill. They want the young bloke who works with you. We don't care about the details of what you two did or why they want him, we just go where they point us and do what they tell us. So save yourself the grief; who he is and where do we find him."

So it was Aiden they wanted. Well there was no way that he would give up his nephew to them. He would tell them nothing no matter what they did to him. He stubbornly stuck to his only line of defense – denial. "You've got the wrong man, I tell you. I don't have a clue what you're on about. Why don't you just take my wallet and bugger off."

His plea only served to increase the ferocity of the beating. Jimmy stoically refused to respond as they fired questions at him. Finally the frustration of the bigger of the thugs spilled over into rage. He grabbed an iron bar that lay on the ground and swung it hard at Jimmy's skull. Jimmy collapsed and lay face down, his head bleeding profusely. The smaller man grabbed the other's arm and began to protest. "What are you doing? You've likely killed him and we don't have any answers yet. Olivadi won't be happy."

"Never mind him; it's Muller that scares me. The Swiss can be meaner than most when things don't go their way. But look we're getting nowhere here. We can find the brat ourselves. We don't need him," he grunted to his partner.

"You're probably right. For sure this is taking too long. Finish him then and let's get out of here."

At that moment a patrol car cruised by the end of the laneway. The officer in the passenger seat caught a glimpse of figures moving in the shadows and signaled his colleague to back up their car to have a second look. The policeman brought up the spotlight attached to the side of their car and began to advance the beam along the cobblestoned paving. He caught a glimpse of figures running away brought the beam up but it was too late. The two heavies had seen the car backing up and as soon as the spotlight came into play they bolted in the opposite direction and disappeared into the gloom. He continued to play the beam up and down the alley and froze it when it illuminated a crumpled shape on the ground.

"Looks like we've got somebody down," the policeman said to his partner. "I think I saw two men running away but it's too dark to be sure that there weren't more. You had better call in a report and get some backup. Better call an ambulance as well."

Within minutes reinforcements had arrived, portable lights had been put in place and the laneway was lit up like a film set. In turn the action had quickly attracted a crowd of rubber-necks. There were now two police cars and an ambulance at the scene and another two patrol cars had been dispatched to scour the surrounding streets.

A local plain clothes detective pulled up and made his way over to a senior constable. "What have we got here Dennis?" he enquired.

The uniformed officer looked up in surprise. "What brings you out here, Bill?"

Bill Kennedy was a veteran of twenty years on the job. He'd built a reputation as a deep thinker and a very shrewd operator. He was also known for his wicked sense of humor. "I was in the vicinity and there's not much on TV tonight so I thought I'd drop by for a look," he answered dryly.

"Glad we can be of service giving you some entertainment," his colleague replied playing along. "Anyway at this point, it looks like we've got a mugging. We think that there were two of them but that's about all we have so far. The injured man is in a pretty bad way. He hasn't been able to tell us anything useful. About all we got out of him is that his name is Jimmy Donnelly, he's a local and he doesn't know who his attackers were."

"Being that I'm here and all, I might as well take a look at him," said Kennedy. He walked over to where two paramedics were strapping Jimmy onto a gurney and examined the injuries inflicted. "They didn't hold back any did they boyo. I don't think they liked you very much."

Jimmy had the wherewithal to not give anything away. He made it known that was in no state to answer questions and without further delay he was loaded into the ambulance and taken to hospital. A search of the laneway showed that the other end opened onto a busy street and from there the thugs could have gone in any of three directions. An hour later after a fruitless search, the uniforms packed up and moved off to attend to other calls. Kennedy left as well but he could not shake the feeling that the whole thing looked a lot more personal than a simple mugging.

Early the next morning Aiden received a phone call from Maureen letting him know the little that she knew about what had transpired. As soon as they finished talking he rushed to the hospital and went straight to Jimmy's bedside. His uncle was propped up on pillows sipping water through a plastic straw. One side of his head was swathed in bandages and the part of his face that was visible was bruised and raw.

"God Jimmy, you look awful. They really got stuck into you didn't they."

"Yeah they had a real go but it could have been worse. They came out of nowhere, dragged me down an alley and started to lay into me before I could even think of reacting."

"Was it a robbery or was something else going on?" asked Aiden tentatively, fearing the answer.

"It wasn't a mugging – they made that crystal clear. They were hired thugs working for that gambling crew. From what I could pick up, it seems like our win on the Derby cost them a very big bet they had on another nag. I don't know how they found me but I always thought that they could track me down if they really wanted to. Anyway, it's not me they're interested in - it's you they're after."

"Me? What could they know about me?"

"I'm guessing it's played out the way we hoped it wouldn't. They've probably been asking around the bookies and with you being the one that picked up the winnings and being known a bit, they must have gotten some sort of a description. How they connected us is a mystery. It might have just been a fishing expedition – just an assumption that two people with the gift would be connected in some way."

As Jimmy spoke, Aiden's could not escape the thought that his recent big betting spree had indeed been the main reason that they were able to get a lead on them. Dismay grew into full-blown guilt as he looked at the mess they had made of his uncle. He wanted badly to give voice to his chagrin but he kept himself in check. Jimmy had not finished describing what had occurred. "They wanted to know who you were and where to find you. I didn't tell them anything. I just kept saying they had the wrong man. But they weren't having any of it. They said that they would find you without my help. Good thing they didn't find us together."

He paused for a sip of water before continuing. "Anyway, they're laying into me and I'm telling them nothing. Then all of a sudden, the bigger one loses it completely and starts ranting about making an example of me to show what happens when people don't cooperate. Then he grabs an iron bar and goes at me. By all rights it should have stove in my head. It was a pure fluke that when he swung it at my head the bar caught the padding in the collar of my jacket before it ricocheted onto my skull. Took a bit of my ear with it. Bled like a tap, so it looked worse than it was."

Aiden could no longer hold back. "God man, it's all my doing. I kept on pushing it and I got carried away. I got noticed and it's led to this. I'm a fucking idiot"

"No need to put on a hair shirt boyo. I know all about the temptation of a big score. Like I've said before, as much as I didn't want to set off any alarms with the gambling crew, the main thing that held be back was feeling uncomfortable dabbling in something I didn't understand. Besides, someone remembering you doesn't lead them to me. Like I said, they must have got on my scent some other way."

Then it was Jimmy's turn to look guilty. "When I think back, it's just possible that I did a little bragging about having a big win on the Derby when I had a few pints in me."

"I suspect you might be saying that just to make me feel better but thanks anyway."

Jimmy didn't reply to that and changed the subject. "One thing I want to pass on in case I forget later. When I was lying there, they thought I was out of it. They probably thought I was done for. Hell, I thought I was done for. So anyway when they were arguing about what to do, they let out more than they should have. They said two names – Olivadi and Muller. The one that counts is Muller. They said he was Swiss and it sounds like he runs the show."

Jimmy's story had shaken Aiden to the core. He fought to remain focused but the image of Jimmy lying in an alley completely vulnerable with two murderous thugs standing over him kept flashing in his mind. It was like something out of a mobster movie but it involved someone he loved; it was real. He was out of his depth and the feeling of helplessness threatened to overwhelm him. "Jeez, this is freaking me out. What a position to be in. How did you manage to get away?"

"I had no doubt that they were going to finish me off. I tried to move but I couldn't. Just then a miracle happens - a patrol car goes by and backs up to take another look at what's going on. The two bastards do a runner and so here I am. Like I said, it's pure chance that they didn't do me in."

They sat in silence, Aiden slowly regaining control, his brain beginning to function. "I'm not so sure. Maybe there's more to it than randomness. Most innate traits evolve as a protection or as something that helps in survival. This thing wouldn't have developed as a gambling aid – that's just something we've learned to do with it. But maybe our luck operates at an instinctive level as well and helps protect us. Like when there's a lone survivor after a ship-wreck or a plane crash - a little guardian angel helping out."

That brought a wicked grin to Jimmy's face. "You might be right boyo. The Lord knows I've managed to get myself into and out of enough scrapes over the years."

"You're amazing you know. Look at you lying here with the shit beaten out of you and you try to make a joke."

"I'm alive aren't I? I survived and that's what really matters."

He gestured toward the tree of drips beside his cot. "And besides, I think there might be a fair whack of some sort of happy juice coming through the intravenous."

Despite everything he was struggling to absorb Aiden laughed at that. And with that the gloom lifted at least for the moment. "Move over uncle. I could do with a hit of that."

CHAPTER 28

Lukas was laying out the priorities for the week for Philippe Durand when one of the secure lines on his desk phone buzzed. He hit the speaker button. "Muller."

"Olivadi, Mr. Muller. There has been a breakthrough."

"Come on up immediately please. I want a full briefing." He hung up and addressed his assistant. "Philippe, we'll come back to this later. This is more important to me. But I want you to remain for the briefing."

Moments later Olivadi entered, nodded to them both and took a chair. "We've identified the younger player," he said without preamble. "The older man is James Donnelly and it turns out he has a nephew - name of Aiden Donnelly. My operatives are certain that he is our target."

"That is excellent news. Let's hope your men have gotten it right this time. My faith in their judgment has been badly shaken."

Olivadi looked uncomfortable as Muller went on. "You know I have no qualms about employing 'necessary force' when called for. But those idiots of yours clearly lost control. Such action only goes ahead on my orders. The time was not right and it could have brought about premature unwanted attention."

"I've taken steps. They know that if there is another mistake they will no longer be part of our operation." Hard eyes and the thin line of his lips conveyed a clear message that the men would not be simply fired.

Lukas leaned back and looked thoughtful. Over steepled fingers he addressed both of his men. "Now that we have our quarry, let me tell you the way we will approach this. No-one goes near him. We will not confront him yet. First I want him to understand that he doesn't have any choice in the matter. He simply won't be able to operate if he is not one of us. As you are aware, we have known for a long time – back to my father's days – that a person with the gift can negate another's power. We don't understand how but one can block the other and render his luck useless."

"Yes," said Olivadi, "Just like we have done before with reluctant recruits. It's very effective."

"Quite so. Now I want you to send two of our players over there immediately – check with Kelly as to who would be best. The job for your surveillance team is to keep tabs on the target. Every time he makes a bet, we need to know the details. And then we will make sure that he collects nothing. When he has had time to understand our power, then we will make contact. He will be much more amenable to our offer. Are you perfectly clear? Any questions?"

"No questions. It is an excellent strategy and implementing it will be straightforward."

"Good. Make sure that the team is equally well informed."

"Yes of course. There will be no mistakes this time."

Lukas nodded. It was clear to all present that he intended to hold Olivadi to that promise.

"Very well. Let's get moving immediately. Report directly to me on everything that happens. If you cannot reach me for any reason, report to Philippe."

Olivadi left the office and Lukas returned his attention to Durand. His expression was reminiscent of a carnivore that had cornered its victim – a look that Durand had come to understand meant that Muller was pleased. "Now let's get back to the other business at hand."

CHAPTER 29

Shock...confusion... a tinge of fear...a whiff of panic. The race was about to start and he felt nothing. The familiar sensation was simply not there. He tried to attain a meditative state but it was too late. The horses jumped and his selection failed to win. He was at a loss. *What the hell just happened? Is this a case of a false feeling that Jimmy talked about. Never had that problem before. It seemed perfectly okay when I made the selection. What's going on?*

The following day he made another wager – same result. Now he was really worried. Are you losing your grip boyo? Next thought - I need to talk to Jimmy. Quick change of mind – What if this involves the gambling crew somehow? Could be. So keep Jimmy out of it – he's copped enough. Maybe I just need to get out to the track. That's where I operate best.

Two days later he attended the Fairyhouse race meeting oblivious to the two men dogging him. He picked out his horse, placed his bet and went to the grandstand. Now the test would begin. He felt confident as he began meditating and quickly reached the desired state where he could 'feel' his gift firing up. He directed his attention to his chosen horse and immediately detected a barrier. Oddly, it did not seem to be the same obstacle that he tackled on Derby Day. The impression he got was that it was more like a screen between him and the action. Even so, his first instinct was to approach it the same way – smash his way through. As before he worked to turn his thought into a bludgeon to use to pierce the curtain. When he had condensed it into a tight hard ball that he felt was right for the job at hand, he readied himself for the onslaught.

Again and again he hurled his thought at the barrier. But to no avail. Clearly he faced a new and different threat and exhausted, he had to admit defeat – at least until after he had rested. As well as being tired he was famished. He surmised that the cerebral exertion was probably accompanied by a speeding up of his metabolism. He made his way to the dining area and settled down with an oversized bowl of pasta. As he forked large mounds of the steaming food into his mouth he mentally chewed over the problem confronting him. *At least I've proved it's definitely deliberate interference. Okay, let's see what they've got.* The meal finished, he set about giving it another try.

Once more he shaped his will into a weapon. He felt strong. No, more than that - he felt potent. *I'm going to blow them away.* He launched his missile – gave it everything he had. If his earlier effort was a Stinger surface-to-air this was a Patriot. Still the barrier held. *No good. Whatever it is, brute force alone is not the answer.* A new strategy was needed but he had no idea what that might be. He left the track deflated, at least for now.

He rarely remembered dreaming in color but that night his sleep was punctuated with a vivid kaleidoscope of nonsensical but somehow sinister dreams. The sequence that burned most intensely when he awoke sweating was centered on a fenced yard, full of horses. Men with grotesque faces and armed with electrified prods surrounded the enclosure. It was clear who the real beasts were. The horses circled the enclosure in a tight bunch, their eyes wide, nickering in fear as they sought an escape. The dream became a nightmare when the horses morphed into a group of men, naked and chained. It ended abruptly when he wrenched himself to consciousness breathing heavily. He had been one of the men.

CHAPTER 30

After the attack on him, Jimmy had taken a number of protective measures. To explain what had already taken place, he put about a story that a bunch of thugs were chasing him for an unfair gambling debt. He added a small piece of misinformation, telling people that the kingpins behind it were English. The immediate connotation was that this was just another case of a good and honest Irish son being harassed by the tyrannical overlord - a surefire way to engender sympathy and support in any fellow Irishman. Under this guise, he had charged his cronies with the task of letting him know should anyone come around asking after him. It went without saying that no-one would give any nosey foreigners the time of day. Next he now made it a habit to take a taxi whenever he travelled anywhere. Finally he had decided that his usual pub was no longer safe and had found another one to frequent. This establishment was decidedly seedier than its predecessor and its regulars included more than a few that would be described as 'likely lads'. But Jimmy was always generous in buying a few pints for the boys and had quickly become a welcome addition to the clientele. If trouble started, he was fairly sure that he would have people to watch his back.

Aiden joined him at his new-found haunt and relayed everything that had happened over the last few days. "Obviously they're powerful and very well organized. No surprise in that I suppose. Biggest issue is that they're faceless. I have to find out who and where they are. Then maybe I can convince them to back off. And there's the next problem. I don't see how we can take them on without a lot more help on our side."

"You're right, no doubt. You and me alone don't stand much of chance against them. I know what you're driving at and I accept the time has come to share our secret. I'm nervous about it but I can't see any other way. Trouble is though, it's an awfully big secret. Outside of Maureen, I don't have anyone that I can totally rely on," Jimmy told him.

"No-one? For sure you have no shortage of friends."

"My mates, they're fine to hang out with but I reckon the greed angle would get to them. They'd want some of the action. Over the years it's been one of the reasons that I've struggled to get as close to some people as I might have wanted; that fear of revealing too much. But, hey, in the end that's my failing. What about you. Do you have anyone in mind?"

"Definitely. I've thought this through and I want to get Dylan, Michael and Shannon on board. You know them and you know they are loyal and trustworthy."

"Yes, they're all good lads."

"And Sharni of course – I know she will want to help."

"She's a fine lass – you'd have to go a long way to do better, boyo."

"Can't argue with you on that score. I'm glad you like her – she's become very special to me. I'm not sure if it's love but if it's not, it's damn close. Anyway, if we've settled on who to involve there's only one more thing that I want to talk to you about. Outside of trying to deal with what's happening to me I have one other main worry at the moment...and that's you."

"How do you mean?"

"Well so far this lot has come after me by trying to make sure my bets lose. The tactic seems to be that if they make it so that I can't operate alone, I'll be forced to work for them. It doesn't look like they mean to do me physical harm – at least not while they think I'll give in and join them. You on the other hand are still in immediate danger. They'd have no qualms in punishing you for my stubbornness. Or as a demonstration to me of what might happen if I keep holding out."

"I want very much to tell you that you're wrong. But as much as I hate to admit it, what you say makes sense. You know I'd be up for a fight but I accept we need time to find them first. So I agree – right now I'm more of a liability than an asset for you."

"Thank you for seeing it my way – I thought I'd have a hell of a job convincing you. You know there's no-one I'd rather have watching my back but for the moment, you need to disappear for a while – somewhere they will not easily track you."

"Well, I still have a few disreputable mates from the old days over in Galway. One of them runs a guest house that would make a perfect hidey-hole."

"You should take Maureen as well. They might try to get to her."

"I wouldn't put it past the bastards either. I'll tell Maureen that after this nasty business with the thugs, she and I need a holiday in new surroundings. I'm sure she'll be happy to go. It'll be good for us and I'll be well out of the way. And while we're away I'm going to find the right moment tell her everything. It's high time that Maureen knew the truth about what's been happening and why."

"I'm really glad to hear that. I know you're a guarded type by nature but I think it will be good for you to have someone in your corner who knows your secret. And when she tells you that you're a delusional lunatic, tell her that I'll back up your story."

"You'll have to, that's for certain," said Jimmy wryly.

"One last thing. I know technology is not your thing but it's time you entered the modern age. I've bought you a mobile phone and I want you to actually carry it around with you."

"Against the grain but okay, I will. It makes sense for us to be able to keep in touch. Anything else you want to cover?"

"Not that I can think of," replied Aiden.

"A last thing from me then. Did I tell you that I had a visit in hospital from that detective who was there after those thugs got into me?"

"So he was following up on it then?"

"Yeah. And I can tell you he's a man with a hell of a lot of questions. I stuck to my story but I know he wasn't satisfied. He's a sharp one and even for a copper he's one very distrusting bugger – knows something is going on but has no idea what it might be. Nothing we can do about him though, so let's get on with what we can do. I'll go make my arrangements and you tee up your friends."

CHAPTER 31

Plan into action...starting with Sharni. She was pivotal. He put in a call to her and after the usual pleasantries, told her he wanted to see her and asked her to fly over the following weekend – his treat. He played it light and bright, just a get together, no big deal – he didn't want to alarm her or raise wrong expectations. She said okay, so next he was on to his three closest friends and invited to come around. He used the pretext of cooking them all dinner while Sharni was in town.

She arrived mid-afternoon; giving him several hours to fill in before the group were all together. He was noticeably distracted, conscious of what he was going to reveal later. He was babbling away to the extent that she commented on it. "Aiden, you're jumping about all over the place. Is there something you want to tell me?" she asked.

He tried to cover up. "I'm just focused on putting together a memorable dinner party, that's all," he claimed.

"If that's all it is, why not let me help with the preparation then."

That offer was a god-send. It kept them both occupied and provided a topic of conversation. They worked well together in the kitchen and as the afternoon wore on, Aiden's tension dissipated and with it his erratic behavior.

His nervousness ramped up again when his mates arrived in the early evening. He made sure that he plied them all with plenty of food accompanied with a liberal quantity of alcohol. It couldn't hurt his mission if they were well fed and feeling mellow. After the meal, as they relaxed with drinks in hand, he decided that the time was right. His frontal lobe had sold him out and refused to summon up the script he had practiced in front of the mirror that morning.

He stewed for a while unsure how to broach the subject and then decided the only way to go was to plunge right in. "Sharni, guys, I have something to tell you. You know that I trust all of you completely. I'm going to let you in on a secret that will sound very weird but all I ask at the moment is to keep an open mind and to let me lay it all out before you say anything."

He then related everything that had happened since that first moment when Jimmy had lit up the monitor at the research center. He finished his story by telling them the little he knew about the organization that was behind Jimmy's bashing and how it was now focusing on him. "Now before anyone speaks, let me say again I'm not psychotic and I'm not hallucinating. You've all actually seen it in action at the races. It was no freak occurrence when those leading horses stumbled and our horse won the steeple chase. If I need to, I can demonstrate again...Well actually right now with that gang queering my bets I probably can't. So I'm simply going to have to ask you to trust me and believe me. I need your help. There's no way I'm going to kowtow to those hoods but I can't fight back alone. I have to find out who's running the show and find a way to confront the head-honcho."

It was Shannon who spoke first. "Well you guys pretty much know that I'm a sucker for anything that touches on the paranormal so maybe I'm an easy sell. The thing is, I might be crazy too but in a weird way, Aiden's story it actually explains a few things for me."

The others joined in with tentative expressions of support. Aiden said nothing, preferring to allow his friends to talk their way through his revelation. The conversation roamed widely as thoughts were aired and questions were raised and resolved. Slowly they debated themselves all the way from doubt to belief.

It was Dylan who injected a necessary dose of lightheartedness into the deliberations. He turned to Aiden and announced. "Okay I'm sold. I've known you most of my life and you don't have the imagination to make up this stuff."

"Thanks Dylan – I think," replied Aiden with a smile, grateful to his pal.

Dylan's remark served to close-off the discussion and it was Sharni who brought them back to the subject of Aiden being in trouble. "So okay," she said. "Right now there's this dodgy group pressuring you to become part of their operation. I'm not sure that I understand what they are doing and how. Can you explain that part a bit more for me?"

"Well I'm guessing that they are keeping very close tabs on me. I haven't seen anyone following me but I'm sure they are. They seem to find out when I bet and their tactic is to have some of their people use their ability to cruel the bet. I don't know the complete mechanics of how they go about it but it's not the same as when I influence a race – I don't think they know how to do that. They don't push for another horse - their way is to put up some sort of interference across the whole race meeting so I can't use my ability. They might not even have to know what horse I'm on – just that I've had a bet. In my mind's eye I picture the obstruction as being like a fine but very strong mesh between me and the race. At first, I had no clue that anything at all was happening. I thought that I was losing it."

"At first...?" Dylan queried.

"When I was betting off-course I had no insight at all. So I decided to go to the track. If I'm there with the horses my method means that I interact more directly and I can sense the barrier they put up. So I deliberately took them on. The mental workout is actually strengthening me. So I threw the kitchen sink at them and for a moment I felt like I was close to breaking through or countering whatever they are doing but in the end, no joy. Brute force doesn't seem the way to go."

"It sounds risky - a bit of a two-edged sword. Presumably if you can sense them, they can sense you. So, on the one hand it might be a good training workout but at the same time it's likely to antagonize them. And judging by their track record, they could become violent if they don't get their own way," observed Michael.

"To be honest, I don't know whether or not my attempts to crash through impacts them in any way – wears me out for sure. Besides I don't know what else to do. I don't want to just sit back and take it and like I said before, I can't try to reason with them because I don't know how to get to the ones in charge. Even if I could find the gofers here, it'd be useless trying to argue with them – they have their orders and that's all they care about."

Again it was the ever practical Sharni who looked to move the conversation forward. "You came to us for help and you know we'll assist in any way we can. Have you got any ideas of what you want us to do?" she asked.

"I've given this a fair bit of thought. The first job is to try to track this gang back to their lair. Between Michael and his knowledge of company law and you with your access to information, I think we have a reasonable shot at it. The organization has been around for a while and I think it likely that it is actually a company – probably a private company. They must be turning over a lot of money so there must be a trail of some sorts. The top man is called Muller. He's Swiss, so that might be where the company is registered. I think that Muller is a common name but I'm hoping that there is something in the company articles that might let us zero in on the right firm."

"What about Shannon and me?" asked Dylan.

"You can help me try to locate the people watching me. I'm going to lay some bets this weekend. We'll map out a plan of where I'll go and when and then you two can take up positions along the way to see if you can spot anyone."

Dylan couldn't help himself. "It all sounds very 'Boys Own' doesn't it?" He held up his hands in surrender and quickly retreated under the looks he received from all but Aiden, who was smiling. "Am I being inappropriate again? Sorry gang. Believe me, I know this is serious and I know that these people are dangerous. Sometimes my humor is my way of dealing with things when I feel out of my depth."

His admission elicited nods and wry smiles. Aiden reached over and clasped his friend's arm. "It's fine Dylan. Your sentiments are spot on. Where would the Irish be, or the Scots for that matter, if not for our sense of humor when we are up against it? We're all the product of generations of survival through tough times. The result being stubborn bastards who won't be downtrodden by those who think their power gives them privilege. Time for me to fight back - with a little help of my friends, of course. So up to a point I want us to treat this as a bit of a lark. But with an important rider - I don't want to put anyone in jeopardy. This is something foreign to us and we all need to be careful. From here on, if you feel threatened in any way, back off and look for help. Paranoia is a sound protective reflex."

"On that note, I have a suggestion," said Shannon. "If you are being followed, they might know where you live. You need to beef up security around here. I can set you up with a first-rate system easily and it might just save you some grief."

"Thanks – that's a great idea and something I hadn't considered. Anything else occur to anyone?"

No-one had more to offer and so they did their best to turn the conversation to more everyday matters. It proved to be a task beyond them so they decided to call it a night. As the boys left their parting handshakes were like a silent pledge.

When they were alone, Sharni took Aiden's hands in hers. "I'm worried about you. Maybe you should just disappear for a while. Maybe they'll just go away if they can't find you."

"I've thought about doing just that. But I keep coming back to the fact that they seem to be very determined. I don't think they will give up and I don't want to hide away in fear forever. I'm not trying to be macho or anything like that. It's not like I want to beat them, I want them to leave me out of their plans and let me live the way I want to live."

She patted his hand affectionately. "That I can understand. Well I definitely can't say life has been boring since I met you. I'm a bit overawed by all this but it's also so exciting. And I'm fascinated by your ability. What's it feel like when something happens just the way you want it to work out?"

"It's hard to describe but I'll try. When the feeling comes into play everything around me looks a little strange – like nothing is entirely stable or fixed – and it feels like time has slowed down. If I can bring about what I'm aiming for, everything freezes for a moment and then becomes incredibly vivid. The rush that follows is pure exhilaration."

When he finished speaking, his eyes were bright and his skin flushed. Sharni too was caught in the moment. She felt a tingle run down her spine and permeate through her thighs. Her voice was husky when she spoke. "Wow. I can almost feel it with you when you talk about it." She looked at him for a time and then with her impish smile firmly back in place, she began to lead him toward the bedroom. "Right now I'm thinking about something that I want. Let's see if I can get lucky."

CHAPTER 32

Michael wasted no time getting down to it and was quick to report back to Aiden. "For a start, I've followed your assumption that this group would not be a public listed company. So I ran a search on private companies in Europe that had a Muller as the head honcho. As you suspected, it's a common name and there are plenty of them. Then I filtered them around keywords in their company articles like 'gambling', 'gaming', 'casino'. That produced a list of a dozen possibles. I even tried 'Olivadi' as well but that didn't help. So that's as far as I've been able to narrow it down. I'm pretty much out of ideas of a next step from my end so I've sent all the details to Sharni to see if she can dig a bit deeper."

"Fine work Michael. I'll wait to hear from her. In the meantime, I'm hooking up with the other lads tonight at my place to figure out how we'll go about playing Spy versus Spy."

When Dylan and Shannon arrived, Aiden set them all up with a beer and they began to toss around ideas. The plan they came up with was uncomplicated – hopefully simple enough to actually work. The following day, Dylan would set himself up in a café across the street from the local Ladbrokes betting shop. Aiden would make his way there by foot with Shannon observing and then tailing behind a minute later. The aims were straightforward – try to spot the ones on Aiden's tail - follow them - report back.

Their first attempt was a mixed bag. When they met up again, Shannon began to explain what had transpired. "The two thugs were easy enough to pick out – they just didn't look as though they belonged. The first one was on to you as soon as you reached the street. Then he peeled off and the second one took over after a couple of blocks. Every few blocks there was another changeover. They were being careful not to be seen by you but that made them look awfully suspicious from my perspective."

Dylan took over the story. "Yeah, so Shannon phoned me with a bit of a description and I had no trouble identifying them. I even managed to get a couple of snaps of them on my mobile phone – I've sent them off to Sharni. They didn't go inside the betting shop and left before you came out, so that confirms that they want to know that you made a bet but don't need to know what horse it was. Anyway, so far, so good. Shannon had arrived by this time and we started to follow them – and I must say, we were feeling quite the pair of gumshoes. Short lived though. They started to walk towards the river but after they went a couple of hundred meters they flagged down a taxi and left us standing around like a pair of shags on a rock."

Their hangdog faces made Aiden laugh. "Don't sweat it. We've made a heap of progress. Next time we'll be prepared for whether they walk or ride."

Two days later they repeated the exercise. But this time Shannon was in support in his car. He parked up the street from the café, in the direction that the goons had taken previously. The lead up scenario was as much as before – Aiden walked to Ladbrokes with his shadows in tow. The heavies confirmed that he was placing a wager and then moved on with Dylan on foot in their wake. They passed Shannon and again walked on only a short distance before looking to hail a cab. Dylan could see what they were up to and as soon as he saw a taxi pulling up, he reacted immediately, dashing back to Shannon's car and throwing himself into the passenger seat. They moved off quickly and managed to fall in five vehicles back and well positioned to keep their quarry in sight.

In a swank suite in Brussels, the conversation between Lukas Muller and his security chief was brief. "All is going according to your wishes," reported Olivadi. "My men have had no trouble keeping under surveillance. The target continues to place bets regularly and our players continue to negate his efforts. The only thing that is a little strange is that so far he is showing no signs of panic. He is either a little slow-witted or else very stubborn."

Muller looked smug as he replied. "No matter. I'm prepared to be very patient. We will continue to play our fish for a while yet before I reel him in."

Olivadi gave no response. His boss was anything but a patient man. Clearly he was enjoying this one-sided contest. But equally he also knew that if things did not continue to proceed in his favor, the veneer of tolerance would be shed in an instant.

CHAPTER 33

The four lads assembled at a local pub. Shannon and Dylan were looking particularly pleased with themselves as they filled in the others about their exploits during the day. "They went straight to a hotel up near Trinity College," related Dylan. "When we got there, I followed them while Shannon found a park. They met up with two other men in the front lounge – presumably these guys are the blockers. They weren't together long – just enough time to pass on their info."

Shannon cut in. "Yeah. By the time I go there, the gathering was already breaking up."

Dylan gestured that he wanted the floor. Shannon relinquished the spotlight. They all accepted that he was the showman of the group - he reveled in the dramatic. "The hoods headed back out of the hotel and the two new guys made for the elevators. I guess they were going back to their room to start doing their voodoo thing. We decided to stick with them. There's no way that they would have a clue who we were so I followed them into the lift. Of course I didn't have a keycard so I made a play of patting my pockets looking for it and that wasted enough time for them to swipe the card reader. I hit a random floor button at the same time as they choose theirs – always works. Anyway, I got off at my floor and left them on their way to the top floor."

"The penthouse level. They're certainly not scrimping on accommodation," observed Michael.

"Yeah. They're living high on the hog for sure." A little nudge to Aiden's ribs. "Hey, maybe you should reconsider joining them – lifestyle of the rich and famous and all that."

The comment earned a playful punch to the upper arm in response. "Funny boy, Dylan. Trouble is you'd be hanging around like a bad smell, polishing off the mini-bar and running up the room service bill."

"You have the right of it there, boyo."

"Getting back on track. You lads have done brilliantly. Now it's a case of what to do next," Aiden was saying when Shannon interrupted.

"Ah but we haven't finished yet. We are in luck in another way," and then he stopped short for a second. "Luck. Now there's a word that I can't say anymore without thinking about all sorts of connotations." A wry shake of the head. "Anyway our good fortune is that my firm handles the security for the hotel. And that means I may be able to access CTV camera footage for the floor and we might be able to see what rooms they are in. And another thought – these guys are probably not Irish citizens, so they would have been required to register their passport details. Unless their papers are false, we should be able to get names for them."

"I don't know what to say," said Aiden shaking his head in gratitude and amazement. "You've done an incredible job. We may not need the names of the underlings – not sure where that would take us - but you never can tell. And it won't hurt to get every bit of intelligence we can."

That night he heard from Sharni. "I've gone through the leads that Michael sent over and based on what I have access to on our intelligence database, one lot stands out in a big way. There's not much about the company in the public domain – virtually zero publicity over the years. They come across more like a secret society than a business."

"Well that fits for sure."

"The company was started by an Andre Muller quite a few years ago – he's now the Chairman and the CEO is his son, Lukas Muller."

"So the time line works then."

"Yes, spot on. Chances are your uncle encountered the father and you've copped the son. But there's more. They list themselves as an investment company. But on top of that there are rather vague and cryptic references to high risk speculation – read gambling. One thing that sticks out is that they have come under investigation in relation to a couple of assault cases but no charges have ever been laid."

"It all seems to fit in perfectly."

"That's the way I saw it too."

"Can you find out more about Muller himself?"

"I don't know. As a type, he clearly tries to keep away from the limelight but nothing ventured and all that...so yes, that's what I'll be on to next. I'll send through whatever I can put together."

"Thanks, you know how much I appreciate what everyone is doing for me. I need to fill you in on what the lads have been up to at this end."

He related their accomplishments, trying to keep everything low key but Sharni saw straight through him. "I'm blown away by how well you've done but I have to say I'm more than a little worried that you are putting yourselves at risk. These men are dangerous and if they get wind of what you lot are up to, there's no telling how they'll react."

"I know. We talked about that before we started and I promise you we were very cautious in how we went about it.

Now we've done what needed doing and gotten away with it. We can probably keep our distance for a while. Okay?"

"I guess so. Just take it very carefully and I'll be happy."

Aiden used the ensuing lull as an opportunity to shift the conversation away from thoughts of peril and on to more everyday things. They spent the next half-hour chatting about whatever popped into their heads. By the time they broke off the call, Aiden was smiling and at least for a while his attention was not consumed by his predicament.

The break was sweet but brief. Alone again it wasn't long before he began to worry. On the one hand with the help of his friends he had already achieved much more than he thought he could. But he was still very much the underdog. It came down to one simple fact. Until he found a way to break through their screen, the group he was up against maintained the upper hand.

His helplessness chafed at him and his frustration grew. He needed to act, needed to try again. They might have stopped him last time but all the same, the race track gave him greatest hope. It was where his strength lay; where he could interact directly with the horses. If he was to have any chance of shifting the balance of power, that's where he would take them on. And he pledged to himself, this time he was going to win.

CHAPTER 34

With the weekend came a race meeting at the Curragh. He made sure he was very visible as ambled down to Ladbrokes and placed a small bet in five of the events on the program. His logic was that he had no idea how things would unfold and he might need a few attempts. He returned home, picked up his motorbike and rode out to the racecourse. There was a modest crowd on hand and it was easy enough to find a good vantage point. He still had no better plan than brute force and as the horses paraded past his confidence began to erode. *Am I wasting my time? Crashing through was not the way before, why is it going to work today? If I fail – then what? Do I give up – not bet again? God I'd miss the thrill of it. There must be a way...think man, think.*

A sudden flash of inspiration. *If you can't beat them, join them. Could that be the way? Maybe, just maybe.* Using his meditation technique Aiden entered a trance-like state. He invoked his ability and immediately felt the curtain descend. As a frame of reference he pictured the barrier as a kind of fine woven mesh. Mentally he pushed against it. He could sense its presence almost as if it really did have a physical structure. He probed around it trying to understand its nature. Satisfied he withdrew the pressure and this time as he re-engaged he tried to visualize his mind melding with it, becoming part of the mesh. A tingle of excitement. It was working. There were no words to describe how he knew but there was no doubt that his mind had become part of the gestalt that was the essence of the obstruction. Paradoxically being part of it meant that it was no longer a barrier to him. The next step was as astounding as it was simple. Metaphorically, he allowed part of his consciousness to pass through.

A feeling of immense satisfaction flowed through him. He had beaten the bastards. He had never felt so sure of himself, so in control and so powerful. He felt like his body was surely glowing and couldn't suppress the urge to take a furtive glance down at his hands and across to the punters standing nearby. No, there was no outward sign of his inner potency. Oddly after all of the hassle it took to reach this point, to overcome this challenge he had no desire to make a show of his triumph; quite the contrary, it made him want to go about his business calmly and efficiently. He did not know if his rivals were able to sense that their block was no longer effective against him, nor did he care right now. This was his moment alone. With clinical precision, he invoked his power and willed his horse to victory. It was done, he had found a way.

He then allowed himself a little bit of showboating by repeating the performance in the very next race and did it easily. Then with a small bow to no-one, he turned on his heel, left the course and made his way home.

CHAPTER 35

Score one point for the good guys. Now where do I go from here...maybe it's time to send a message to Muller. Yeah, let him know that he can't control me so it's time to let it go. Not through the thugs though...they might react badly. Better to use the players to get to him...yes a visit to their lair is the way to go.

He put in a call to Shannon and outlined how he'd beaten Muller's blockers. "Time to up the ante. I'm going to make contact with Muller through his boys at the hotel. But I'm going to need their room number. Have you been able to get a look at the CTV footage?"

"You're moving very fast Aiden. And no, I don't have access to it yet. I need to wait until it's been archived – that'll be in a day or so."

"You can't speed it up? I want to get cracking before I lose my nerve."

"No can do, I'm afraid. Security around the footage is tighter than a duck's arse until it's been put into archive. You'll have to hang tight. I'll call you as soon as I have something."

"Shit. I was really hoping to get stuck into this right away."

"Look, you know full well there's no point in you spending your time stewing over a small delay. But we both know that's exactly what you'll do if I don't force you to chill out for a bit. So tell you what - I'm going to round up the other lads and we're going to have a few pints tonight. And after you've brought them up to date, it'll be time out. There'll be a total ban on any mention of gambling and luck for the rest of the night. The conversation will be around football and women, just like pub night used to be."

"I have been obsessing haven't I? But you have to admit that it's been a very weird time. That said I really could use a break from it so for sure I'm up for it and I promise I'll behave."

They met up at their usual haunt in Temple Bar. Aiden now thought of the pub as the place where he first met Sharni. He suppressed a pang of loneliness – he missed her badly – and greeted his mates. It didn't take long for Aiden's forced joviality to transmute into the real thing. The night was just the tonic; filled with good-natured banter and a healthy slab of carefree laughter. A night of camaraderie and above all a regular, normal get-together. *This is how my life should be...not that other crap going on. Those bastards...appearing from nowhere and stuffing my life around.* For a fleeting moment Aiden questioned whether he would be better off if he'd never discovered that he possessed a rare ability. But no, it was an integral part of him now. He might just as well contemplate giving up one of his other innate senses.

Back home and bolstered by a fine night with his friends, Aiden waited with something approaching patience until at last Shannon phoned him with the information he needed. *Right let's get to it. Time to get a message to Muller.*

He booked a room at the hotel online and checked in early in the afternoon. With the room came a keycard and with it access to the elevators, all the way to the penthouse floor. He spent time in his room rehearsing his speech and getting himself prepared. When he felt ready, he made his move. Not allowing himself time for backsliding, he was all briskness as he marched up to the suite, rapped sharply on the door and called out 'housekeeping' before ducking to the side out of view of the peep-hole.

As the door opened he moved quickly to take up position in the center of the entrance and wedged his foot against the door. It was encouraging that the man facing him was several centimeters and many kilograms smaller than he. The man's eyes widened in recognition and involuntarily his mouth fell open in bewilderment. Aiden was the last person he had expected to encounter.

"I have a message for your boss," announced Aiden.

"I don't understand," was the hesitant reply.

"Forget the bullshit, okay. I can see you know who I am; probably showed you a photo of me before you were sent here. More to the point, I know you work for Muller and I know what you've been up to. So let's not bother with games. All I want is for you to tell Muller that I want to talk to him. Got that – him – nobody else. Tell him to call me. No doubt the snooping around that was done included getting my mobile number."

Soon after Aiden returned home his phone rang. A glance at the screen determined that the caller number was blocked – no surprise that he didn't recognize the male voice on the other end of the line.

There was no preamble. "You will join us. No, you must join us. Only we know how to properly harness your special gift." The manner was brusque. The voice sounded educated and conveyed an accent that was European but impossible to pin down more precisely.

"Harness? I'm not a plough animal and I have no intention of working for you or anyone else. Look I'm happy to keep out of your way. I just want to be left alone."

If the man on the other end listened to what Aiden said, he showed no sign. "You will fail without us. You cannot survive as a lone wolf. You must realize that by now."

The uncompromising arrogance in the man's tone carried clearly through the phone speaker but still Aiden tried again. "It's over Muller. You can use a roomful of your people against me and it will make no difference. Your barrier won't work. I found a way around it."

This time the voice was a sneer. "That cannot be true. No-one has told me of this."

Aiden stifled his mounting frustration. "Your lackeys are probably too scared to admit anything. Or maybe they don't want to believe it either." A spur of the moment idea. "I'll give them and you a demonstration. Let's see...a pause as he chose at random. "Okay...make a note of this – the next race meeting at Leopardstown is in three days. I'll be there and I'll put money on horse 2 in race 2. Have your goons try to block me and when it wins, you'll know it's over."

With that Aiden hung up without another word.

With no fuss Aiden duly delivered on his promise at Leopardstown. *Chew on that you bastards.* He felt the pressure of recent times receding. Finally he could see an end to it – soon he would take back control of his life. His emotions were running high and his immediate thought was that he wanted to share it with Sharni. *It's about time I paid a visit to Glasgow.*

He called her straight away and happily she was as keen as he. Sharni lived in a rented share-house and so as not to complicate matters he insisted that he get a room. He took her recommendation and booked a room at a boutique hotel right in the heart of the city. She had laughingly advised him that the daily tariff included the contents of the room's mini bar.

"Are you implying that I might be someone who likes a drink or two?" he asked feigning outrage.

"Now what on earth would give me that impression?" she replied laughingly. "I just happen to know you're a man who enjoys a challenge."

CHAPTER 36

David Lawson slinked tentatively into Lukas Muller's office. He knew that Muller had become obsessed with bringing to heel the Irishman and he'd heard about the latest failure. He sat down. One brief glance at the blazing fury in Muller's eyes had him cowering in his chair looking down at his hands.

"You cannot begin to know the extent of my displeasure with the fiasco that took place in Ireland. We were made to look impotent," said Muller through gritted teeth, his lips barely moving.

Lawson started to respond, his words mumbled and incoherent. Muller cut him off with an impatient hand gesture. "I don't want lame excuses. I want an answer to one question only. How could your training be so inept that this upstart - hardly more that a boy - is able to prevail over two of my most seasoned players?"

Trying to muster a defense, Lawson replied hesitantly. "I spoke with our men and they have no clue as to what happened. They were not even aware that he had broken through their block. I can only guess that this man is more powerful than anyone we have come across before."

The attempt to deflect blame proved fruitless. Muller was not inclined to listen. He wanted an outlet for his anger and Lawson was it. "I have had reason previously to doubt your capability. You have disappointed me before. You are pathetic and your weakness offends me. Get out of here now while I am still able to control my rage."

As Lawson scurried from the room, Muller could almost smell the man's fear and that served to incite him even more. Like the parable of the scorpion and the frog, he followed his nature. He reached for his phone. "Philippe, please locate Renzo and would both of you to come to see me."

As soon as they arrived Muller issued his orders. "Lawson will be leaving us. Philippe, can you begin looking for a replacement – a much more effective replacement. Renzo, I want you to see to finalizing his severance. Thank you, you may leave now."

Both men understood Muller's meaning.

CHAPTER 37

Aiden was looking forward to getting at least a small taste of Glasgow and reflected again about its historical similarities to his own home town. Both had declined from prosperous industrial cities to ones struggling with mass unemployment, poverty and crime. And how in recent years they were recovering. In the case of Glasgow it was by reinventing itself as Scotland's financial hub and as a center of art and culture.

Sharni was to meet him at his hotel in the evening after she finished work. He had a few hours to fill in so after checking in and picking up a map of the area, he went for a walk around the surrounding streets. By the time he returned to his hotel it was only another 30 minutes before his room phone rang and the desk advised that a Ms McLaren was waiting for him in the foyer. He was down there in a flash. Two beaming smiles converged on each other and they showed admirable restraint in limiting themselves to a hug and a quick kiss. Still it was enough for Aiden to experience a small thud in the region of his solar plexus. The amused looks from the concierge and one of the bell-boys suddenly had them feeling like they were center-stage so clasping hands, they moved over to a couch in a less conspicuous part of the foyer.

"It's so, so good to see you Sharni. I've missed you – a lot."

"Me too. Talking on the phone is one thing but it's a poor substitute. I'm so glad you came over. I love spontaneity in a man – especially if it's something romantic."

That brought a laugh from Aiden. "I don't think I've ever been called 'romantic' before. I'm beginning to wonder if you've bewitched me. And I know just how you did it, devil woman."

She gave him a look that was all innocence and wide eyes – and at the same time very sexy. "Who me? I surely don't know what you mean, sir. I'm just a humble little Scots girl."

"There's not a humble bone in your delightful body. Now for some reason my mouth has gone dry. Let's adjourn to a pub and talk there."

"What about the free mini bar in your room?"

"I thought I'd keep that for a nightcap later."

"Oh and what makes you think I'll be coming up to your room later."

The way she liked to tease him was irresistible. A hint of a smile played at the corners of his mouth as he glanced at the small overnight valise she had brought with her.

"A man can only live in hope."

After dropping her bag in his room, Sharni led the way to a nearby bar that was clearly a popular after work watering hole. It was populated with office workers of the twenty-something age group. The building was Georgian architecture; possibly it could have been a bank in its past life. The interior had been modernized – thankfully not in the ultramodern minimalist style that Aiden found stark and cold. The décor was more in the style of shabby chic with couches and oversized armchairs. The crowd was chatty and upbeat; happy to have put another day's toil behind them. It was the kind of place that made it easy to settle in and relax.

Over a drink Aiden was relaying his first impressions to Sharni. "So far I like the feel of Glasgow. The vibe in town is definitely a lot like Dublin. Oh yeah, and that reminds me.

Some of the sights are just as quirky as well. When I was out exploring earlier, I went past the Gallery of Modern Art. What's the story with the statue of the guy on a horse with an orange traffic cone on his head?"

Sharni laughed. "It's actually quite famous – at least around here. The statue is the Duke of Wellington and that's its usual headwear."

"Doesn't the city council take it down?"

"They try every so often but it's become a challenge that they can't possibly win. A couple of weeks ago they removed it and by next morning some wag had adorned Wellington not only with a cone on his head but also with another one placed like a megaphone between the horse's ears up to his mouth."

"Classic."

"I like to think of it as symbolic of the youth of Glasgow. It's not destructive but it does make a statement about challenging the status quo. And that's something a lot of us applaud in this town."

As time slipped by hunger pangs turned their conversation to food. They checked out the bar menu. There was nothing wrong with it but it just didn't quite hit the spot with them. Neither knew what type of cuisine they felt like eating; just that it needed to be something casual but intimate - a tavern or café rather than a restaurant. So they were forced to stir from their comfortable nook and go in search. There was an abundance of dining options in the vicinity; it was a matter of finding the one that called to them. The mild evening was beginning to turn cool as they walked arm in arm around the area browsing menus posted in the windows of the various eateries. The increasing chill in the air turned their fancy toward food of substance. In the end they settled on a steak-house that specialized in Angus beef and fat chips – perfect.

Back in his room, they did manage a small nightcap before other possibilities became much more pressing. Next morning they ate breakfast in bed before Sharni had to head off to work, leaving as she put it, his 'lazy Irish arse' in the bed; a slightly disheveled bed but one that was still warm and redolent with the heady scent of her. He burrowed down in the blankets, luxuriating, lost in thoughts of her. He dozed for an hour before concluding that he had milked the situation as far as possible. Housekeeping would be knocking on the door soon so it was time to hit the shower.

A fortunate thing too that he was up and functioning because it was at that moment his mobile phone rang. His first thought of course was that it would be Sharni but the suppressed caller ID sent a small tingle of anticipation through him. *Okay Muller, time to get my life back.*

Again Muller was straight down to business. "Your display was impressive but in the end it is of no consequence. It changes nothing."

Exasperation surged in Aiden. "Let me say it again and this time pay attention to what I'm saying. It's over. Just understand that. You have no hold over me. Your lackeys can't block me. And everyone who matters to me knows my secret, so you can't blackmail me either. "

He hesitated momentarily when he realized that he had not yet told his parents. He promised himself he'd set that right as soon as he could. Knowing how practical they were, they would struggle to accept the truth. He'd have to go down to see them and tell them face-to-face – and he'd take Jimmy with him as back up. That settled, his attention returned to the job at hand and when he spoke again, he kept his voice even and controlled. He needed to try to take emotion out of the conversation and appeal to logic.

"Please understand where I stand. I am not a danger to you. I have no interest in your business. Outside of horse racing, I have no interest in anything to do with gambling. And when it comes to the horses, I only care about the races here in Ireland. So I'll keep out of your way and you keep out of mine."

"You speak of understanding. It is you who fails in this. I don't care who does or who doesn't know about you and your ability. But I care greatly who knows about me and my organization."

"I've already told you that I don't intend to cause trouble – I just want to be left alone. I have nothing to gain by telling anyone about you. You'll simply have to trust me."

Muller could not keep the sneer from his tone. "Ah, yes – trust. I'm afraid trust is not something that comes easily to me unless I have a strong hold over someone."

"That sounds like a threat. You don't need to threaten me. You have my word and I keep my word."

The sneer was replaced by an attitude of distain. "How noble of you. But that is not how I operate. I want your talents under my control and I am used to getting what I want. Now this conversation grows tiresome. You can have a few days to think it over. But when I next contact you I expect you to agree to my terms."

An abrupt silence on the line signaled that the exchange had been terminated. Shit. The man really is barking mad. He won't stop unless I find a way to make him.

He resisted putting through an immediate call to Sharni and over coffee in a nearby café, tried to come up with a way out of this nightmare. His imagination conjured a myriad of confrontation scenarios each one more fanciful than the last. Most of his ideas bordered on the ridiculous. He was floundering. His mind in turmoil, he abandoned his plans for a day spent sightseeing and returned to the sanctuary of his room. An hour's fruitless pacing and he was still nowhere. He couldn't fathom a feasible course of action. Trying to deal with this lunatic was beyond him. For the first time in months, he could feel the dark tendrils of depression tugging at him. *I am so over this whole mess – I just want it to end.* He forced himself to rally. *Fuck it. Fuck you, Muller. I'm not going to give up. That Aiden doesn't exist now.* He began deep breathing exercises and eased into a meditative state – not to invoke his ability but to regain control and bury negative thoughts. Calm now, he phoned Sharni. "Any chance that you can get away early? I don't want to say much on the phone but Muller has made contact and I'm right back where I was."

"Bugger – poor love. Give me an hour to reschedule a couple of meetings and I'll be there. Stay strong, whatever it is we'll figure out something."

A geological epoch passed and finally she was at his door. The look of love mingled with concern and empathy touched him to the core. Suddenly his frustration boiled up inside and he found himself on the verge of tears. He realized how vulnerable he felt right now and how very much he loved her and needed her. He pulled her to him to gain a moment to compose himself. She sensed he was close to the brink and swallowed the words of sympathy that she wanted to say. He needed help not coddling.

After a tender kiss, she assumed her professional guise. "Okay my sweet. Tell me what's going on."

Aiden relayed the essence of his phone conversation with Muller. He outlined some of the hare-brained ideas he had come up with and business-like or not, Sharni could not hold back a giggle. In that instant his spirits lifted. She was like a tonic. They talked over possible courses of action and finally reached the same conclusion. Logic was a waste of time. Aiden needed something over Muller to force him to back off.

Aiden pointed out what was to him the obvious problem. "Trouble is we're out of our depth. We did well to follow his men around but that's pretty much the extent of what we can do in the sleuthing department."

"Don't underestimate the resources that I can tap into," replied Sharni. "More to the point, while I was investigating Muller I was thinking about what we could do with whatever we discovered. I came to the conclusion that the threat that we know all about him might be just as effective as having something concrete.

"Not sure I get what you mean."

"Let me try to explain. We know that he's an arsehole – and about one rung above your common crook. As you say, getting proof of dirty dealings is probably beyond us. But we should be able to put together a profile of Muller. Who he is, where he stays, how much his company is worth – that sort of thing."

"Okay I get that. Sort of an unauthorized biography but what does that do for us?"

"His Achilles Heel is his almost obsessive need to keep out of the limelight. We need to make him think that we have more on him than we do. And that we'll use it. We'll make him think that we can shine a light into those dark corners where he hides his crimes."

"Whew. You're scaring me a little – remind me never to get offside with you."

"He threatened the man I love, so for me it's no mercy."

His world tilted on its axis. *She just said she loved me.* His response was as spontaneous as it was heartfelt. He took her hands in his. "I love you too," he said.

There was a second's hiatus. A fleeting moment of embarrassment from saying it aloud. It passed. Practical when it mattered, she put them back on track. "Business now, fun later," she declared – sparkling eyes and warm smile. "So crimes aside, I think we can be sure that he fears anyone knowing anything about his operation. It would hurt him in badly. His business couldn't function if it became known that he used special operatives. Casino managers especially would freak out. They're a paranoid bunch - they might not believe that some people have a special gift but they'd ban Muller's boys anyway - just in case."

"You really are one clever lady."

"And you've only just come to that conclusion?"

Aiden was excited now. "I can do this - with you and the lads helping me. We already have quite a bit on his operation and of course I know the secret of how he makes his money. That's a good start. But thinking about it, I wouldn't want to go too much into his men having special powers in a public document. Don't want to sell the farm. I'll just hint that they have an unfair advantage."

"Good point. But to pull it off, we really need to get some more information on his players. That's what you need to threaten to show to the casino boys. Getting anything there, I'm afraid is a much harder assignment."

"Maybe not. Shannon's firm looks after security at the hotel where a couple of them were staying. He thought that he might be able to get their passport details. I told him not to bother because I couldn't think of a use for the information. But that's changed now. I'll give him a call and get him back onto that angle."

Sharni was proud of the way he had bounced back. His earlier helplessness touched her but the inner core of resilience he was now showing was what she wanted to see in her man.

"I didn't know about that connection through Shannon. If he can get names it would be just the ticket," said Sharni.

"I'll get him on to it first thing tomorrow and I'll start to write up the information that you and Michael uncovered about Muller's business."

"And I'll see if I can get a better lead on where to find him. But you're going to have to be patient. The intelligence system is not particularly user friendly so it is most likely going to take me a while to chase down any leads," she added and then changed tack. "There's nothing more we can do for the moment and that's just as well 'coz I'm famished and I've arranged for us to meet up with Jen and Kate at an Indian place near here. I for one am looking forward to a good curry nosh-up."

Aiden's smile was a little forced. "It'll be nice to catch up with them. I just hope I won't be bad company."

She put on her mock-stern voice. "You better put your best foot forward mister. I've done a fair bit of skiting about you – so don't let me down, hear."

Instinctively she knew exactly how to get around him. His smile was now genuine as he gave her an exaggerated salute. "I promise I'll be the embodiment of wit and charm, ma'am."

"No need to shoot for the unachievable," she replied cheekily and ducked away as he pretended to make a grab for her.

"Some sassy minx is looking for a spanking."

"Yeah...yeah...later...later. Right now, this girl needs to be fed."

CHAPTER 38

An almighty crash and the sound of shattering glass exploded in the room. Jimmy froze momentarily and then relaxed as a boisterous caterwauling erupted from a dozen voices - telling him that one of the bartenders had dropped a tray of glasses and was now suffering a bout of good natured ribbing from the patrons.

It was their third day in Galway City. They both much preferred the freedom and privacy of looking after themselves rather than staying in a hotel or guesthouse and so Jimmy had arranged to rent a little cottage from a friend from the old days. On the first night after they had settled in he'd made them both a cup of tea and as they sat across from each other at the kitchen table, he told Maureen everything; about his gift; about Aiden and their discoveries and about the group pursuing them. She'd surprised herself in two ways. Firstly she'd believed him immediately. There was something about the sincerity in his eyes and besides, it was simply too far-fetched a story for Jimmy to invent. Moreover, the truth of the matter was that at its core they had a strong and supportive relationship. True, she often declared him 'touched in the head', but that was only to keep his feet on the ground when he came up with one of his more outlandish ideas. In reality he was a very intelligent and capable man – if just a tad eccentric. And she loved him completely. Secondly, although she was hurt and annoyed by the fact that he'd kept his secret from her until now, she'd let it slide – not something that was in her nature really. In this case she'd put aside her feelings because she'd decided that it would be a little self-indulgent to dwell on them now given that threat hanging over Aiden and Jimmy. That said, she told herself, she reserved the right to return to the matter when all this was behind them.

Maureen reached across to where he had clenched his fist on the top of the table and gently put her hand over his. "You're still wound up tight as a spring, aren't you? Not surprising though, it hasn't been long since you were attacked. Never mind, love, we've left that behind us now, so try to loosen up."

He returned her warm smile with a wry grin and let his hand relax. "I'm pretty much over it or at least that's the way I feel most of the time. But I have to admit that a sudden loud noise or movement gives me a bit of a jolt."

"Time will heal," she assured him.

They'd been trying hard to pretend they were having a recuperative holiday. During the day they took leisurely strolls, arm in arm through the rejuvenated quay area; stopping for a bite to eat or a coffee or a beer as the mood took them. In the evenings they played cards on their kitchen table or at the local, making use of a pack of cards and a Cribbage board they'd found in a drawer at the cottage. But the reality of the situation they'd left behind was never far from their thoughts.

"That and seeing the back of those bastards that are going after Aiden. I don't have to tell you I'm frustrated with being away from Dublin laying low while the lad's in the firing line."

"I know it's not like you to step back from anything but Aiden was right sending us away. We might well have turned out a liability instead of a help if we were still over there."

"I understand that and did when Aiden raised it but understanding doesn't make it chafe any less. But look, I'm not going to sit on my hands while we're here."

"Oh? And exactly what is it that you're up to then?" She asked giving him a quizzical look, head tilted down, eyebrows arched and looking at him over her glasses. It was an expression that she adopted often with him. One he had come to know meant she had already decided that she most likely wouldn't like his answer.

He raised his hands, palms outward in supplication. "Hear me out darlin'. Not all of my ideas are harebrained."

That brought forth a wry smile from Maureen. "Alright, I'll hold off on my judgment. Let's have it," she said.

No-one in the pub was paying them the least bit of attention. Nevertheless, Jimmy leaned forward and signaled for her to do the same. He lowered his voice. "I know some people from the old days that know their way around a bit."

Maureen looked like she was about to jump in, so he gave a 'let me finish' gesture before she could speak and hurried on. "They're not big time crims or anything. More like, you might say, very flexible entrepreneurs. They might be rough types but that are very loyal to their mates. I'm sure I've mentioned them before – the O'Flaherty brothers."

"And just what is it you want of them?" Her tone said that she was not at all sold on where this was going.

"A couple of things," he replied. "I want to tee up some muscle in case we need it. And I want to hire some of their Dublin contacts to try to uncover where those thugs are staying."

Maureen considered what Jimmy had proposed, turning it over in her mind looking for anything about it that bothered her. There was nothing. "I like it - it's a fine idea. We have to be ready to fight fire with fire if it comes to that," she said, nodding to emphasize her support as she spoke.

"That's good then because I've already arranged for the boys to swing by the cottage for a chat tomorrow morning.

Now, don't you be given me that look. I've not kept anything from you have I? Just like I promised t'other day – no more secrets - an open book."

Maureen tried for exasperation but failed. "You old rogue. You truly are incorrigible. You're supposed to tell me what you're up to before you go and do it, not after. You'd best be off to the bar and buy us another drink before I hit you over the head."

The O'Flaherty pair arrived at the cottage a couple of hours after breakfast. Jimmy greeted them warmly and led them into the parlor where he introduced them to Maureen. Physically Martin and Frank couldn't have been more unalike. Martin was the oldest and he was a wiry whippet of a man, whereas Frank's build was intimidating; he was a hulking individual. They were half brothers. Martin's mother had died in childbirth and their mutual father Danny had remarried a year later with Frank born a year after that. Half-kin or not, they had been inseparable their entire lives. They came from a long line of laborers on the land where along with hard muscles and calloused hands, they inherited a deep distrust of landlords and the landed gentry. However as young men they left that calling and made their own path - all the way to the docks of Galway City. Over the years both had worked themselves into positions of authority. They were known as tough negotiators who could be ruthless when forced into a corner. But regardless of how their stature and power grew, they never lost their misgiving about the motives of the moneyed class. Viewing life as being a constant struggle of the worker against oppression provided them a ready-made excuse for all manner of dubious behavior. Consequently, it was rumored that there was nothing that they could not procure given a loose justification of a cause being noble or failing that, the cash to make it so. Of course the advent of sealed shipping containers made life a much more complicated but apparently even that was not an insurmountable obstacle.

When Jimmy had arrived on the docks as a young man from Dublin looking for work and adventure, the O'Flaherty's were also just starting out. The three of them being green as grass in the workings of a major port had naturally gravitated together and happily, they had hit it off immediately. From Jimmy's standpoint, having a couple of locals watching out for him had been a godsend. After Jimmy had returned to Dublin, they continued to keep in touch, albeit sporadically. Now here they were, meeting up again, years later. Their bond was still strong; only separated by the irrelevant influences of distance and time.

Maureen had laid out morning tea for them and their fulsome praise for the spread brought a touch of color to her cheeks. She scolded them for their blarney but was still beaming when she took her leave declaring that she was off to take in some sea air. Some things remained firmly entrenched in a by-gone era and she knew the business to be discussed was considered not for a woman's ears. Jimmy stuck to the story he had concocted in Dublin about an unfair gambling debt an unscrupulous English bookmaker – exactly the kind of mistreatment of the underdog that incensed Martin and Frank. They gravely shook their heads in unison muttering the word 'bastards' when he told them about the attack on him; aghast at the inhumanity of some. When Jimmy outlined the help he needed from them they couldn't wait to lend a hand. Indeed, in view of the righteousness of the cause and of course their friendship, they assured Jimmy that their own commission would be kept at an absolute rock bottom price.

CHAPTER 39

Back home in Dublin again, Aiden compiled the dossier. Item by item it came together. He intentionally kept it concise and to the point – the better to get the message through. It began with a list of facts about the company history and the business it was in; naming Muller and his father as the kingpins. He included specific references to the company backing a group of gamblers who had an unfair advantage but did not elaborate on the nature of their advantage. Muller would understand the meaning. He knew that Aiden could choose to reveal more if it became necessary. Shannon succeeded in getting hold of copies of the passports, so Aiden now had names and photo-id of two of Muller's players to add to the document. He read through the finished product and was pleased with the result. *Okay Muller, I'm ready to play. Now I just have to find you.*

He managed to get back into his standard routine of training, reading and cooking. His social life consisted of a daily call with Sharni, a beer with the lads and football. He found himself missing Jimmy and took to calling him for a brief chat every couple days. Even though things were quiet on the Muller front at the moment, they agreed that it was better for Jimmy to stay away. In any event, it sounded like he and Maureen were still having a fine time in their temporary home away from home. His only activity out of the norm was a series of large bets both on and off course to build up his bank balance. His adversary had access to significant funds and he wanted his own sizable war chest of cash in easy reach.

Finally Sharni had something to report – but not exactly the news Aiden wanted. "Sorry my love but Lukas Muller is proving difficult to pin down. He seems to move around quite a lot and appears to have no permanent home."

"Bugger. Where do we go from here?"

"I don't how much it helps but I have a location for Muller senior in Nice."

"Let me think. Maybe...could be that I can get through to the son via the father. If we're lucky he might be a bit more reasonable than his lunatic offspring."

"Worth a try at least," replied Sharni.

"Definitely and it's the only avenue we have. I'll organize to fly there as soon as possible."

"Okay but give me time to arrange some time off."

Time for him a do a little teasing for a change. "Oh, it hadn't occurred to me that you'd be coming as well."

She took the bait. "Listen mister, if you think that you are going to take a trip to Nice without me, you're clearly a bit soft in the head...and not safe to be let loose travelling alone....Are you laughing? Oh, it's like that is it? You cheeky sod - you're going to pay big time for that. I'm the one who does the messing with your mind in this relationship, not you."

They took a room at a hotel located a short distance up the road from the establishment where Muller resided - it would be just a little too cozy to be in the same digs. As a bonus, their hotel's position was ideal for a little sightseeing around Old Nice if the opportunity arose. It was the first time either had visited the city and they were immediately enchanted. After checking in, they took a stroll along the promenade by the sea. The weather was warm and the

Mediterranean sparkled in the sunlight, its color an exquisite shade of deep blue that was unlike any other stretch of water in the world. The beach is one of coarse pebbles rather than fine white sand. But this did nothing to deter the beachgoers. There were plenty of people sprawled on hired sun beds or swimming or playing ballgames along the shorefront. Sharni was obliged to reward Aiden several times with an elbow to the ribs when his attention lingered a little too long on one of the many dark-haired beach-beauties, skin the color of honey, basking in the sun. The defense's proposition that he 'was just admiring their tans' did not sway the prosecution.

Getting to Muller proved more difficult than anticipated. As a gatekeeper, the concierge was up there with some of the velvet-rope-door-bitches he had encountered outside bars that had become the latest hot-spot for the beautiful people. Eventually he convinced the concierge to let him leave a note in Muller's pigeon-hole. Aiden took the proffered pen and ornately embossed hotel note paper and sat down in a leather armchair and thought about what he should write. There was a good chance that the functionary at the counter would take a peek at his note – he looked a nosey type. Aiden decided to make the message cryptic enough to appear innocuous but mean something special to Muller. He settled on a simple statement: 'I've come here from Dublin and I have the Gift. Call me' and then added his phone number. His thinking was that Muller would have some awareness of recent events courtesy of his son and the keywords of 'Dublin' and 'Gift' should do the trick.

The call came the following day. The voice on the other end was cool and clipped, with a slight accent that to Aiden's ear was identical to that of Lukas Muller. *Spare me from another 'I'm-all-business' Swiss capitalist.*

"I will see you in my suite in one hour. Henri on the desk will be expecting you and will bring you up."

Muller answered the door and led Aiden to the sitting room of the suite that was Muller's home. He couldn't help being impressed by its opulence. He was no interior designer but because it was a style he liked, he recognized that it was rooted in the Art Deco period. The carpet, a muted pastel shade of mint in color, was deep and so plush that he could feel his feet sinking into it. The furniture was French Art Deco – he had no doubt they would all be authentic pieces. They comprised a low couch and two armchairs with small side tables. These surrounded a low coffee table and opposite lay a desk – probably a concession to the lack of a separate den. The walls were a neutral ivory tone on which several original paintings were strategically hung. The whole was capped off with a floor to ceiling bay window with a view to the sea. Aiden's thoughts roamed. *Is this what I want? I have the power to make as much money as I please. I can have wealth and all the trimmings. But no, it's not who I am. All this is tempting but I'd feel trapped in no time. Give me the simple life any time.*

He snapped out of his reverie when Muller spoke. "Your note was quite ambiguous. Please explain the nature of your business with me."

"I think you understand perfectly or you wouldn't have agreed to see me. But I'm happy to spell it out. I believe that you met my uncle years ago. Well I too have the same ability. And because of this I am being hounded by your son. I want you to intervene and have him stop."

Muller said nothing so Aiden went on and told his story of all that occurred. When he was done he handed Muller the dossier and the mailing list that he had put together. "To help him make up his mind, I've prepared this for you to give to him."

The man quickly scanned the papers. "This is very sketchy but I get the message. It could be very damaging."

"I told your son many times that all I want is to be left alone. But he refuses to hear me – refuses to except the simple truth. I am not a threat to him but at the same time I have absolutely no intention of being part of his organization."

"And yet here you produce a document that proves his concerns to be well founded."

Aiden felt anger rising and tried to hold his temper. "Only because your son would not listen to reason. He forced me down this route...to hell with it...I'm not here to defend my actions. It's gone way past that."

Muller relented when he heard the sincerity coupled with a degree of desperation in Aiden's tone. "Remain calm. I will do what I can. I'll make sure Lukas gets this and it will be my advice to him that he cut his losses and desist in pursuing you."

Aiden was thrown by the rapid shift in attitude from Muller. He stammered a reply. "Well...er...yes...it would be best all round if you could do that. And I give you my word that if he goes away, the file will never see the light of day."

"Be aware that I can promise nothing. My son can be very driven and does not always follow my counsel."

He emerged from the hotel satisfied that he had done what he could. Evening was coming and the promise of a warm fine day tomorrow was written in pink by the setting sun on the clouds that dappled the sky. *Life feels pretty damn good right now - a small step forward, a beautiful woman waiting for me and this stunning place. I couldn't possibly want anything more.*

Knowing that they had achieved as much as they could reasonably have expected, Aiden and Sharni treated themselves to some time-out. They started out early to explore the Old Nice precinct and came across the Cours Saleya, an open-air market that has a bit of everything. They browsed the diverse array of bric-a-brac, admired the beauty of the flower stalls awash with color and bought bread, cheeses and wine for a picnic lunch. Walking on they set about making the long climb up Castle Hill. When they finally reached the top, the effort was worth it. They were rewarded with stunning picture-perfect view across Nice and the crescent curve of the bay. After a rustic lunch they lay back in the grass under the canopy of a large fig tree, holding hands and at peace with the world.

Over the next few days they used the coastal rail line to venture further afield. First they took the train west to Cannes but not being film festival time all was very quiet and their hoped for game of star spotting was a complete wash-out. Next they travelled east to Monaco. They were not dressed appropriately to gain entrance to Monte Carlo casino so instead skirted its perimeter. They came upon a patio area with a large balcony overlooking the harbor, its moorings brimming with a flotilla of outrageously expensive luxury yachts and cruisers. Across the bay, the pink palace was visible in the distant hills. They sat down in the shadows of the casino with a cool drink, amusing themselves by pondering which of the craft they would prefer to own – oblivious, of course, to the seminal role that the hulking building behind them had played in the genesis of their troubles.

CHAPTER 40

Lukas slammed the dossier down on the table. His face blazed with fury. "How dare that insignificant nobody try to intimidate me?"

"Try to calm down Lukas," said Andre, hands spread in a gesture of conciliation.

"Calm down? Did you not read it? If he sends this out it would be very damaging to our business."

"Yes, I know that. But he swears that he will not use it if you leave him alone. And I believe him."

He studied his son. Lukas looked haggard. His eyes were wild, ringed with dark circles and the whites streaked with red. There was a slight tremor in one of his hands as he gripped the desk with an intensity so fierce his knuckles had turned white.

"Lukas, I'm worried about you. You don't look at all well. This thing is beginning to become an obsession and that's not healthy. It has taken control of you and that lessens your capacity to think rationally. My advice is to let it go. Why not take some time out for a vacation – time to gather your equilibrium."

What his father said was true. He had not been sleeping well and his temper was like a malevolent beast crouching in his brain, ready to lash out at the slightest provocation. He had noticed that even his own advisors seemed to be keeping out of his way. And when they were unable to avoid him, the wariness they exhibited as they figuratively tiptoed around him was enough to trigger his anger. Merely thinking about it was causing the creature to stir. His father's homespun wisdom and unasked for advice irritated him even more.

"I appreciate your views," said Lukas but his tone gave lie to the words. Clearly he did not care one iota for his father's opinion. "But I am now in charge of the business and it is I who decides when and if I let this go."

Andre suppressed his own rising exasperation. "I can see that you need some time alone so I'll be leaving now. All I ask is for you to consider what I have said. I know I am not good at showing it but I do have your best interest at heart."

CHAPTER 41

If Lukas did take some time to consider what his father had to say, it failed to sway him. Two weeks after returning from Nice, Aiden was heading home on foot in the early evening twilight after a workout at his dojo. He turned the corner into his street and could see Muller's two hired thugs waiting outside of his house. His first thought was that they had a message from their boss and so whilst he didn't like seeing them there, he wasn't overly concerned. He approached them and saying nothing, waited to find out why they had come.

The smaller of them spoke gruffly. "Mr. Muller does not like to be blackmailed."

Without a further word, he produced a baton and swung it overhand aiming for Aiden's head. His reflexes and martial arts training were enough to enable him to block the blow and shove the attacker backwards. His training also meant that he was under no illusions as to the level of his proficiency - he was no Bruce Lee and you simply don't take on two professional enforcers. Fight or flight? Easy question - he took advantage of the time his block had bought him and bolted off down the street. If nothing else, he was entirely confident that he could outrun the heavies.

An hour later, having taken a circuitous and extremely cautious route, Aiden made it home. He double checked the locks on all doors and windows and made sure the alarm system was active. Aiden didn't call the police but they came anyway. Detective Inspector Bill Kennedy arrived just as Aiden was about to make some telephone calls to his friends. Now he was seated across from Aiden and explaining that a neighbor had seen some of what happened and phoned in a report.

"This would normally be handled by the uniform lads but when it came to my attention that the victim was a relative of Jimmy Donnelly, I decided to look into it personally. I can see that you're wondering why that might be. Well, the thing is, I wasn't convinced that the attack on your uncle was a random mugging. And now here we are with a situation of a couple of heavies trying to have a go at you. And I can tell you that I definitely don't believe in coincidences. So perhaps you'd like to tell me what's going on."

Aiden tried to come up with something plausible but making things up on the fly was not his forte – he was not a good liar. Tall stories were Jimmy's territory and that's where he pointed Kennedy. "I don't know what it's about. Maybe they do have a grudge against my uncle. He's out of town and I guess it's possible they thought I could tell them where to find him. I didn't wait to ask them. I did a runner as fast as I could."

"Good attempt son but I think you know more than you're letting on," Kennedy said and then went quiet, sitting back a watching Aiden. It was a technique he used often. Let the interviewee fill the silence. It worked more times than not but Aiden kept his mouth shut. Eventually Kennedy sighed and stood up to leave.

He gave Aiden his card. "When you decide you're in too deep, call me."

True to the knack that the police have, Kennedy's prying left him feeling exposed and vaguely guilty even though he hadn't actually done anything wrong – ironically in fact, he was the victim in all this. He called Jimmy and filled him in on all that had transpired.

"Bastards. It's high time they got theirs."

"Agreed but what can we do about them?"

Jimmy's response surprised him. "Just you leave it to me. I might have left town but I've had the feelers out for the whole time I've been away. I pretty sure I know where they are staying. It's a rooming house not far from where you live. I've not done anything with the information till now. I didn't want to make things more complicated."

Aiden was becoming a little alarmed. "What are you planning to do?"

"Don't you be fretting about it. You know very well I'm an easy going man by nature but now with them going after you, they've made me an angry man. They think they're hard men. Well they'll fuckin' well need to be. They haven't run into an Irishman who been pushed too far. I'll show them hard men, made that way through years of struggling to just to stay alive and build something for their families."

"Just go steady Jimmy. I don't think I like the sound of this."

"Never you mind okay. I don't want you involved in any of what might go down. It's my backyard they're in now. Besides that copper is one very nosey bugger and I don't want him getting his hooks in you. All you need to know is that couple of Galway boys will be visiting Dublin and a couple of visiting foreigners will be leaving Dublin."

The doorbell chimed and when Aiden looked through the peephole he was greeted with fish-eye view of the craggy face of the diminutive DI Kennedy. Only a few days had passed since his last visit and Aiden's talk with his uncle and he suspected that Kennedy's return had something to do with Jimmy and his friends. His heart-rate went up several notches as he opened the door. *Jesus Jimmy, I hope you haven't gone too far. Stay calm Aiden, stay calm.*

Kennedy did not make a move to enter and Aiden didn't invite him in. "Ah, Mr. Donnelly. Good morning to you."

"Inspector. What can I do for you?"

"Thought I'd swing by and share a bit of news with you. Last night two men were found unconscious in a ditch just outside of the city limits with hessian bags over their heads. They were admitted to hospital having sustained a variety of injuries from what looks to me like a systematic beating – likely carried out by parties who know a bit about inflicting pain. Not life threatening but enough damage to have the pair of them on crutches for months. Haven't seen the likes since the bad old days when this sort of thing was done to warn someone off."

"Why are you telling me this?" Aiden managed to get out. His heart was pounding now and he could feel the blood rushing to his head. He was sure that his face was a bright crimson and he looked as guilty as sin.

"Just hear me out, okay?"

Aiden nodded - mute.

"Now there are several unusual facts associated with the case. The men are visitors to our fine shores – they had their passports with them - and it's difficult to imagine how a couple of innocent tourists managed to upset the sort of men who would mete out this kind of payback. That said, it is most interesting to note that these two fit the descriptions of the men who tried to assault you. And coincidentally it seems they arrived in Dublin only a few days before the attack on your uncle. Now, strangest of all, they both claim to be suffering amnesia as well and can't remember anything at all about what occurred. Certainly the sort of thing that piques this man's curiosity."

Kennedy stopped talking. Aiden stood statue-like trying to harness some semblance of calm. The inspector gave it another try. "Like I said – rather an odd set of events.

Anyway, I was wondering Mr. Donnelly, if you have any thoughts on the matter?"

"Are you saying that you think I did this? That's ridiculous. I'm not some sort of standover guy."

"No I don't see you having a direct part in this. But I do think that it's connected to the attacks on your uncle and on you. And I'll repeat what I said to you the other day. I'm pretty sure you know what's going on."

Aiden was impressed. Even though he had no proof Kennedy had put a lot of it together. Fortunately the key to resolving the puzzle was so extraordinary that he could never make the leap solely based on experience and intellect.

Kennedy started to leave and then turned back with a parting remark. "Let me tell you one thing lad, I've been in this caper a long time and I can tell you, I've come across a lot of people who find themselves caught up in something that gets out of hand. It gets to a point where they don't know where to turn. You seem like a good enough young fella and I want to help you if I can before it's gone too far. So I want you to think it over and then call me alright."

He left without waiting for a response – not that Aiden had one to offer. He was just glad to see the back of the overly insightful copper.

CHAPTER 42

Olivadi completed the uncomfortable task of telling his boss that their men in Dublin were out of action and waited for the tirade that he was sure would follow.

Instead Muller spoke through clenched teeth in little more than a whisper. And the effect was all the more chilling.

"Those bungling imbeciles have botched every single task that they have been given. I sincerely hope that they are in a great deal of pain."

The head of security could think of no response and so sought to move the conversation forward. "What do you want to do about the target now?"

Muller brooded over the question, scanning in his mind's eye a catalogue of failures and disappointments. His face was a window to his thoughts as his expression went from petulance to anger finally settling on raw hatred. When he spoke, his eyes were on Olivadi but it was as if he was talking to himself. "I want more men. And not Englishmen; it would appear that they do not have what it takes. I want specialists for this assignment and I'm prepared for you to pay over our usual going rate to get the right sort of operatives. Donnelly has proved most obstinate. No doubt he will continue to defy me and so I have decided to end it. I intend to cut him loose – or more precisely, to rid myself of a gross irritation. He is to have a motor accident and sadly one that he will not survive," instructed Muller.

Pleased with the plan he had hatched on the spot, he allowed himself to smile. His bared teeth conjured in Olivadi's mind the image of a circling shark.

"I'll see to sourcing the appropriate types...shouldn't take too long."

"Good. This time I'm taking no chances. When your end is organized, I'll be travelling to Dublin to personally supervise."

CHAPTER 43

Aiden was returning from Wicklow. He'd made good on his promise to himself and had gone to see his parents to tell them what had been happening in his life. As anticipated, when it came to revealing his ability they took a mountain of convincing that Aiden had not lost his marbles. And the tactic of getting Jimmy on the phone had almost scuttled the 'tell all' completely. His folks came to the conclusion that they had cooked up this story between them as some sort of elaborate ruse.

Or as his father succinctly put it, "You two are just having a laugh. Well your mother and are having none of it."

In the end, it was Aiden's tenacity and sincerity that swayed them. He repeated his story. He offered to give them a demonstration. Finally he asked them to trust him and believe in him. That simple plea was the turning point. They began to ask questions and he answered openly, holding nothing back. He tried his best to put into words the mechanics of his gift and what it felt like. He won them over - to the point that his father offered the opinion that it was just possible that he had experienced the lucky feeling once or twice in his life. His claim was greeted by his mother patting his arm in a 'yes dear, of course you have' gesture as her eyes were raised to the ceiling.

He left later than planned. Night was falling and before long the darkness deepened as the weather turned nasty. Drizzle set in just as he got beyond the town limits. It mixed with the oil residue built up on the road and creating a greasy slick film on the surface of the road. Aiden could feel through the bike's handling that the grip of his tires was becoming more tenuous.

The downpour steadily increased its intensity, graduating to a full-blown storm. With it a strong squally wind blew in from the east, buffeting him as he rode. His headlight reflected off the wet bitumen surface making it hard to see. All he could make out were eddies of rain swirling across the road and as he cut through them, icy water whipped up around his legs. The sharper bends were now difficult to negotiate. *Damn it, I knew those tires were about due for replacement. Why did I keep putting it off?* He throttled back to a more modest speed.

An automobile appeared behind him, closing quickly. The driver kept his headlights on high beam bathing Aiden in light and worsening the already poor visibility. Aiden edged as near as he dared to the shoulder of the road and waved that the car should overtake him. *If you're in that much of a hurry, go around you arsehole.* Instead the car stayed behind him, pushing up closer and forcing him to quicken his pace. He was travelling faster than he considered safe but could do nothing about it.

In the distance ahead another set of lights emerged from the darkness; this time coming towards him. He could tell it was bigger than a car – more the size of a small truck or large van. This diver too failed to dip his lights. As the gap closed he could clearly gauge that the lorry was headed right for him. Comprehension hit him with an almost physical force. *These bastards are out to get me.* Whether the plan was to manufacture a head-on or to force him off the road, there was no doubt they wanted him hurt or dead. And he could see no way out. With the realization of the situation, fear gripped him and he gasped aloud.

In the time it took for that sudden intake of cold night air the scene changed completely. Because of his training regime, Aiden had developed a deep intimacy with the workings of his brain. He was able to feel it clearly when his ability kicked in. It was happening right now. The difference was that he had not consciously invoked it – this was spontaneous. At that exact moment with a sound like a small explosion, the lorry's front left tire blew out. Now instead of hurtling like a missile towards him, it lurched wildly to the other side of the road. Aiden fancied he could see the wide-eyed expression of the frantic driver as he struggled to gain control. In his panic he over-corrected causing the vehicle to fishtail down the road. It was only meters away when Aiden assessed the trajectory and throttled hard as he aimed his bike at a spot where he judged a gap would open up. He made it through but it was a near thing – he'd been close enough to have counted the scratch marks in the lorry's paint work.

A moment later the cacophonous crash of metal on metal assailed his ears as the two vehicles collided at full speed. He brought his bike to a stop, got off and turning, took in the tableau of twisted metal. It looked as though an ultra-modern sculpture had been dumped on the side of the road. *They couldn't have survived that.* Any doubt there might have been was snuffed out when an explosion ripped through the night. The ruptured fuel tanks had gone up and flames erupted twenty meters into the air.

His emotions were in turmoil and he stood frozen beside his motorcycle while fear and anger jostled for supremacy. *I should go back. Shouldn't I?* At last he gave a violent shake of his head. The storm had passed and the clouds were breaking up. He took off his helmet and looked to the sky as the moon emerged from the clouds. His posture was animal-like as shouted passionately into the wild night. "FUCK YOU MULLER."

His roar of defiance strangled into a sob of despair as his voice broke. The futile loss of lives hit him hard. He cried, his body heaving with anguish. He'd never seen anyone die. Why was he being put through this? Eventually the tears stopped and he regained at least a veneer of composure. From that flimsy platform fury started to build anew. *I didn't do this. None of it. I don't deserve any of this shit. To hell with all of you – fucking greedy, murderous bastards.* The powerful emotions helped to steel him but in truth he was operating mostly on nervous energy when he remounted his bike and headed for home.

Safely back in his house, the adrenalin rush was abating and his hands were shaking. He recognized the classic symptoms of mild shock. He wanted badly to talk about what had just happened and how his gift had saved his life. But it was too late at night and would only serve to give someone else a sleepless night. Come the morning he would get in touch with Sharni and Jimmy. In the meantime he poured himself a solid shot of Bush Mills. By the time he'd finished his drink he felt numb but not from the alcohol. It was caused by the physical knock-on effect emanating from his emotional exhaustion. Bone tired, he stumbled to his bed and was asleep as soon as his head touched the pillow.

CHAPTER 44

Aiden woke early and was showered and dressed by dawn. In his head, the anthemic song 'What's Left of the Flag' did nothing to raise his spirits. He was tense and unable to stomach the thought of breakfast as he waited for the paperboy to deliver the morning edition. Eventually a dull thud on his small veranda signaled its arrival and he was there in an instant, snatching it up.

He spread the paper across his kitchen table and there it was. The crash had made the front page under a banner headline that screamed 'FIREBALL'. Below was a photograph of the burnt-out wreckage. Aiden scanned through the story looking for anything that might point to his connection to the carnage. 'Horror crash...sometime last night...bad weather conditions and poor visibility...at this stage police had little to report with any certainty...two men had been killed in the head-on collision...the severity of the impact suggested both vehicles were travelling at speed...most likely that the occupants died on impact...an ensuing fire had incinerated the bodies... identification was likely to take time...no witnesses had come forward'.

Aiden relived the terror as he read the article. His heart rate rose and a sudden feeling of nausea had bile rising from his gut, scorching his esophagus. He resisted the panic attack, his training taking over. It passed and with it went the sense of guilt that until then he hadn't realized had been lurking insidiously in his sub-conscious. Now he could eat. In fact he was surprised to find he was suddenly famished. He made himself a breakfast of mammoth proportions – bacon, eggs, fried tomato and avocado on the side. As he savored his meal he mulled over what to do next. Between Muller and Inspector Kennedy he felt threatened from both sides. He needed to contact his friends but he didn't want to say anything of consequence over his phone – somebody might be monitoring his calls. He tried to talk himself around. *You're being paranoid Aiden old son. Been watching too many crime dramas.* But it was no use. Over-reaction or not, his strong desire was to play it very safe. Nor did he want to go outside to find a public phone box. He was not about to leave the security of his home fortress alone. It was highly unlikely but there might be other homicidal thugs out there keeping him under surveillance. The upshot was an impasse.

It took some minutes for him to conquer his dithering and decide what he would do. He called Shannon and, giving no explanation, asked if his friend would be able to drop over during his lunch break. Probably because of the business he was in, Shannon was quick to read between the lines. "I'll be out and about near your place a little later this morning," he remarked, keeping his voice casual. "I'll see you then."

Thirty minutes later Shannon was with him and Aiden unloaded. Of necessity he kept his voice level and the description matter-of-fact. He feared that he'd break down if he didn't. Nonetheless, by the time he was done, Aiden was sweating and Shannon's face was ashen as he spoke. "God man, I don't know what to say. This is serious shit. Should you call the police, maybe?"

"Can't see how it would help. What would I tell them? How could I explain what's going on without them locking me up as a lunatic?"

"You're right, I guess but still...I mean...where the hell do we go from here?"

"Right now I have no idea either but one thing is, I need to tell the rest of the guys. Will you drive me somewhere? I know a boozer nearby that has a public phone in the back and out of hearing of the punters at the bar."

He finished his calls to the lads and then got on to Jimmy. He gave them all a bare-bones version of events – the front page story in the paper was a result of two men trying to run him off the road. And yes, he was absolutely sure that it was a deliberate attempt on his life. He didn't look for ideas from them, nor did they have any to offer. His world had been shifted and he simply needed their friendship to help him regain balance. Dylan and Michael announced they'd be over after work with sleeping bags and a crate of beer – an idea that got a thumbs-up from Shannon as well. Jimmy declared that he and Maureen would be back home by the following afternoon and be around to see Aiden as soon as they could.

Now for the most important call. While talking to the others, he had been rehearsing what he might say to Sharni. He started poorly with the commonly used but completely useless expression: 'I don't want you to worry'. More than any other, this is a phrase designed to cause the person hearing it to mentally cringe with images of all manner of death and mayhem instantaneously flashing before them. He did better as he got going, desperately trying to sound in control and resolute.

As he had expected she declared that she'd be on the first available flight. He launched into the response he'd been practicing. "No...please. I know you want to be here for me but I couldn't cope if you got hurt. I'd be so worried about you that I wouldn't be able to function. The guys are coming over to stay with me. And Shannon says he's going to beef up security – and the house is already like Fort Knox. Oh and Jimmy is coming back from Galway. So all in all, I'll have plenty of back-up."

"But I need to be doing something or I'll go spare."

"The best way you can help me is to keep up with the research. The men who were killed; the police will be trying to identify them. Are you able to get any visibility of the investigation?"

"I can try. If they're not Irish nationals – and that's most likely - the police will put it out on the wires looking for help from the international law enforcement community. Then I'll be able to see it."

"Nothing else has worked against Muller so the only idea I've come up with is to get something illegal on him and try to put him away. I don't have a clue where it will lead but if you can connect these guys to him, at least it's a start."

"It's under strong protest but I'll do it your way. You stay very safe and you call me every day, okay."

"You know I will and thank you for going along with me. I know it's for the best."

Back at Aiden's house, Shannon went over the array of security settings and declared it satisfactory – short of installing electrified fencing. They settled in to watch a corny old black and white BBC movie while awaiting the arrival of the other pair and more importantly the liquid refreshment they were bringing. Aiden was sorely looking forward to unwinding with his friends and when they arrived the night didn't let him down. The beer stocks began to disappear at an alarming pace and the level of machismo was rising in inverse proportion. At heart they all knew that their bravado was a defense against sure knowledge that they were in a situation that was beyond them. But inside their fortress they could assert their invulnerability. Those heavies wouldn't know what hit them if they were stupid enough to show up now.

The next morning four much more circumspect lads emerged from beds and sleeping bags. The living room looked like a small cyclone had been unleashed and then morphed into a tornado as it passed through the kitchen. There was no shortage of groaning and incoherent muttering as they stretched out the kinks in their muscles and scratched in all manner of places as men are wont to do on rising. By silent consent the morning called for a fry-up of sausages and eggs – plenty of grease, held by some to be an effective remedy for a hangover. At the very least it was a kill or cure treatment: if you could keep it down, chances were you were going to survive. After breakfast, they put in two hours of solid penance, otherwise known as cleaning up.

After his friends had left for work, Aiden received a call from Jimmy letting him know that he'd be back in town in the afternoon and intended to come by as soon as he dropped Maureen at their house. A few hours later his uncle was at his door and he was not alone; he was flanked by two big, big men. *Whoa, these two buggers are a couple of attack dogs,* was his first thought and it was an apt enough description. He'd never seen a more imposing pair. Facially, they were not alike but their bodies were from the same mould. They seemed almost as wide as they were tall and the thickness was all muscle bulk. They were bull necked with broad shoulders and Popeye forearms. Their legs looked as if they could be used to anchor a hammock. They were of average height but their breadth gave them an overall appearance of being taller than they were.

Jimmy introduced them. "These likely boyos work for the O'Flaherty brothers over in Galway. Right now they work for us. This is Mick," he said gesturing towards the man on his right and this is Andy," he added nodding in the direction of the other fellow. Aiden noticed a glimmer of amusement in his uncle's eyes as he reached out with some apprehension to shake their hands - anticipating he was about to have his own mangled. He need not have worried. Their grip was firm but nothing more. These were men who were very aware of their power and saw no need to show off.

"The lads are going to be staying with you for a while," announced Jimmy. "Can you show them through to your spare room so they can stow their gear?"

Aiden hadn't noticed until now that each had a large backpack slung over his shoulder. "What? Er, sorry...I mean, come in," he stammered, momentarily flummoxed. "It's down the hall, second door," he managed to get out, pointing the way.

Aiden made way for Mike and Andy and as they went through to the room, he pulled his uncle aside. "I'm not at all sure about this, Jimmy," he whispered, not wanting the men to overhear.

"Don't judge them by the way they look. When you get to know them a bit, you might find that you get on pretty well with them. Their appearance is one reason they are so good at their job. Frank O'Flaherty told me that they rarely have to use their muscle. An angry stare from them and most people back off right quick."

"But what am I going to do with them here at home – you know to entertain them?"

"Nothing – pure and simple. They are ex-military, so they don't mind bunking in together and they can fend for themselves for meals and all. You just have to point them to what's what in the kitchen."

Aiden remained unconvinced the arrangement could work. He was used to having his place to himself and he was not comfortable sharing his space with strangers.

Jimmy firmly put down the last of his resistance with a reminder of the reality of the situation. "You'll get used to it. The lads know how to be unobtrusive. And the truth is that when you wake up tomorrow and want to nip out for bread and milk you'll be pretty pleased that these guys are watching your arse. Now come on, let's show them where everything is and then the four of us will nip round the pub to seal the deal."

It only took a couple of days for Aiden to acclimatize to having housemates. Much of the time he hardly noticed them at all and when he did spend time chatting with them, the conversation flowed easily. Andy was quiet and thoughtful but when he did have something to say, his ability to get to the nub of the subject and his bone dry sense of humor hinted at an intellect that Aiden had not expected from someone with his physique. Mick was more of a talker; a man given to expansive gestures and punctuating his statements with a booming laugh. In another life he might have made a fine standup comedian. He managed to extract an element of absurdity from most events and his observations when reading the newspaper were hilarious, especially when he became fired up about politics. Moreover as Jimmy predicted the feeling of security made any minor discomfort worthwhile. Without them around there had been a real risk that he'd have become a prisoner in his house.

There was one further change; whether due to their presence or the passage of time he didn't know. On top of the rest of the pressure he was under, he'd been sleeping badly. His nights were interrupted by the same vivid dream full of the sight and sound of that horrible smash. Perversely his imagination had exacerbated the torment. In his nightmare he could hear the trapped men screaming and smell the stench of burning flesh. But last night his subconscious had not subjected him to the ordeal and he woke fresh and rested for the first time in days. He hoped fervently that perhaps this particularly distressing phase of his life was now behind him.

Sharni called to report what she had found. She sounded slightly breathless in her excitement and eagerness to share. Her words spilled out. "The police have identified the two men. They were a couple of Russian standover men and both have long and particularly vicious records. I know I sound terribly hard but frankly the world is better off with them gone."

"God I'm so pleased you said that. After what they tried to do to me I've been thinking it but haven't been game enough to say it out loud," Aiden replied. "So here it is – I'm glad the bastards are dead." He felt a lessening of tension that he hadn't even known was there. Admitting what he had been holding inside purged him of it – one more plank in his recovery.

Somehow on the other end of the phone she sensed it. "I wish I was there right now to hold you my love."

"I know. I want it too but it just can't be. Not until we're free of this mess."

"I want to argue but I won't. You have enough on your plate," said Sharni, acceptance tinged with exasperation coming through in her tone. He heard a distinct huff and in his mind's eye could see her give a little shake of her head.

"I've more to tell you," she said returning to the reason for the call. "The Russians arrived in Dublin a couple of days before they came after you – she couldn't bring herself to say 'tried to kill you'. I was able to get a copy of the passenger manifest and one of the other names is very interesting – a Renzo Olivadi."

"Olivadi – the ones who attacked Jimmy used that name. It can't be a coincidence."

"That's my thought as well. So we have a link from the hit men to Muller through Olivadi. But...and it's a big but, you and I know it's real but I doubt that it's strong enough to take directly to the police."

"So what do we have then?"

"Another piece to add to your profile on Muller. And from this end I can put some notes into the intelligence database. I'll list Olivadi and Muller as possible associates of the Russians. Maybe it'll pique someone's interest and focus attention on them."

"I have a feeling that the 'someone' is likely to be the inquisitive DI Kennedy and that might not be a good thing."

"Do you want me to back off then?" asked Sharni.

"No, go ahead with your plan. Who knows, it could work in our favor and it beats doing nothing," Aiden replied. "And speaking of the good inspector, we know he's like a dog with a bone. He won't let this drop, so I've been working on a story – it's partly the truth and it might satisfy him. I'm still filling in bits but the gist of it is to tell him about Jimmy and I winning big on the Derby. Then out of the blue this lunatic standover merchant comes on the scene. He's lost a bundle on the race. Somehow he finds out that we won money and demands we make good on his losses. We don't want to go to the police because we're worried about what the hoods might do to our families. I know it's a bit lame but what do you think?"

"Well, like you said there's a kernel of truth in it. And there are plenty of extortion rackets around. It might fly."

"Yeah, maybe. Let's face it, the real truth is even more implausible. Anyway, I'm not planning on rushing down to see him. It's more like having something prepared if I'm pushed into a corner."

CHAPTER 45

"Tell me Olivadi, just where do you find these idiots? Are they half-witted cousins of yours in need of work, perhaps? Or do you have a pipeline straight into some special camp in Siberia that houses imbeciles? Tell me – I'd really like to know." Muller began with sarcasm but as he spoke he became more agitated.

They were in an office at the back of what once had been some type of workshop. It was located in a slightly run-down part of west Dublin. The surrounding buildings in the area were mostly storage facilities.

Now Muller was waving his arms around and his speech degenerated into a rant. "Maybe you enjoy seeing me fail. Is that it? Are you laughing at me behind my back? All of you – is that it? Do you all hide in corners plotting and then pointing and snickering?"

Like his father, Lukas Muller's demeanor had always been much more aligned with the Germanic influences on Switzerland rather than that of the French. Now in the face of yet another disappointment, his histrionics had Olivadi silently drawing a comparison further east to Austria – or more accurately one psychotic piece of effluent that seeped out of that country.

He chose his words carefully seeking to calm his chief and at the same time mask his concerns as to Muller's sanity. "Sir, I assure you that it's not like that at all. All of the men respect you and know well that your leadership and business acumen is the reason for their success. And as for me, I've always acted with total loyalty."

He hurried on before Muller could launch again. "And with respect sir, the Russians came highly recommended. Their careers as mercenaries and enforcers are rock solid. I can't understand why in this instance they have so utterly ineffective. I am beginning to wonder if something is at play here that we don't comprehend."

Muller seemed calmer now but his eyes still smoldered, a clear signal that he was barely in control and could erupt again at any time. "Are you implying that the Irishman possesses some sort of paranormal powers?" Muller scoffed. "Utter nonsense. This luck ability is useful for gambling and nothing more. So please spare me from ridiculous suggestions about hocus-pocus."

Olivadi wisely chose not to pursue the point and waited for him to go on.

"Well, let us see how this magician of yours copes with a bullet in the brain, shall we. It ends now and it's obvious that to get it done I'll have do it myself. I suspected that it would come to this. That's why I had Philippe source this place to rent as well as the van out in the alley," said Muller, indicating the office and workshop with a sweep of his right arm. "This is part of my backup plan, in the event that your men failed me. It is the perfect spot. The place is virtually soundproof and there are not many people about in the street. I can finish it right here and easily dispose of the body. Yes it will be quite simple and then we will be gone before anyone even knows what happened. And one more thing, I know you want desperately the chance to prove you are as reliable and loyal as you profess, so you will help me do it."

Olivadi drew back. Muller's attitude and words scared him. His breath caught and there was a thrumming in his ears. His way was to act through others, not to be directly involved – it had always been that way. He'd joined the police force as a young man and soon discovered he was adept at reading the mood of the bureaucracy. He sensed the right thing to say in forums and gave an impression of progressiveness and efficiency. His superiors anointed him a rising star, one of the new breed set to modernize policing. He quickly rose through the ranks without actually achieving much at all. His skill was to stay out of the firing line but to be on hand when a successful operation was finalized and accolades were being handed out.

When his standing was at its zenith and before anyone figured out that he was a fraud, he secured a position with Interpol. It was a perfect fit. He thrived as an administrator and a manipulator, again keeping well away from the front line of operations. He quickly saw the potential to make the most out of the intelligence that passed across his desk and before long he was running numerous sidelines that were extremely questionable but also extremely profitable. He left when one of his cronies let him know that he was the subject of a clandestine investigation.

Next as Muller's Head of Security he'd been a party to actions that had gone from increasingly dubious to outright illegal. But again he'd acted as the enabler, an invisible organizer. It was one thing to arrange things to be carried out at a distance but a very different matter to be directly involved.

"But...but...I've never actually shot anyone," he stammered. "To be honest, I'm not sure I can."

His protest was dismissed with a wave of the hand. "I'm sure the size of the bonus I'm offering will overcome your squeamishness. No, I'll hear no argument; my mind is made up. I want to look into the face of the man who thinks he can deny me and see it in his eyes when he realizes the consequences."

"But I don't understand. How will you be able to convince him to come to you?"

"Leave that to me. He will come," said Muller, a self-satisfied smirk on his face. "Your job right now is to secure us two silenced hand guns. Can you manage that small task?"

Olivadi was stung by the sarcasm but he only nodded, saying nothing.

CHAPTER 46

An annoying trill on Aiden's phone signaled an incoming call. He reacted immediately, wanting to silence the irritating warble. *I really must get a decent ring tone.* When he saw that the caller's identity was suppressed, a flush of red colored his neck and cheeks; an outward sign of his inner anger.

But unlike previous calls, this time Muller's tone was cajoling, almost unctuous. "Please hear me out Mr. Donnelly. Those men acted grossly beyond their instructions. They were meant to intimidate, not to attempt to harm you. That has never been my intention. And even that action was a mistake on my part. I am a business man and this entire episode has not been good business."

"Why should I believe anything you say to me, you bastard?"

"I don't blame you for feeling that way. I have acted appallingly. My father warned me that I had become obsessed with winning. I refused to listen at the time but he was right. Perhaps it is a trap that any of us could fall into given the nature of our mutual endeavors. In short, I can only plead temporary insanity. But this event on the highway shocked me to the core and I've regained my senses."

Aiden was skeptical – Muller had proved again and again that he was a low-life and lying would be the least of his sins. But he wanted very much for it to be true and it was swaying his gut instinct. If Muller was speaking truthfully he would finally be out of Aiden's life.

"Let's pretend I accept what you say; then okay, I'll hope to never hear anything about you ever again. So I'll hang up now. You go your way and I'll go mine."

"No, no, please, there is one more thing that I need to put an end to this."

Aiden's heat was rising again and he cut in. "You have the nerve to ask me for something. What a load of bullshit." Aiden snapped.

"Please stay calm. I understand your anger but my needs are simple. I only wish to meet with you so that I can apologize in person. I am a proud man and it is hard for me to admit that I am wrong. But I feel obligated to do this as a kind of self-punishment, a way of ruling a line under all that has transpired."

"And you think I'm about to jump on a plane and come to wherever it is you're hiding out."

"Not at all. As a matter of fact I have come to you – hat in hand as they say. I've rented an office in Dublin." He gave Aiden the address.

"I know the area. I'll be there tomorrow morning at 11 o'clock."

Aiden had no idea what motivated him to agree. Perhaps he needed some level of closure as well. Or perhaps he wanted the satisfaction of witnessing this haughty bastard humbling himself. Maybe it was the lure of seeing in the flesh the shadowy manipulator so elusive when Aiden was trying to track him down who was now suddenly on his doorstep and readily accessible. Most likely it was a combination of all these things.

Next morning Andy and Mick drove him to the building in their rented BMW. The dirty white-washed façade with its grime smeared window gave no visibility as to what was within. Aiden asked them to wait in the car while he went inside. The entire setup had their antennae twitching and they were distinctly unhappy about him going it alone.

Aiden tried to reassure them. "Guys I know it's your job to protect me and I really appreciate it. This meeting is about trying to get my life back but it's confidential and I can't have you there. I'm sorry but that's the way it is. And I'm definitely not expecting any trouble whatsoever."

This was a circumstance they were familiar with in their line of work. However they remained hesitant, knowing Aiden was not the seasoned professional they usually worked with.

"Here, take this," Aiden said handing over DI Kennedy's card. "If I'm wrong and we need the police, this is the man to call. He's honest and he knows some of what's gone on."

In the end they agreed but only on the condition that if he was not back with them in 30 minutes, they would come for him – and come hard.

Aiden pressed on the buzzer next to the single door to the building and heard an old fashioned clapper and bell sounding off somewhere deep inside. While he waited he began to rotate his shoulders and open and close his hands to ease the tension that had begun to seep through his body. *Just got to keep myself together. It'll all be over with soon.*

Moments later the door was opened by a tall gaunt man with an olive-brown complexion. He looked as though he hadn't shaved in a couple of days. Underneath the stubble his face was lined and his forehead glistened with sweat that he dabbed at with a striped handkerchief. He was clearly jumpy and his eyes slid away from Aiden's as he introduced himself.

"Mr. Donnelly, my name is Renzo Olivadi. Mr. Muller is waiting for you. Follow me please."

Aiden trailed him around what had once been a service counter, through a doorway into to a narrow corridor that led towards the open workshop space at back of the building. The property was showing signs of dilapidation; there were holes in the plywood walls and patches of the cream paintwork had peeled and flaked onto the concrete floor. Just before the passageway ended they came to a widened section of the corridor with closed doors on either side. The one on the right was labeled 'Toilet' and the one on the left, 'Manager'. Olivadi rapped on the manager's door, waited briefly and then opened the door to the office. Aiden followed Olivadi inside. Seated behind a desk was a man of average build, fair of skin and hair. Like Olivadi, he looked haggard but Aiden could readily see that his facial structure was similar to that of Andre Muller. He had the same chiseled, aristocratic features, the same straight-backed posture and bore the same expression – mouth set in a perpetual sneer and jaw thrust forward. It was a look that you associate with money, privilege and arrogance. Muller did not rise and Aiden chose not to sit. The tableau remained that way while each appraised the other in silence.

Then Aiden looked into Muller's eyes and knew he'd made a serious error of judgment. Those eyes reminded him of photographs he'd seen of Rasputin and Charles Manson – they exuded such malevolence that Aiden had to fight to stop himself from taking a step back.

Finally Muller spoke. "Mr. Donnelly, thank you for calling by. I'm afraid I may have been a touch disingenuous when I asked you here on the pretext of offering to grovel before you in apology."

"Muller, I'm really not surprised. It was stupid of me to believe anything that comes from your mouth. An arsehole is always an arsehole. So what is the purpose of this farce? Surely we don't have to rehash this bullshit again and again. You can't still think that there's any chance I'd agree to join your circus."

"No. It took some amount of time but I finally accepted that it would never happen and it was time for me to move on."

There was something in the way Muller spoke that set Aiden on edge. "And what does that mean, exactly?" asked Aiden.

"Well as it happens, part of what I told you yesterday was the truth. I said that it was time to put an end to this and that is exactly what I intend to do."

With that, Muller rose from his chair. A gun was gripped in his right hand. The weapon was equipped with a silencer that doubled the barrel extension and made it look even more menacing. Aiden took an involuntary step backwards.

"Mr. Donnelly, I recommend that you remain very still. Both Mr. Olivadi and I can be a little trigger happy," Muller's tone was jaunty and conversational as if he was commenting on the weather outlook. He was enjoying himself.

Aiden forced his eyes from the gun in Muller's hand and slowly looked back over his shoulder. Olivadi's weapon was a twin to Muller's but unlike his boss, this man was not enjoying himself. His fear was evident in his eyes and in the tremor in the hand that gripped his gun with white-knuckled intensity. But with all of that Olivadi stood resolute. Whatever he might have been, he'd been broken by Muller. Now he was merely a puppet and would do his master's bidding. Aiden returned his attention to the scornful face of Lukas Muller and stood unmoving in full knowledge that he was in mortal danger. As harrowing as it had been having vehicles bearing down on him, trying to maim or kill him, that was a trifling matter compared to standing helpless with two guns pointed at him.

As hopeless as the situation looked, the will to live surged inside Aiden. And with it came something else. Deep, deep in his brain something stirred. It was happening at a level of his psyche so fundamental that it contained the very essence of Aiden's 'self'. Aiden sensed it but was not controlling it. To say it was akin to what he experienced on the road was to compare a wave to a tsunami. This was an arousal of pure power of a raw, primeval kind.

Multiple things happened simultaneously. Behind him, Aiden heard Olivadi gasp. He saw Muller's finger squeeze the trigger of his weapon even as his eyes widened in shock. Aiden's world exploded in a burst of noise, excruciating pain and blazing, incandescent light. His brain had gone nova.

CHAPTER 47

After precisely 30 minutes Andy and Mick slipped quietly into the building. They were both armed. Their agility belied their bulk as they moved stealthily down the corridor with Mick leading the way. When they reached the manager's office he signaled a halt with a hand movement. They positioned themselves on either side of the door and listened. There was not a sound coming from the office but they both detected the distinct smell of weapons having been fired. They prepared to force their way inside. Mick kicked the door down and Andy went in fast and low, his partner at his back covering the high view. With well-drilled efficiency they panned their weapons around the room while taking in the minutiae of the gruesome scene that greeted them.

Aiden lay on the floor, unconscious or dead. Blood was pooled around his head like the nimbus of a saint but rendered in grisly carmine. Muller was sprawled in his chair behind his desk, clearly dead, a bullet hole in his forehead. If a face could portray both outrage and surprise at the same time, he had achieved the feat. Olivadi was slumped in a corner, his gun lying at his feet. He looked almost catatonic. Mick went to Aiden while Andy saw to Olivadi. He kicked his weapon aside and with brutal effectiveness, knocked him out. At first sight, it looked bad for Aiden. When Mick found a pulse he felt a wave of relief. Both he and Andy had formed quite a bond with him. On closer inspection it was apparent that the wound was caused by a bullet grazing the side of Aiden's head. The shell had also taken a tiny piece of his ear with it. Both injuries were superficial but were the kind that bled profusely. The bleeding had stopped and Mick was puzzled that Aiden had not already come around. So for safety's sake, he carefully maneuvered him into the recovery position. Then while Andy went out to their car and brought it around back, Mick used the desk phone to make three calls; the first was to Jimmy, next to arrange an emergency ambulance and finally one to DI Kennedy. When they heard sirens approaching they exited through the rear door and melted away.

Aiden remained in a coma for two weeks. The hospital medicos were at a loss to explain why. His wounds were not the issue so they speculated that perhaps he had sustained a severe concussion when he hit the floor. When he finally clawed his way to a state of semi-consciousness, it was the middle of the night. In the muted night light he could see that he was hooked up to a monitor and an intravenous drip. The medication being fed to him made him feel as though he was floating and it was difficult to focus but he eventually worked out he was in a private one bed hospital room. His hazy memory was slowly returning but he could not summons any clear view as to what had taken place after Muller produced a gun. As he lay there he took inventory of his body. He felt the bandages around his head but the only physical discomfort he could detect was a mild throbbing along the side of his skull, around the area of his temple and ear. Nonetheless he had an overwhelming feeling of 'wrongness'.

He tentatively probed his brain and almost immediately recoiled in shock. In the place where normally he could sense his ability he could detect nothing. He tried again and a mental picture flashed into his mind of what looked like a charred walnut in seated at the base of his brain. As he lay motionless trying to comprehend what was happening, he began to hyperventilate. It progressed rapidly to a full blown panic attack. His heart rate skyrocketed and in turn triggered the alarm on his monitor. The night nurse responded immediately and assessed the situation with a practiced eye. It was common for patients to be frightened when they first woke from a coma in a strange place and she tried to calm him, telling him that he was being cared for and that everything was okay. Her words of reassurance had no impact because for Aiden, unquestionably, everything was not at all okay. Finally she administered a sedative and Aiden drifted off. At times he drowsed close to wakefulness and during these periods he pondered his predicament. Maybe because he had been in control of his ability for only a short time and maybe because the whole experience had been so surreal, he was surprised to find that he was moving already from mourning his loss to at least a degree of acceptance. He drifted back into a deep dreamless sleep.

When next he woke, he was not alone. In what was a Bizaro World replica of an earlier scene, it was now Aiden in the bed with his head swathed in bandages and Jimmy standing at the foot of the bed looking on with eyes full of concern. Jimmy recognized the irony. "God man you look awful," he said with a wide grin. Jimmy loved trench humor.

"I'll laugh at that when it won't hurt me to laugh," Aiden replied, managing to summons a small smile.

There was another thing different from when Aiden was at Jimmy's bedside and it was a wonderful difference. Sharni sat in a chair by Aiden's side, holding his hand.

Between them, they built a picture of what had transpired. Aiden explained how he came to be at the workshop in Muller's office and Jimmy detailed the aftermath. Muller was dead. Olivadi was still incoherent and under police guard on another floor of the hospital. The gap was the shooting itself.

"I've tried," said Aiden, a little exasperated, "but it's no good. I can't get any vision in my head as to what happened at the very end."

"Somehow you lived through an impossible situation and that's all that matters," observed Jimmy.

"There's no doubt that the gift saved my life. Remember when I suggested that it might be a survival tool. Well I know for sure that I was right. I was totally up shit creek in that office. I had no way out and I froze. But my ability didn't. Whatever went on, it was instinctive and it was massive."

It was time to tell them of the awful aftermath. Aiden took a couple of deep relaxing breaths, steeled himself and began to speak. He stared into the middle distance and kept his voice a detached monotone lest he faltered. "Too massive, I think. I can't sense the feeling at all. There's nothing there; it's gone. I think that it was cooked in the effort."

He stopped and closed his eyes. It had been one thing to philosophically mull over the loss when alone and floating in a semi-stupor. But the emotional effort of saying it aloud had suddenly left him completely drained. There was not a sound in the room. Sharni squeezed his hand trying to convey her love for him and that he had her unbridled support.

CHAPTER 48

Because he was out for so long, the hospital insisted that Aiden remain in hospital for a few more days while he underwent a barrage of tests. Nothing untoward was found. While he was confined, aside from family and friends, he had two visitors of note. The first was expected - Detective Inspector Kennedy. Aiden told him the background story he had come up with to explain Muller's pursuit of he and Jimmy. He added that he had gone to see Muller because he'd been deceived into believing that he could negotiate a way out.

Kennedy sat for a while, chin resting on steepled fingers, digesting Aiden's explanation. "You and your uncle are in possession of something these people wanted. I'm sure of that. I have no clue what it is but other than personal curiosity, that doesn't really matter right now. So I'm prepared to accept that what you've told me is the whole story even though my gut tells me there's a whole lot more to all this. What's important is that it's clear to me that you two have acted on the up and up. I can't say the same for the other mob. Olivadi will be charged with attempted murder. As for you two – you have nothing to answer for."

His other visitor was completely unforeseen. Much to Aiden's extreme discomfort Andre Muller appeared in the doorway to his room. Aiden's first instinct was to send him away immediately but for some reason that he couldn't explain, he relented and allowed the man to come in. In the end he was glad that he had.

Muller stood somberly with his head bowed and his hands clasped in front of him. "I wanted you to know firsthand that I do not blame you in any way for what happened. The fault is entirely mine. From a very young age I worried about Lukas. He was too quick to anger and seemed to have no capacity for compassion. When perhaps I could have done something about it, I was too wrapped up in my own pursuits; too self-centered. As a father, I failed him."

"I'm trying very hard to find some compassion but the truth is that your son cost me something very special. Whatever happened in that room, it did something to my brain. My ability is gone."

Aiden saw no point in telling to Muller that he was convinced that luck was a force and obeyed the natural law that action demanded reaction. For different reasons they both had discovered that luck is a capricious mistress and once it is unleashed no-one can control all of the consequences.

EPILOGUE

Andre Muller addressed what was left of his son's organization. "I'm not a gambler and never have been but chasing profits from it has produced nothing but bitterness, grief and loss. It cost me the two most precious people in my life. The pursuit of wealth from poison fruit is cursed and I want nothing more to do with it."

He waited for a response but with none forthcoming. He continued. "I am dissolving the company. All of you will be paid handsomely. My lawyers will be in contact with each of you over the coming weeks. I wish you all well – not luck, not good fortune, but well - for the future." And then he turned and walked out of the room.

Philippe Durand remained silent and tried to mask the rapacious gleam in his eyes. He was already beginning to scheme.

Aiden had recovered physically but lacked his usual spark. For the most part he had moped around his house. Sharni had stayed on hoping to be able to see him through it. She was just starting to become frustrated but that morning he had bounced out of bed full of cheer. It was just possible that the old Aiden was back and Sharni was not going to question the change in him nor was she about to permit any back-sliding. She arranged to meet Jimmy and Maureen for lunch at their local, forced Aiden to spruce up and had him out the door and into the pub by midday.

Over a round of beer and a rustic serve of pub grub she broached the subject. "Okay mister, what's going on? You've had a secret little smile on your face all morning. Not that I'm complaining but it's a big turn around."

"To answer that I need to take you all back to when I woke up in hospital. My head hurt, I felt nauseous and my vision was blurred. And the knowledge of how close to the end I'd come with that bullet grazing my skull certainly didn't help. All up, I felt like shit. When I tried to connect to that spot in my head where my ability lies, there was nothing there and I went into melt-down. My first thought, when I could think again was that the final effort might have completely blown the circuit. I tried to tell myself it was okay – I was alive and should be grateful for that. But it was like a core part of me, something that makes me who I am had been taken away."

Sharni reached out for his hand. "We understand, darling. Of course you have every reason to be sad. But that doesn't explain why you are suddenly more upbeat. Not that I'm not happy about it but I am curious. Have you found a way to accept it – is that it?"

"Well not exactly. Now I've had a good rest and some time to recover, I started wondering if maybe it was more of a kind of temporary protective shut-down caused by an overload - more like a fuse going than the whole shebang."

Jimmy jumped in. "What are you saying boyo? Does it feel like it's coming back?"

"Not positive but there are signs. When I was in hospital, I kept trying to probe at that part of my mind; like when you have a toothache and you can't stop worry at it. But all I got was the impression that it was like a lump of burnt coal. I gave up because it was too depressing and hadn't tried again for days. Last night I gave it a go and it felt different; like there was a little splutter and a spark. And this morning, I'm sure I felt something. It was much more tangible."

Aiden eyes went out of focus and they knew he was looking inward, mentally touching and probing at his brain. Then he re-focused, flashed a cheeky grin and a wink at Sharni before addressing his uncle. "Hey Jimmy, would you happen to have a form guide with you?"